wait

a BLEEDING STARS *novel*

A.L. JACKSON

Print ISBN: 978-1-946420-00-8

eBook ISBN: 978-1-938404-89-4

wait

MORE FROM A.L. JACKSON

Bleeding Stars
A Stone in the Sea
Drowning to Breathe
Where Lightning Strikes

The Regret Series
Lost to You
Take This Regret
If Forever Comes

The Closer to You Series
Come to Me Quietly
Come to Me Softly
Come to Me Recklessly

Stand-Alone Novels
Pulled
When We Collide

More Bleeding Stars Novels Coming Soon
Stay
Stand

A.L. Jackson

wait

prologue
FOUR YEARS EARLIER

"Shh…" he whispered into my hair as he pulled me closer, chasing away the lingering fear from the nightmare. The residual anxiety slicked my skin with sweat and I hiccupped over the sobs I tried to keep contained.

Quiet and hidden where they belonged.

Yet he had heard.

The arm wrapped around my back drew me to the haven at his side, while he lifted the other to hold a small hoop over our heads.

In the darkness, my eyes adjusted to make out the circle covered in brown suede that dripped with beads and colorful feathers, the center woven in an intricate web.

I stared as it swung, enraptured by the movement, by the calm of his voice as it murmured close to my ear.

"Shh…" he said again as he scattered a mess of light kisses to my temple. "See. You don't have to be afraid. This…this will hold all your dreams. They have no power over you. They can't hurt you."

Pain clenched my heart, and my fingers dug into his shirt, fisting it tight.

It was what I had buried inside that held all the power. But when I was with him, it somehow lost some of its strength.

He nuzzled his nose into the flesh along my ear, whispering ease.

"You can trust me, Edie. Trust me. Whatever it is, I get it. I get it." His voice dipped even deeper. "Talk to me."

Trust.

I did.

I trusted this broken boy.

So I whispered my secret.

Offered it to him.

To hold it.

Protect it.

Until the day he crushed it in his hands.

one

AUSTIN

*D*rab, yellow light filtered in from overhead. Squinting, I fought the stir of panic that had my heart going double time as I read my older brother's words scrawled across the letter.

> *Three years, Austin. Three years gone. I gave my life to you, and then I gave you the space you asked for. Now I need you. It's time.*

It wasn't like I didn't have it memorized. I'd read the tattered letter what seemed a thousand times. I just didn't know if I had the strength to do anything about it.

"You about ready?"

Startled by the voice coming from behind, I sucked in a breath before I gathered myself, quickly folded up the letter, and shoved it into my back pocket.

"Yep," I said. Turning around, I found Damian standing in the doorway to the dressing room that was nothing more than a glorified storage closet.

But hey, what's that old saying about beggars can't be

choosers?

His grin was wide. "Good. 'Cause it's a damned madhouse out there tonight."

Unease rolled through me.

Madhouse.

Seemed crazy there'd always been a part of me that'd craved it. The part of me that had hungered to be on the same stage as my brother, Sebastian, and his band *Sunder*. To be a part of that life. Bringing the thrashing hard rock alive for the fans who ate it up. Giving them an outlet and a voice.

But I knew I could never really fit into that world or fill those kind of shoes.

It'd been nothing but foolish…stupid to even entertain the idea of being a part of something so big. Of something so *important.*

God knew, I wasn't even close to being worthy.

Still, I couldn't kick the need that pooled in my belly, begging for that extreme high I would never get enough of.

It was better than any drug or vice.

The innate need to play and the rush I felt when I gave into the urge.

So I'd settled on these small venues where it was safe and far from the limelight and fame of my brother's world.

But the longer I played here, each week the crowd seemed to grow.

"Dude…don't look so freaked out. A crowd is a good thing. You do realize that's what the whole performing *thing* is all about, don't you?"

Asshole had the balls to throw his fingers up and air quote *thing.*

I huffed a response.

His grin widened as he cupped both his hands on the outside edges of the doorframe, letting the wood support him as he rocked back on his heels, just as casual as could be. "Cory's wrapping up his last song then you're on."

Playing at *The Lighthouse* really wasn't all that bad of a gig. It provided enough money to get me by, since I sure as shit wouldn't accept any more money from my brother.

I'd stopped letting him take care of me the moment I walked out his door three years ago.

But more than that was the thrill of stepping out on that tiny stage. The freedom I found in the song.

And if I was being honest? Maybe...maybe some part of the name reminded me of her. A beacon casting its light on murky, dangerous waters. Calling the lost from the storm.

"All right, then. Let me grab my stuff."

I went for the old acoustic guitar set in its case and carefully lifted it from the maroon felt. The grainy, worn wood felt like relief in my hands.

It had been my fifteenth birthday present from Sebastian, or Baz like everyone called him. He'd told me music was in my blood. That it bound us together in some way. And no matter how fucking far I'd run from it, I knew he was right.

That he and I were somehow bound.

Just the same as I was bound to the sea.

Damian lifted his chin. "You in for Saturday?"

I shot him a frown as a reply.

"Come on, man. Quit being a goddamned buzzkill. You could at least come with me this one time. I mean, it's no Hawaii, but the waves around here are killer. Fucking cold as shit, but you can take it."

Humorless laughter slipped out beneath my breath. "What makes you think anything has changed? Told you before, I'm not interested."

He shook his head. "That's what makes no sense. You've been up and down the coast, hugging the ocean the whole damned time because you refuse to go anywhere else, and I'd put down bets you haven't even dipped your big toe in the water. Not once. You scared or something?" He asked it with a sly grin and a taunt, like that could get me to change my mind.

Scared.

The word didn't come close to describing what the thought of getting in the ocean did to me, the confused torment that would forever keep me attracted and repelled.

I shrugged like it didn't matter when it mattered more than anything. Like he hadn't just scraped right across a wound so raw it would never heal.

"I'm just not interested."

I kept it as vague as I could, refusing to get into some heart-to-heart with Damian Rodriguez. Not because I didn't trust him. But because there wasn't a soul in the world who could truly understand. Not one who would get why I was compelled to stand at the ocean's feet, bound to it like a prisoner.

Just the same as I was forbidden from it like a castaway.

The only *soul* who could was gone.

Guilt threatened to rise like the blackest storm. Sent to swallow and devour.

Clenching my jaw, I beat it down.

Since I'd left L.A., I'd gotten pretty good at it.

Pounding it back.

Pretending I wasn't consumed by the memories of what I'd done. By what I'd destroyed. By every fucked-up mistake I'd made since.

God knew, there were too many to count.

You'd think I'd learn. That I'd figure out a way to stop ruining all the good things I was given.

That hollowed-out vacancy in my chest throbbed like a bitch.

You had to wonder how many holes could be torn into your spirit, gouged into your heart, until there weren't any pieces left to hold you together anymore.

Damian groaned, but with zero frustration behind it. Instead it was packed with a load of careless ease.

Not a care in the damned world.

If I didn't like the guy so much, it would drive me straight out of my mind.

"For real, man, it's a good thing that brooding shit looks so good on you, or I'd call you hopeless. Hell, I bet it's just an act.

Everywhere we go, the girls go crawling all over you. Think you've perfected tall, dark, and mysterious. I'm about to start asking for pointers."

With a forced, teasing grin, I glanced his way. "Hey, I can't help it if the ladies love me."

"Totally unfair. You just sit back, not saying a word, and they start orbiting like you're the goddamned sun or some shit. While I'm over here working my ass off to get one to look my way."

I stifled a scoff.

More like a black hole.

But whatever.

Just because I was a loner didn't mean I didn't enjoy a little *company* every now and then.

I'd purged a lot of vices from my life. That was one I wasn't giving up.

Learned the hard way…in the long run making attachments just turned around and bit you in the ass.

Or you just destroyed them yourself.

You crushed the flickers of joy because you couldn't be trusted to keep them safe.

To keep *her* safe.

Because you were a failure and all your good intentions turned to shit.

So you just slid through life pretending you didn't hurt and miss and wish you could go back to the beginning. Make it right. All the while knowing you'd probably turn around and fuck it all up again, anyway.

Damian rapped his knuckles on the outside wall. "Do me a favor and think about Saturday at least, all right? You're going to turn into a vampire or something equally as scary if you keep wasting around in this dive night after night."

He started to head down the hall, then paused and poked his head back in. "Oh, dude, almost forgot to tell you. My cousin's place in San Francisco is totally chill for you to come out and play next month. August 14th. It's pretty kickass. Good money. You game?"

I did my best not to cringe at the question. Did my best to ignore the way the letter folded up in my back pocket suddenly felt like it weighed a million pounds.

Three years.

Three years since I'd seen my brother's face. Three years since I'd seen the guys in the band.

So much had changed in their lives since I'd left.

And God, I wanted to be different, too, but I was a whole lot of the same. I mean, that's what this whole journey had been about.

Finding myself.

Becoming something better.

Someone stronger.

But even though the outside had changed, there were too many moments when I didn't feel any different than the eight-year-old boy huddled where he hid on the beach.

That was the day I'd torn my soul in two.

The same day Sebastian first lied for me.

The day he'd stepped up to take care of me because he knew I wouldn't make it any other way.

Didn't think anyone could understand just how damned bad I wanted to be there for him the way he needed me to be.

I just didn't know if I had anything to give without it costing both of us more in the end.

"Don't know," I answered.

Damian shook his head. "They need to know, man. Can't hold your spot forever."

"Something might have come up."

"Something might have come up?" He drew out the words like a question then sobered as his voice dropped low. "You know you can't keep doing this forever."

"Doing what?"

"Running."

I scowled. "I'm not running."

"You sure about that?"

"What about you?" I shot back. "You're the one who just

packed up on a whim and took off with a complete stranger. I could have been an axe murderer, for all you knew."

Since I'd left L.A. three years ago, I'd been traveling up and down the shores of the Pacific Ocean. When I'd been exploring the northern coast of Washington, I'd played a few times at a small club in the town he was from. He and I had become friends, and by the time I was packing up my stuff and heading south, he'd been packing up his and insisting he was coming with me.

He grinned. "Nah...you might be a morbid son-of-a-bitch, but I'd know a killer if I saw one." He raised his brows and fluttered his fingers in front of his face. "Spidey senses."

But that was the thing. He didn't really know me. Not at all.

"Besides," he continued, "I might be along for the ride, but that doesn't mean I don't know exactly where I'm heading."

"And just where is that?"

He lifted his hands out to the sides. "Somewhere badass. Some place where I won't be stuck in a small, dead-end town. I'll know as soon as I get there."

If only it were that easy.

Applause echoed through the walls. He gestured with his chin. "Get your ass out there before Craig starts to wonder if his headliner has gone MIA again. Oh, and you should totally ditch the hoodie, man. Girls wanna see what's hiding underneath."

I resisted an eye roll as I shrugged out of the thick material I wore like a shroud, fighting off the stir of unease I felt in doing it. Hiding behind it was just so damned much easier. "Yeah, yeah, I'm coming."

I slung the strap of my guitar over my shoulder and trailed Damian down the dark hall. A dark hall so much like the ones I'd spent growing up in, where I'd lived on the outskirts of my brother's band, lost to the music and the vibe and the revelry that ruled our worlds.

The disasters we caused.

The continual trouble we found.

Now, the type of music and the places I played were a

world apart, a distance that didn't quite touch, yet I felt stitched to it all the same.

Drawn and repelled.

I guess I should have known I'd never get far.

Dimness held fast to the room. The upscale bar in Santa Cruz, California was set up with round tables in the open space out in front of the stage that took up the right side of the room, and the area was rimmed by secluded booths with a long wooden bar taking up the far left side. The entire back wall was made of glass, the accordion panes pushed to either side, opening the entire bar up to the patio area that overlooked the sea during the day.

Night had taken hold, and strands of twinkle lights were strung up on the lattice-roofed patio where they extended all the way inside. People were packed into the space, a crush of darkened silhouettes sitting beneath the counterfeit stars donned by the club ceiling.

The din of voices grew quieter as I took the stage and settled myself on a short stool. I situated my guitar on my lap and pulled the mic stand closer.

My heart sped while my spirit swelled, and I was hammered with a crushing wave of fear, regret, and some kind of agonizing joy.

The mess of it damned near made my head spin.

Because in truth? I wasn't there for any of the people packing the space.

I was there because just like every night, this was where I felt that fragmented piece inside stretching out its fingers. Searching for all that had been lost. For that piece of me I could never reclaim.

Still, I'd spend the rest of my life chasing it.

In the distance, my ear tuned into the sound of waves crashing on the beach.

Letting my eyes drop closed, I strummed a quiet, subdued chord and pressed my mouth to the mic. On a breath, I let the words bleed free, and my voice filled the confines of the quiet club.

It seeped out into the darkness.

When I sang…I always felt so incredibly alone.

Just like I deserved.

Because this nightly tribute was nothing less than a penance.

A fucked-up retribution.

Atonement I would never earn.

Yet tonight, when normally my spirit would feel like it was detached, hovering somewhere afar, I felt grounded.

Wound up in a calmed frenzy.

Tied to a violent peace.

Shivers slithered across my skin, and my throat grew tight as I was hit by wave after wave of a severity I couldn't shake. Something deep and compelling and just out of reach.

I struggled through the lyrics. Ones that were intensely private, yet blameless to the innocent ear.

I guess there was typically comfort in that.

I was nothing more than a stranger who sang his forgettable song. One he personally would never forget.

Could never forget.

But tonight I felt exposed.

Pried open and picked apart.

Awareness pricked at my subconscious. It grew dense. Thick. Like I was rushed with an undercurrent of energy that pounded in my ears and thundered my heart.

No longer able to fight it, my eyes flew open while I did my all to keep playing *his* song.

And it didn't matter that I stared out into a dusky haze where the lights were cast low, faces lost in shadows and bodies obscured in mystery.

It was unmistakable.

The horror and pain that watched me from where she'd stumbled to standing next to one of the tall, round tables.

She clutched her stomach.

Like she could shield herself from my assault.

From my presence.

And it felt like torment and fate.

My throat finally fully locked up and the song came to a jilted end.

She exhaled a tortured breath that I swore I breathed.

Those pale blue eyes glittered in the light.

Edie.

two

EDIE

Do you know what it feels like to stand at the precipice of life?

Teetering on the edge of the here and now?

You know in your gut you're only one fumbled step away until you're in a free fall.

Tumbling down, down, down.

On a direct collision course with your past.

Even when you've done everything in your power to leave it behind.

So damned careful not to travel the same roads littered with mistakes and regrets and unbearable pain.

And there those roads were.

Circling right back around again.

Bringing you face to face with the past you'd give anything to forget.

Forcing you to face everything you'd ever wanted and the one thing you could never have.

Hit with a wave of weakness, my legs trembled and shook as I tottered right at that sharp, craggy ledge.

Feet slipping as the world crumbled out from under me.

My hand shot out to the back of the chair to keep myself from falling.

To keep from falling just as fast and hard as I'd so naively done before.

Only this time I knew firsthand how bad it would hurt when I hit the bottom.

Strains of his guitar moved through the suffocating air.

But it was his voice...that unforgettable voice that washed over me exactly the way it once had.

With comfort and joy and an aching hope.

Yet at the same time, it sounded so different.

Deeper.

Darker.

Raspier.

A voice that held the power to slow my movements. As if all things were set to pause, and I was caught up in a time and space that didn't move.

A space that contained only him and me and the heartbreaking song he played.

"Edie." Jed just barely broke through the trance, through *his* voice and *his* song and the thunder *he* had pounding in my heart and in my ears. Jed tried to get in my line of sight as he leaned forward in his stool. "Edie, tell me what's wrong. You look like you've seen a ghost. Are you not feeling well?"

I almost laughed.

Because Jed was right.

I had to be standing at the feet of an apparition.

The boy was all aglow in a halo of light, his melodic words a haunting harmony that wrapped me in tendrils of languishing comfort.

The way they always had.

Soothing while I got caught up in his snare.

I hadn't seen him since the night this broken boy had crushed the fragile piece of myself I'd given him.

Only Austin Stone was no longer a boy.

A desire I had no right to feel burned bright in my belly and thrummed through my veins.

Like a simmer of sin.

Forbidden and foolish.

As a teenager, Austin had been tall and gangly.

Like he was just itching to grow into his skin.

And God, it seemed almost cruel in the way he had. Like he'd been sent with the sole purpose to torment my judgement and resolve.

The lanky boy who'd towered over me had to have gained at least another two inches. His light brown hair was still short on the sides and back, longer on top. Like it'd done before, it hinted that frustrated fingers had been tugging and pulling at it for most of the day.

But it was the way his shoulders had filled out and now pressed and bunched beneath his fitted T-shirt that screamed he was all man.

The way his wide chest expanded with each breath.

The sultry twist of his full lips and the sharp curve of his jaw.

The way those big, strong hands wrapped around his guitar.

Not to mention the intricate ink that now covered the exposed skin of his arms.

His powerful presence slammed into me like a dark storm.

Ominous. Sinister. Threatening.

The room spun again. Or maybe it was my head.

Four years gone.

Four years of heartache and hiding and regret.

And there sat the only boy I'd ever loved a handful of feet away.

"Edie...goddamn it...you're scaring me. Tell me what the hell is going on."

Jed was suddenly standing at my side, at the ready to chase away any threat. To take care of me the way he had when I'd come crawling into this city.

But it didn't matter.

The only thing I saw was *him*.

I knew it the moment he felt me. It was as if I'd pried his

eyes open with the mere strength of my presence. Those earthy, poetic eyes that didn't know if they wanted to be green or grey.

For the briefest flash of a second, they widened in shock, before the moment was gone and awareness took hold.

Even from across the darkened space, that roiling grey shouted a thousand secrets and concealed a million regrets.

My chest squeezed. Painfully. In want and hate and horror.

How was it possible he still made me feel this way?

Grasping my stomach, I took a fumbled step back.

Away from that ledge.

Just as his song came to a staggered end.

"Edie." I could hear my name escape as a breath from Austin's lips, an echo from the mic that reverberated from the speakers.

A ripple of confusion rolled through the bar as his stool screeched when he pushed to stand.

That was my cue.

I had to get out of there.

Protect myself the only way I knew how.

I turned and ran.

Because running was what I did best.

I shoved through the groups of people crowding the tall round tables at the foot of the stage, and escaped out through the accordion wall of windows into the night.

Cool air whipped across my face as I hit the wooden planks, and I gasped for a breath, ignoring the stares of those who were trying to enjoy the quiet where they relaxed at the secluded tables outside.

Ropes of globe lights were strung up beneath the trellised patio that overlooked the churning sea.

The sea.

An ache I could only feel for this boy slammed me hard, just as hard as the realization.

Those old, old wounds that locked up his tongue but were still so blatantly clear.

God. How badly had I wanted to wipe them away? To fill

up the hollowed out hole that gaped from within him, insert myself as a balm the same way as he'd sought to heal me?

But that was before he'd turned right around and thrown all my hurt back in my face.

Above me, the strands of lights twinkled and danced, as if they were one with the stars that shimmered from above.

Beneath them I felt so small.

Exposed.

"Edie."

The desperation in his voice hit me like fiery darts, and I gasped out a breath and pushed myself harder. I rounded the side of the patio and hit the walkway that led to the parking lot out front.

Where I was going, I didn't really know.

Away.

That was it.

Just *away*.

"Wait."

The anguished call pelted me from behind.

Wait.

Oh God.

I gulped, trying to fight the moisture I could feel welling in my eyes. The helplessness that set in as I fought for that elusive escape.

I should have known. Should have known one day it would all catch up to me.

"Edie…please…just…wait."

I gripped the railing as if it might propel me forward. Instead, my footsteps faltered and slowed. I stood facing away, my back heaving as his consuming presence rose over me from behind.

"Please." This time it was a whisper. A plea.

Sincere.

Slowly I turned.

Drawn.

He'd always been my weakness.

Austin stood at the end of the walkway, just outside the

reach of the lights, his body obscured in shadows.

Even larger than I'd imagined when I'd first seen him up on stage.

So foreign.

So familiar.

My heart ached. Because I was looking at the boy who'd been my best friend. The one person who I'd thought would completely understand. One who wouldn't judge or make it hurt more than it already did.

He'd been my safety.

My haven.

Until he'd dragged me right back into hell.

"Why are you here?" My words cracked. "H-h-how…how did you find me?"

I saw the shake of his head, and he took a single step forward, out of the shadows and into the glow of the single lamp attached high on the exterior wall that lit the way.

It hit him like a spotlight.

The boy was so beautiful.

It was a threatening kind of beauty, a whorl of mystery and pain, sharp lines and corded muscle.

It almost dropped me to my knees.

He fisted his hands at his sides. The question was strained, hard as it pressed from his mouth. "You believe in fate, Edie?"

Old grief I'd bottled for so long burst. It came out as some kind of maniacal cry. Incredulous. Oozing disbelief. "After everything that happened…that's what you're going to ask me?"

"Edie…I—"

"Do you have any idea how badly you hurt me?" I cut him off, my own hands fisting as I took a single step forward. "The damage you caused? Careless words, Austin. So fucking careless, thrown out there without a single thought to the repercussions, without any consideration of how they would affect me. How they would change my life. *You promised.*" My brow twisted with the accusation. "And now you have the nerve to stand there and ask me if I believe in fate?"

I swallowed hard, shook my head. "You can go straight to hell, Austin Stone."

When I was fourteen, I'd promised myself I'd never give up control again. Never would I put myself in a situation where I was helpless. Powerless. I'd never again allow myself to be left without a *choice*.

And Austin Stone had whittled me down until I'd relinquished it all to him.

I trusted him.

He laughed, but there was zero humor behind it. "Come on, Edie. You can do better than that, can't you? Considering you know hell is exactly where I've been all along, and you and I both know I deserve so much worse. And yeah...those words were reckless, but you know they weren't heedless. You couldn't expect me to just stand there. Not with *him*. Not with what he was saying. Implying. I *couldn't*." The last cracked on the emphasis.

I felt as if every cell in my body was being crushed. Squeezed so tight there was no chance but for everything to implode. "And because you lost it, I lost it all. You. My home. My future."

His big hands fisted. "I know. I...I fucked it up, Edie. Warned you, I do. That I would."

But what he failed to say was he'd *promised* he wouldn't fuck it up with me.

I couldn't tell if I was relieved or terrified when Jed suddenly rounded the corner. His sister, Blaire, was hot on his heels.

Knowing her, she'd been trying to hold him back, to give me the moment I so clearly needed.

"Edie," Jed gushed out in relief when he saw me. He came to a stop a few steps behind Austin.

As if he'd just stepped into the bristling intensity and it tripped up his feet.

The stand-off.

The war.

Austin standing there? I knew that's exactly what this was

going to be.

"What the hell is going on here?" Jed demanded. His voice twisted into a threat. He glared at the back of Austin's head, worried eyes flicking to me, hardening when they snapped back to Austin.

Blaire tugged at his arm. "Jed...I told you to give her a minute. Sometimes you need to let people sort out their own issues."

Jed just grunted and shrugged off her arm.

Refusing to budge.

Austin swung his head to look behind him. When he did, his face shifted to the side, all those hard, beautiful lines exposed in profile. His expression wound into a bitter sneer. "Nah, man. All's good here. Just telling an old friend hi. Isn't that right, Edie?"

Aggression curled between them.

Alive and raging.

Jed was a burly, beefy, hulk of a man. A full beard covered most of his face, his brown hair cut short at the sides and longer on top.

Had I ever imagined him and Austin going toe to toe, I would have put all my money on Jed.

Now I wasn't so sure.

Jed lifted his chin, as if for the moment he was standing down, turning to me as his tone softened. "You okay, Edie?"

I nodded. "Yeah, I'm okay."

Lie. Lie. Lie.

I was shaken to my core.

"I just want to go home." It left me on a desperate breath.

Desperate to run.

Desperate to hide.

Because I didn't know how to face *this*.

All the memories we'd made. The hurt he'd inflicted. The hope he had crushed.

The love that had never dimmed.

It all stared back at me now, held in the depths of those tumultuous eyes that always saw far too much.

Jed pushed around Austin and stalked my way. "All right, let's get you out of here."

As she passed by Austin, Blaire cast a searching glance in his direction, before her attention flickered over to me, a ton of worried questions moving across her expression.

Questions I didn't know if I had the strength to answer.

With an arm wound around my shoulder, Jed spun me, breaking the spell Austin had me under, and tucked me into his side.

Protecting and shielding.

He began to lead me away, down the planks and toward his car waiting in the parking lot out front.

With each step we took, I could feel the heat of Austin's stare. That burning intensity I wasn't sure I could ever escape.

The hurt and the hatred.

I just couldn't tell where the hatred was directed.

If it was aimed at him or me or the rest of the world that had threatened to choke the life out of us.

The world we were supposed to take on together.

Just as we started to round the corner, I paused because I just couldn't stop myself, turned to look back at the man who stood there staring back at me.

Emotion gripped his expression just as tight as the clench of his fists.

Hard and tortured.

As if I was the one inflicting the pain.

I choked down the sorrow that rose like a cyclone, spinning and spinning, whipping up the old affection that longed for that soft, understanding boy to take me in his arms and sing in my ear.

Dangerous.

I searched inside myself for the shelter that secured my heart. The flimsy cover I wore that just barely kept me together. I forced myself to speak the words I knew would drive him away, as much of a lie as they were. "And for the record...no, Austin, I definitely don't believe in fate."

three

AUSTIN

*M*otherfucker.

My fists pummeled the bag. Hit after hit. Sweat slicked my skin and my heart thrashed in my chest.

On the other side, Damian held the bag, pushing back.

I drove into it as hard as I could. Pounding and pounding. Like I might have the chance of beating out all the frustration—all the confusion—that licked at my insides.

"Whoa, man, not sure what the hell is going on with you, but just an FYI...you're about to kick *my* ass through this bag here, which is totally not close to being the point of this exercise. This is a no-contact sport, meaning I should have a safe, cushy spot over here. If I didn't know any better, I'd think you were pissed at me. But considering I'm your favorite person in the world, we both know that's not the case."

I just grunted.

Smack. Smack. Smack.

My taped-up fists slammed against the vinyl.

So yeah.

Maybe the whole damned time I was imagining it was that big, burly motherfucker's face.

Sue me.

I laid into it harder.

Damian pushed back. Hard. "You 'bout done?"

I gave it one last good hit, before I stumbled back, panting like a damned dog. I yanked at the tape around my wrists. "Fine."

I began to pace the garage floor that had been turned into a makeshift gym, sucking deep breaths into my too-tight lungs.

Damian sauntered into the middle of the room, wearing that smirk that claimed he knew too much. "I'm going to go out on a limb here and guess this sour-puss mood you've been rocking for the last two days has something to do with that chick you went and ruined your show at *The Lighthouse* for on Tuesday night. And by the way, Craig is so not impressed. You're totally on probation. Said one more fuck up and you're out."

Like I gave a shit.

I gave him an answering scowl. "Fuckin' up seems to be my forte, now doesn't it?"

"Whatever, man. Use that as a bullshit excuse. *You just can't help yourself.* Sound about right?"

"Sure does."

He shook his head. "God, you can be such an asshole. You do realize taking it out on me isn't going to change anything?"

Dropping my head, I set my hands on my waist, trying to suppress some of the bullshit emotions doing their best to escape.

Because he was right.

None of this had anything to do with him.

I managed to fuck shit up all on my own.

His voice quieted in caution. "You about ready to tell me who she is?"

I swallowed over the lump that suddenly felt prominent in my throat. Like that regret was compounding. Growing bigger. Pressing. I wondered just how long it would be until it exploded.

"An old friend."

Labeling her as only that? It felt like another damned betrayal.

Because she'd been *everything*.

But betraying?

That's what I did best.

"A friend?" His tone was all kinds of incredulous. "Sure didn't look that way to me." He tossed it out like an accusation, his words like darts nailing me to the wall.

I spun toward him. In surrender, I threw my arms out to the side. "Fine. You want to know who she is? She is someone *important*. Someone I *hurt*. Two nights ago was the first time I've seen her in years."

Not since she'd packed her things and ran. It was the night I'd gone and taken the secret she'd offered me like a gift and tossed it out like it was yesterday's news.

I was supposed to protect it.

Protect her.

Instead I hadn't done anything but leave her to be trampled underfoot. Revealed what *he* was never supposed to know.

It was my fault.

I knew it. Losing my fucking head the way I had.

And there was nothing I could say in her panic to get her to stay.

I can't believe you would do this to me. After everything I trusted you with. Just…stay out of it. Stay out of my life and my business because I can't trust you. Don't make this any worse than you already did.

That's what she'd left with me, the words forced out through her sobs, horror in her eyes gleaming through the tears staining her face.

Then she'd vanished into the night. Days had turned into weeks and weeks had turned into months.

It was the years that had passed that assured me I'd lost her forever. I'd been so damned careless. Taking the fragile and tossing it around. Stupid enough to think when it fell, it wouldn't break.

Her parting words spun through me.

Stay out of it.

Unease swirled. A sudden onslaught of nausea.

Maybe I should regret it. Regret the fact I'd ignored her final plea. Sticking my nose deeper into her business than I'd ever allow her to know.

But I couldn't.

Couldn't find any remorse for making that *bastard* pay.

Of course she had no clue it was me.

That I was responsible.

That was something that would only hurt her more. The girl was too kind and too good to understand that sometimes the right thing to do most people would consider wrong.

You know the old rule.

An eye for an eye and a tooth for a tooth.

Only thing I regretted was I wished I could have taken more from him.

God knew he'd just about *ruined* her.

In discomfort, Damian shifted, hesitant as he hedged the subject. Like he was trying to get to the heart of it all without uttering it aloud. Figuring he would set me off.

Smart boy.

God knew I was one misstep from coming unglued.

"She's really pretty, yeah?"

A disoriented chuckle rumbled in my chest.

Pretty.

Not even close.

She was fucking gorgeous.

It was like the girl had been created just for me. A replica of my every fantasy.

But it was the inside that left me a jumbled mess.

The gracious and the good.

The girl was the only one who shed a light strong enough to pull me from the dark. The one who held the power to call me from the blackened waters where my lungs were filled. At

31

the cusp of succumbing.

Right where I belonged.

But that girl…that girl had given me air.

A reprieve from the unending storm.

I raked an agitated hand through my hair. Fuck. Just the memory of her standing there two nights ago threatened to harden my cock, and that right there should be warning enough.

Here I was again. Wishing I could plow right through all those lines I was forbidden to cross.

Itching to taste. To touch. To take.

My stomach twisted, thinking about the way she'd looked when I'd seen her Tuesday night.

How she still managed to affect me.

My dick had gone hard while all the hard, brittle, broken places inside wanted to go soft.

To melt beneath the sweet and the pure.

My fingers twitched with just the idea of diving into those waves, now longer than before, that beautiful mess of hair so blonde it was almost white.

My mouth watered with just the thought of getting one more taste of those soft lips that always rested in a seductive pout.

Guess I shouldn't have been surprised when that asshole had swooped in like some kind of glorified deliverer. Staking his claim. Taking what should have been mine.

But I was the one who was the fool. The one ignorant enough to let her go.

It was jealousy that had gotten the best of me the first time. I wasn't about to let it win twice.

That didn't mean watching him tuck her close to comfort her didn't sting like a bitch.

Did he get her the way I did?

Had she let him in?

Did he know?

Thinking about it had me antsy, fingers twitching with the urge to yank out all my hair, my masochistic mind hung up on the idea of another man touching her.

God, I was a selfish prick.

Had been for my whole damned life.

Taking the good and crushing it in my hands.

Shit.

I didn't want to be.

I didn't want to continue to be a failure.

But it seemed impossible to right all those wrongs.

Because this disaster I'd caused?

It'd rippled wide with a devastating effect.

Ruining lives.

I'd forever regret ruining hers and destroying the last good in mine.

"Come on, man. Just...go...talk to her." Damian shrugged like the solution was simple.

I huffed. "Talk to her? She made it pretty damned clear she didn't want to see me, let alone talk to me. And it's not like I have her phone number and can just dial her up."

With his index finger, Damian scratched behind his ear and averted his gaze to the floor. The way he always did when he was feeling guilty. Finally, he looked up. "You know Deak knows her, right?"

I froze. A scowl marched across my face as his words sunk in. "What do you mean, Deak knows her?"

Deak was the owner of this house. Three months ago, Damian and I had come to Santa Cruz with the expectation of passing through, not staying for longer than a week or two, the way we always did. But on the night I'd first played at *The Lighthouse*, he and Deak had struck up a conversation. Didn't take them long to realize they were both addicted to the sea and the surf, Deak growing up on the big waves of Australia while Damian had braved the freezing waters of the Washington coast.

That night, Deak had offered up his place. Said he'd been looking to let out a couple rooms in the house he'd inherited from his grandparents. He'd been living here alone for the last two years since he'd moved to the States.

I'd told him I couldn't promise how long we'd stick around, because I wasn't about to get myself tied to one place.

Not when I had no idea where I belonged or where I was headed.

Still, we'd been hanging here for the last three months.

The house was perched on a cliff that overlooked the ocean. Night after night, the sound of the waves filled my ears, calling to me just the same as they pushed me away, *his* presence strong and profound. Same way it always was anytime I was up close to the sea.

Precisely the reason I never got far.

I'd thought that's why I felt incredibly bound to this place.

But I guess I'd been tied to it in a way I didn't get.

Not until now.

Not until *her.*

And fuck, if it didn't feel like fate.

Eyebrows drawn, Damian cocked his head as he began to explain. "That guy? The one you looked like you were about two seconds from tearing apart?"

I gave a short nod.

Like I could forget.

"He owns the surf shop where Deak helps out sometimes. Name's Jed. Turns out your girl works there too, works the register at the shop. Rooms with him and his sister at a little place a couple miles from here. Apparently Jed said something to Deak about her freaking out about some guy playing at *The Lighthouse*. Deak put two and two together. Asked me this morning if I knew how you knew Edie Evans. Said something about her being a sweet girl who didn't need any more trouble."

Anger burned through my veins.

Rooms.

Was she sharing his bed?

Turning away, I raked a hand down the back of my neck, rubbed at the tight muscles, not sure if I had it in me to process what that fact meant.

Maybe fate was too damned late.

"Never seen you this spun up, man. She's different than the rest?" Damian asked.

I knew what he meant. Wanting to know if this was just about me wanting to get my dick wet. If she was like the girls I blew through town after town.

Wishing for someone or something to fill the void.

Knowing it was impossible.

But at least for a few sex-fueled moments I could forget.

It'd never been about that with Edie. Even though that's what had fucked it all up in the end.

My need for her had grown to a place where I couldn't see straight. Couldn't think straight. Because of it I'd burned what we had straight into the ground.

"Yeah, man. She's different."

So different.

So different and perfect and right.

Too perfect for me.

But that didn't mean I didn't ache for her with every messed-up part of me.

He huffed out a sigh. "Seems to me you have some amends to make."

Guilt throbbed in my conscious, heavy and hard and suffocating. I looked toward the ceiling, the words raw when I forced out the confession. "I've made more mistakes than I could ever make up for."

There were some mistakes you couldn't take back.

Damian might think I was a good guy.

He was wrong.

"Then you'd better get busy, my friend, because hanging out here acting like a straight-up asshole isn't going to win you any points."

Her fragile voice echoed through my mind. Touching me like it used to in the dark, her hands fisted in my shirt like a plea.

When I'm with you, it doesn't hurt so bad.

Hope sparked in that dark, dark place.

That place only her light could reach.

There were so many mistakes I'd made that I could never redeem.

But maybe...just maybe...this one I could vindicate.

four

AUSTIN
AGE SEVENTEEN

I tossed and turned. Kicked the covers from my body. Stared up into the darkened ceiling of my room.

Everything felt too close and too tight, my skin slick with sweat, my heart beating too goddamned hard.

A creeping dread sank into the pit of my stomach as my ear tuned to the quiet sobs that seeped through the wall from the room next door.

Fear and sorrow.

I felt it. *Recognized* it.

Even when the sound was muffled by her pillow.

By the walls and the distance.

I *recognized* it.

I slid from the confines of my bed. I gripped handfuls of hair as I paced and listened some more.

What the hell was I supposed to do?

This was the girl who'd been too shy to even look at me earlier when she'd stood in the front doorway, while her brother had grinned like a fool at her side, all too eager to announce his baby sister was staying for the summer while the band was on break.

God. Even with her head cast low, she had to have been the best thing I'd ever seen.

Girls came and went in this house.

All the damned time.

Sex and sin.

Fucking easy.

No one seemed to mind when I just reached out and took my share, like I was some kind of twisted, fucked-up partner to the band.

Those chicks were always game.

Good to get whatever taste they could.

Even if it was just me.

An outsider who wished he was good enough to step into the ring.

But this one? She'd all but ignored me when it felt like for the first time in my life, my eyes were open and I could finally see.

Because I'd felt them. Fuck. I'd *felt* them. The quick peeks. The stolen glimpses fueled by the strange curiosity that neither of us had seemed able to shake.

Sure. I'd met her a few times through the years when we'd been nothing more than little kids.

Then?

It'd seemed like nothing.

Now?

It felt like everything.

Now I knew something profound was prodding at me. Calling to me from that room.

A room that was clearly off-limits.

Another stifled sob that hit me like a dagger to the heart, and that was all I could take. I didn't even take the time to think it through, the rash decision made somewhere in my subconscious when I dropped to my knees to dig into the back of my closet.

I rooted out what I kept hidden in a small chest and clutched it in my hand, welcoming its relief. For the flash of a second, I let my grandma's voice caress me like a song, the same as it'd done when she'd given it to me when I was eight.

Pretended like I might possibly deserve it.

Keep it close, sweet boy. Whenever you're scared or the dreams come, cling to it, and it will hold them for you. It will give you peace and safety. Whenever you need it, think of me and remember what I told you.

I knew with every part of me this girl *needed* it.

That she deserved it.

I edged out the door, slinking slowly with my back pressed against the hallway wall, hiding in the shadows.

Like some kind of sick, perverted fuck sneaking around.

Some part of me was screaming that I was doing something wrong.

Crossing a line that'd been invisibly drawn right in front of her door.

The rest of me just didn't care, and I was slowly, quietly, turning the knob and stealing into the darkness of the guest room.

Moonlight filtered in, lighting up her white hair in a soft, milky glow, her skin an almost alabaster white.

Damn it all if my breath didn't hitch. My stomach was twisted in a thousand knots.

I took a cautious step forward.

The floor creaked and my spirit thrashed.

Her little body froze, no doubt sensing my approach, her back to me where she quaked and clung tighter to the blanket covering her face.

So goddamned much fear trembled from her, it chipped out another fragment of my brittle, broken heart.

It seemed impossible.

That this virtual stranger could possibly make me care.

But I couldn't stop the intrinsic need to soothe her pain. To take it away.

Everything else faded away and my sight narrowed on one singular goal.

I couldn't get my fingers to stop shaking when I tentatively brushed them through her hair, couldn't ignore the surge of energy that flashed through my veins. "Shh…I've got you."

She gasped at my touch. And maybe we both were shocked by it, but there was no missing the way her tensed up body relaxed, the way she shuddered out a relieved breath.

Like maybe she got I was there to hold her.

Never to hurt her.

That was all it took for me to go crawling in behind her.

Pulling her into my arms.

At the contact, I sucked in a sharp gust of air. Like I was taking the first real breath I'd breathed since the day I'd stolen *his*.

Light.

It strobed against the blackness obliterating my heart.

God. Who was this girl?

Hesitantly, she turned in my arms.

Aqua eyes, wild and bewildered, stared at me through the subdued light.

Still, they glinted like the sharp cut of diamonds.

Everything trembled and shook.

My heart and my spirit and my mind.

Fear and awe.

It reflected between us, like two mirrors that went on forever.

Eternal.

My throat was tight, and I pulled her closer, my mouth pressing a bunch of kisses into all her wild hair, to the soft skin at her temple. I lifted the hoop with the tangled web over our heads. My words were a strained whisper. "See. You don't have to be afraid. This…it will hold all your dreams. They have no power over you. They can't hurt you. Keep it with you always, and it'll give you peace and safety."

I couldn't help hoping she'd allow me to give her a little bit of it, too.

five

EDIE

Waves rolled against the sand. They came as a quiet thunder as the tide ebbed and waned. The familiar rhythmic lurch of the sea filtered in through my open window, and the flowy drapes framing it blew in the gentle breeze.

Peace.

It's the one thing we all hunger for. The innate need to feel safe and protected against the storms raging around us.

Yet I felt farther from it than I'd felt in a long, long time.

Hugging my blanket a little tighter to my chest, I tucked my trembling body into a tight ball.

Still a prisoner to the night.

To the dreams that would forever keep me in their hold.

They were always there. But somehow they had shifted since Austin had made his unexpected reappearance in my life. As if the nightmares were taunting me with the moments of peace he'd provided. With the compassion and tenderness only he could provide.

Like tendrils of his comfort stretched out their spindly

fingers, winding and whipping, just out of reach.

When I awoke?

I'd never felt so alone.

I choked over the sob I held in my throat, keeping my torment secret while the loss hit me like a silent hailstorm.

My heart thudded violently.

Torn in every direction.

Desperate for connection.

For the one person who'd ever truly understood.

I knew I shouldn't go there—shouldn't torture myself this way—but I found myself untangling my body from my twisted covers. Through bleary eyes, I leaned over to my nightstand and opened the bottom drawer, rummaged through to the back, knowing exactly where it was considering I found myself clinging to it almost every night. The second I held it in my hand, tears streaked free.

Unchecked but restrained by all the walls I'd had to force into place in order to protect the one thing that would always matter to me most.

Taking in a shuddered breath, I rolled onto my back and lifted it above me.

Let it dangle in the air like a silent promise.

Feathers danced in the breeze, and the colorful, shiny beads threaded on the leather strings glittered in the rays of sunlight that slanted in through the window.

The hoop weighed so little. Yet it felt anything but light.

Memories spun, just like the web that was supposed to catch my dreams.

You're safe. You're safe. Nothing can hurt you. I won't let it.

How many times had he uttered that promise?

An old pain twisted through my insides. I'd always known I could never leave it behind. That it would haunt me like a ghost. I'd just never believed those ghosts would have the chance to catch up to me.

Two knocks thudded at my bedroom door. For two

seconds, I clung to the sorrow, to the memories, to the hope that seemed nothing more than a dream, before I shoved the dreamcatcher under my pillow.

I did my best to push off the grief, to pretend everything was just fine, the way I always did, swatting at the tears I'd feign didn't exist.

For so long, it just seemed the right thing to do. To put on a brave face and a fake smile. To shove it all into the past and forget, just like my mother had promised me one day I'd do.

Forget.

But I was beginning to wonder if striving for that distance made me nothing less than a fool. Because that distance was insurmountable. Unpassable. Just a girl looking up at a vast mountain range that could never be crossed.

The door swung open.

Blaire poked her head inside, giving me a wide, innocent grin that was every kind of devious as she entered.

Without an invitation.

Not that I was surprised or anything.

Barging in was kind of her MO.

Funny, it just made me love her all the more.

I donned a bright smile which never felt all that forced when I was around my best friend. She just had this way about her, pulling smiles and laughter from me with ease.

Her huge mass of brown hair was bundled in a messy bun on the top of her head, and she wore an old tattered sweatshirt with the neck ripped out that dipped off one shoulder, her shorts so short she didn't appear to be wearing any.

"Hey," I said. I cleared my throat when the word cracked. Doing my all to keep it cool and even, hoping it revealed nothing. Because the last thing I wanted was for her to worry. For her to dig and prod into the places I couldn't allow her to go.

I sat up and crisscrossed my legs.

A rush of unease stirred. I totally recognized the look in her eye.

Blaire hopped onto the bottom of my bed, facing me as she

mirrored my position. "Spill," she ordered.

I crossed my arms over my chest. I hoped it appeared defiant, when in reality I was trying to keep myself from crumbling. "I don't have any clue what you're talking about."

Her eyes narrowed. "I call bullshit. You are totally holding out on me, Edie Evans. And you know just how much I really hate being held out on."

Subtly, I laughed, shaking my head. I'd been holding out for a long, long time. "There just isn't anything to say."

Her brows drew tight. "Did you know you're probably the worst liar in the history of all liars?"

She cocked her head, edged a fraction closer to study me as if she were trying to decipher some kind of riddle.

"I'm not lying," I mumbled.

The corner of my mouth trembled. Just a little.

"See." She jabbed her index finger twice toward my mouth. "That. Right. There." She swished her hand in front of my face as if she were offering it up as evidence. "You do this little twitchy thing every time whatever is coming out of your mouth isn't the whole and complete truth. It's actually kind of adorable."

"Not true."

Another tremble.

"Ha!" She pointed again, all too happy to be catching me in the act.

I bit my bottom lip.

Hard.

God. When did she start seeing straight through me?

She pffted, catching that too. "I seriously doubt that's going to help. Just give it up and 'fess up. I know you better than you think I do. And what I know is you waltz around here with a smile painted on your face, pretending like you're the happiest person in the world when it's so obvious you're missing something. You have a great job. You live on the beach. Not to mention you have a *really freaking awesome* best friend."

Okay. So maybe humility wasn't exactly her strong suit.

She kept right on talking. "And let's not forget about Jed.

You know, my big brother who's been in love with you since the second he saw you, and you won't even go as far as to throw the poor guy a bone? And considering just about every last girl within a hundred-mile radius would probably throw down to get a piece of my brother and you do your best to avoid him..." She circled her index finger around my face. "I know there's something going on in that pretty little head of yours."

"I like my job."

No lip tremble. Let's hear it for small victories.

The truth was, I loved my job.

So what if I'd basically ignored all Blaire's other overt insinuations? The ones about her brother and my joy?

That wasn't a topic I relished tackling.

Four years ago I'd come to Santa Cruz.

Lost.

Heartbroken.

Scared and alone and vulnerable.

Right back where I'd promised myself I'd never be again.

But at least I'd had the *choice* to leave. The *choice* to protect the little I still could.

I'd never allow anyone to steal my *choice* again.

Jed had hired me on the spot when I'd seen the *Help Wanted* sign tacked on the door of his shop. Blaire and I had become fast friends, and it wasn't long until I was renting out the third bedroom of the beachside condo Blaire and Jed shared.

Blaire scoffed. "I didn't say you don't like your job. But you've been moping around for the last two days like you're some kind of emo chick. And seriously, it's not a good look for you. I mean, come on, you don't even have black hair."

Oh, the sarcasm.

She tsked. "Seems to me super-hot singer guy has your panties all in a twist."

I struggled to keep my breath from catching with the blatant insinuation.

She sobered at my reaction, her voice softening. "You haven't been yourself since, Edie." She lifted a brow. I couldn't tell whether it was knowing or accusatory. "Or maybe you're really just acting like yourself because you found the missing piece."

This time my breath did catch.

Sometimes she was a little too insightful.

But that was the problem. There were so many missing pieces I'd been left a hollowed out shell.

"And I totally dig the tats, by the way. It makes him seen so...dangerous."

She had no idea.

"And those lips...did you see those lips?" She gave an exaggerated groan and waved her hand at her face as if she were overheated. "No man should have lips like that. That's an injustice."

Yeah. I'd seen those lips. Had felt them brush my cheek as they'd quietly sang me to sleep at night. Had felt their soft, tentative exploration across my skin.

Slowly I shook my head. "I told you...he was just someone I knew back in L.A. I wasn't expecting to see him. We didn't exactly part on the best of terms."

"Lover?" She actually had the nerve to sound hopeful.

I sighed. "No."

It was so much more complicated than that.

"Friend?" she prodded.

Resigned, I looked at her, swallowed around the lump so big I was sure it was cutting off air flow to my lungs. God knew admitting it made me lightheaded. "He was my best friend."

She waggled her eyebrows. "So it sounds like you two need to kiss and make up."

Ugh.

Only Blaire.

I shook my head. "Aren't you supposed to be on your brother's side?"

Nonchalant, she hiked a single shoulder. "Oh come on, Edie. My brother might follow you around like a lovesick fool, but neither of us needs to pretend he has any claim on you when all of us know he doesn't."

Guilt throbbed, and I rapidly blinked. "I've never been anything but honest with Jed."

Brutally honest.

While still keeping all my secrets.

I'd done my all to keep Jed in the friend zone. Still, he'd pushed and pushed with zero pressure. Thinking one day he would wear me down.

He'd just never accepted the fact that day would never come.

She pointed at my door. "Night after night, my brother sleeps right across the hall. Not once have I caught either of you sneaking out of the other's room. I bet you haven't even done the dirty deed with him, have you?"

In discomfort, I glanced away, out the window to the toiling sea beyond, knowing she was just goading me. Trying to get me to open up. To tell her all.

Because she was no fool and, even though she'd become my closest friend, she was well aware I hadn't let her completely in.

My brow pinched in something close to offense. "You know we haven't."

Her head tipped as she tossed out the accusation. "And why's that?"

Digging deeper.

Shaking my head, I looked back at her. "I already told you. I don't do flings." Only I had.

Once.

And that *fling* had been my demise.

Then when I'd sought refuge in the *Sunder* house years later, I'd gone and gotten foolish. Tried my hand at love. Opened up and gave Austin the broken pieces that had remained and trusted him to hold them together.

Sadly, the only thing that'd managed was blowing the rubble to tiny bits of dust.

She threw up her hands.

"Oh come on, Edie." Her expression morphed into

something serious. "I know you're not shutting my brother out based on virtue. Otherwise you'd have a ring on your finger and would already be riding toward happily ever after because you know my brother would one-hundred percent be on board for something more than just a fling. So you might as well concede and tell me the truth, because I know that ridiculously delicious boy with a guitar was not just some random guy you had a little tiff with and you parted ways."

I twisted my hands, saying nothing.

Disappointed, she shook her head. "You're my best friend, and I don't even *know* you. I don't know who you are, where you're from, or why seeing some guy has sent you into a complete tailspin. But what I do know? I know you're hiding and you've been since the second you came here. And despite all those things, I really care about you. And I can't be there for you if I don't know what we're up against."

Trust.

It was something I didn't give easily.

Something I hadn't truly granted in what felt like forever.

Not since Austin.

Fear closed in like a shroud. Chills skated down my spine. I fought it back, forced the words to form on my dry tongue, because maybe Blaire was right. Maybe it was time I gave her more than just tidbits into my past. God knew I didn't know how to manage this disaster on my own. "His name's Austin. Austin Stone."

The broken boy who'd become my life. My safety.

But I should have known sometimes wreckage cannot be salvaged.

This was a crushed-up boy who'd been messed up in the kind of trouble that leashed you like a dog then led you down a path of destruction. A boy who'd filled his veins to cover up the pain he wore like a second skin, all in an effort to pretend his own demons didn't exist.

Dark, dark demons.

By the time I met him? I'd already invented my own ruin.

I should have known combining the two would ravage and

destroy the little bits we had remaining.

The admission cut to a whisper. "He's Sebastian Stone's younger brother."

Confusion hovered around her as she tried to make sense of my statement, before her mouth dropped open. "Hold up. You mean *the* Sebastian Stone. Lead singer of *Sunder*?"

Warily, I nodded.

She slapped the heel of her hand against her forehead. "Oh my God. How did I not recognize it? I thought he looked familiar. I mean, he looks *exactly* like him. And that voice and the way he plays guitar? Oh. My. God."

It was the truth.

I'd been a little bit taken aback, startled by the fact Austin had changed so much and now so closely resembled his older brother. Though somehow I wasn't surprised at all that my beautifully broken boy would turn into a devastatingly gorgeous man.

Mine.

Hurt slammed me from all sides.

That's what he was supposed to be.

And here I was.

Alone when I didn't have to be.

Blaire was grinning, her excitement barely contained. As if she'd momentarily become completely oblivious to my turmoil. "Holy shit. This is huge. So huge. How the hell did you meet Austin Stone? I mean...have you met his brother?" She bounced on the mattress like an overeager groupie. "Oh my God, tell me you've met the rest of the band."

Discomfort gripped me tight, my throat raw as I worked myself up to making the confession.

As I worked up the courage to let her into all those places I never let anyone else go.

I'd endured so much loss.

Every single thing I had loved.

Every person.

Family, hopes, and dreams.

All of it had hinged on one mistake.

One mistake I'd made when I was fourteen.

Just a naïve, stupid, foolish little girl.

Ash had just been another casualty of that fateful night.

One that had followed me like a landslide, devouring everything important to me in its path.

The confession came out choppy. "Blaire...Ash Evans is my brother."

Blaire's eyes went wide. Shocked and hurt. "What?"

My mouth opened, an explanation on my tongue, when a soft tap sounded at my door. Jed peeked in. He wore a gentle, hesitant smile on his face. "Can I come in?"

I swallowed hard, hoping the words didn't crack as I forced a smile onto my face and said, "Of course."

He sauntered in. Crossing to me, he placed an innocent kiss against my forehead, lingering just a little longer than necessary, his thumb brushing across my cheek. The kind of affection he always gave. Chaste but always hoping for more.

"How are my girls this morning?" he asked.

Sadness swelled around me.

Any girl would be lucky to be called *Jed's girl*.

But I think I'd known it the second I'd seen Austin sitting on that stage.

Imperceptibly, I shook my head, refuting my own damned lie.

Because I'd known it since the moment he'd crawled into my bed and whispered his ease. Since the moment his spirit had sank into my soul.

Even if I could never have him, I would always belong to Austin Stone.

six

AUSTIN

*F*lames leapt toward the darkening sky. The bonfire cracked and sparked. Twilight clung to the heavens like a fiery blanket of red woven with purples and blues, the sun dipping out of sight at the sharp, silver edge of the ocean. Waves subdued and quieted. Like they gave way to the peace of the night.

Eyes dropping closed, I breathed it in and let the sensation wrap me whole. Take me under. My spirit trembled and thrashed. Like this moment was shared with *him*. Like that connection hadn't been forever severed.

All because of me.

I could almost hear his laughter riding on the waves.

It'd been different than mine.

Lighter. Kinder. Innocent.

Good.

My chest squeezed and that vacant space moaned in agony.

I'm so fucking sorry, Julian. So sorry.

My phone buzzing in my pocket pulled me out of my trance. Suddenly I noticed the carefree voices surrounding me as I came back to the here and now.

Next to me, Damian sat on a piece of whitewashed driftwood, laughing with Deak as they tossed back beers.

My phone buzzed again.

Then again.

Sighing, I dug it out.

Guess I already knew who it would be. For years, he'd given me space. Time to grow and figure out shit for myself. Seemed his patience was wearing thin.

Hesitantly, I thumbed into the waiting messages.

Know you're not a little kid anymore. Shit...I haven't seen you in three years. I probably wouldn't even recognize you. But I know you, Austin.

And I know you're out there beating yourself up, holding yourself responsible when the fault is mine. It's always been mine. Have you figured that out yet? Because I need you to.

This is important to me, Austin. Come home. Back to L.A. Where you belong.

But that's what my older brother could never understand.

It was my fault.

Baz hadn't snuffed out *his* last breath.

That unbearable weight came crashing down. The weight I'd so foolishly thought putting space between the guys, my brother, and me would somehow erase.

Like the distance could fill the chasm.

But I should have known that abyss was bottomless.

I wavered on what to say. Because I wanted to give a solid answer. To stop being a pussy and own up.

As usual, I took the coward's way out. I tapped out a reply.

Trying to figure stuff out. I am, Baz. I promise, I am.

Funny, because things seemed more complicated now than they'd ever been.

I went to slip my phone back in my pocket, when it buzzed again.

I figured it was my brother with a response.

But no.

My heart skidded.

Nerves pricked at my flesh.

Ash.

Sunder's bassist.

Edie's older brother.

Guilt tried to weigh me down.

Always did when I thought of him.

Knowing the secrets I'd kept.

The fact I was responsible for Edie taking off the way she had.

Lying through my damned teeth when he'd demanded information, the guy quick to the hunch that I'd been involved more than I'd let on.

Did he know she was here? Did he wonder and worry? Toss and turn at night, not knowing if she was okay?

Band's suffering, man. Your brother needs you. Think it's about time you return the favor, don't you?

Blinding guilt.

I sucked in a breath.

"Who's that?" Damian asked.

"No one," I said, quick to stuff the phone in my pocket. It was best for now not to go down that road with Ash. I wasn't sure how to deal with him right now.

Not with Edie here, invading every thought in my mind.

For a fleeting second Damian frowned, before he shrugged, dropped the issue, and gave in to the light mood drifting in the cool air.

"So how's it feel to be climbing that hill? Gonna be hitting the top pretty damned soon." Damian smirked, taunting Deak from across the fire.

Rubbing it in just a little bit deeper.

Like the dude turning twenty-seven today made him old.

"Aye, mate," Deak said with the thick Australian accent he never could shake, which apparently was nothing less than bait. Anywhere we went, the second he opened his mouth, women flocked.

The brunette hanging on his side who he'd met five minutes before seemed proof enough.

He shoved the shaggy locks of his sandy-blond hair he wore to his shoulders behind his ears. The guy was surfer through and through, his body lean from the time spent in the waves, skin dark from the sun. He wore a short-sleeved button-up shirt, board shorts, and bare feet.

Deak smirked at Damian from over the top of his beer. "You should know better than that by now. This boy here just gets better 'n' better and the ladies love him more and more. Some things just get better with age."

I sat on another large piece of driftwood that had been hauled up to this section of the secluded beach that few houses overlooked, including Deak's. The brunette's friend had taken a spot next to me.

She slanted me a timid smile.

A month ago, I'd have been game.

But not now.

Not with Edie.

Even if I couldn't have her, that devotion ran deep.

I was getting ready to figure out a way to blow the girl off when I froze.

Tension surged.

Swift and thick and suffocating.

Like a direct kick to the gut.

A gust of wind whipped through.

Stoking the flames. Heat pulsed. Fire against my skin.

I pulled in a deep breath in an attempt to steady myself.

Seeking control when she'd always made me want to lose it.

Slowly, I turned to look over my shoulder, already knowing who I'd find.

"Ah…you made it, mate." Deak's voice barely penetrated in my periphery.

"Yeah, man. You should've known I wouldn't miss it."

Deak's friend Clay kicked up sand, quick to make his way toward us, grinning like a fool who had no idea he was ushering in my complete and utter demise.

He hooked his thumb to the side. "Figured I'd grab some more friends to come out and play. It is your birthday, after all."

Striding along right beside Clay was the girl I'd learned was Blaire.

The asshole's sister.

And the *asshole* was trailing right behind the two of them.

But it was the one at his side who locked the breath in my too-tight lungs.

All that hair flew around her like white flames.

Light. Light. Light.

Did she know?

Did she have the first clue what she did to me?

How she rushed in like swelling waves. Sucking me under. Dragging me to the darkest depths that were lit up with her presence.

Like rays of sunlight that pierced the abyss.

Where she comforted and crucified.

The girl was my own perfect torment.

Shadows danced and played across her face that was both slender and soft. High, defined cheekbones tapered down, giving way to her sweet, pouty mouth.

That sweet, sweet mouth I wanted nothing more than to devour.

My dick twitched and my hands fisted.

Every rational part of me flailed around to find some sort of restraint when every other part just wanted to go for her.

To drive my hands into lush, soft hair.

Kiss her mad.

Take back what always should have been mine.

Fuck. She made me insane. Crazy with lust and delirious with devotion.

So damned beautiful.

But what cut me all up inside was the bottled terror she tried to contain in her expression.

Like maybe she'd forced herself to come along to celebrate Deak's birthday, doing her best to convince herself she had nothing and everything to prove.

A million different emotions glinted in her eyes. Old, old wounds ripped open and raw, and soft, soft affection she'd give anything not to feel.

Like shards of broken glass lighting up in the flames of the fire.

Diamonds.

Transparent.

Through them? I swore I could see directly into her soul.

It seemed that hungry gaze had no place else to settle because she couldn't look away.

Just like me.

Because God. This girl was the only thing I could see.

Jed set his hand on the small of her back.

Possessively.

Aggression curled through my body. It took about all I had to coerce myself to sit still. To not fly to my feet and stalk across the space so I could rip it from her body. All those irrational, foolish places were demanding to be heard.

Maybe it was wrong. But I couldn't help the flicker of satisfaction I felt in the fact she cringed away.

It was barely noticeable.

But believe me.

I fucking noticed.

I was betting Jed noticed, too.

Jealousy was an ugly, nasty beast.

And that monster was rising up, gripping my insides. Spurring me forward.

My knee bounced like a motherfucker as they approached. Jed shook Deak's hand and wished him a happy birthday.

Clay and Blaire both did the same.

Then Edie stepped forward and embraced Deak, her voice both the worst and the best thing I'd ever heard. It was a soft melody that touched me in all the places that it both soothed and hurt for her to touch. That voice so kind. Gentle and good.

It prodded and nudged at all the places that'd gone dim when she'd walked out of my life.

The places only she had lit.

It was kind of sick how bad I wanted that voice whispering in my ear.

How bad I wanted it screaming my name.

Damian nudged me, gave me a knowing eye, a silent warning as he passed me a fresh beer.

Keep your cool.

I twisted the cap and took a deep pull. Cold liquid sloshed down my throat and pooled in my gut, a clashing contradiction to the fire burning inside.

Just as hot as the fire that licked and danced and sparked in front of us.

Edie sat down as far away as she could. Directly on the opposite side of the roaring flames.

Did she really think she could hide?

I studied her through them. The way they glowed and flickered against her snowy flesh.

Hell.

That's exactly where I had to be.

Not being able to touch her.

The forced silence.

Knowing she hated me and had every right to.

Knowing she wanted me just the same.

It was fucking excruciating.

As if she were my long lost friend, Blaire plopped down beside me, on the opposite side of the blonde chick who I'd never gotten around to catching her name.

Blaire's smile flashed bright. Her brown eyes danced as she looked me up and down.

No doubt, she had gotten some kind of dish on Edie's and my past and was ready to dig in.

I would have thought she'd hate me for it, too, especially considering she was Jed's sister.

"So you must be the infamous Austin Stone."

Leaning my forearms on my knees, I clasped my hands and dipped my head, inclining it her direction. "Infamous, huh?"

"I might have heard a few stories about you."

"All bad, I presume."

Her head cocked in question. Like she was seeking an answer in my expression. "I'm not so sure about that."

Conspiratorially, she leaned in with a whisper. "I have to say, it's very nice to meet you. Any friend of Deak's is a friend of mine. He's kinda great, right?"

Confusion left me on a shot of puzzled laughter. This girl was kind of crazy. Because she was clearly not really talking about Deak, and I was honestly kind of surprised she didn't give me a wayward wink.

I shook my head, doing my best to play along. "Our boy here is pretty nice to have around. You know…offering up his house that overlooks the ocean and all."

"Only in Santa Cruz," she said. "You must be happy you came." Sarcasm widened her eyes. "It's just full of all kinds of great surprises, right?"

I chuckled. "Tons of surprises. Really unexpected, amazing surprises."

My attention darted to Edie, then right back to her friend, letting free a telling smile.

Making my intentions clear.

I had every intention of taking back my girl.

I sucked in a breath when that intensity suddenly surged.

The feeling welled firm.

Alive.

It ricocheted between us. A no holds barred ping pong match.

Volleying that need back and forth.

Determined to fight it.

Desperate to cave to it.

Drawn and repelled.

And I was totally giving into the *drawn* side.

Canting my head, my attention latched right back onto Edie.

Just as quick as I'd looked, she dropped her potent gaze, quickly lumbered onto unsteady feet. Like she was weighed down.

Her words were a mumble under her breath, uttered to Deak like they were some kind of dark, dirty secret.

"I need to use the restroom."

Running.

Because that's what my girl did.

Deak pointed toward our house tucked on top of the hill where it was situated right behind me. "It's all yours, gorgeous. Back door is unlocked. Make yourself at home," he told her.

Home.

The word struck me.

That's precisely the way she'd felt.

Like home.

Looking up at her from where he sat, Jed touched her forearm. "Do you want me to come with you?"

She shook her head. Almost emphatic. "No, I'm fine. I'll be right back."

She wove around the fire. I knew with every single step she took she was battling not to meet my gaze.

I felt it.

The turmoil.

The push and the pull.

Drawn and repelled.

Both of us so damned scared of what we might fall into.

It'd always been this way.

I couldn't find it in myself to care how blatantly obvious it was to everyone that I was staring as she went. Didn't even try to hide the way I turned to look behind me, eyes intent on that sweet body that slugged through the sand, while every inch of mine hardened and coiled with need. My muscles flexed and twitched, like they already knew we were giving into what I was craving and were urging me along, my gaze hungry as it trailed her hitting the worn path that led to the back of the house.

Fuck.

I wanted to touch.

To taste every inch. To explore every curve. To dip into the ecstasy I knew without a shadow of a doubt lurked beneath distrust and fear.

She wore dark skinny jeans that came to her ankles, accentuating long, defined legs, hugging the flare of her hips and ass, a flowy white shirt that was meant to be modest yet still clung to those perfect round tits.

There'd always been something about her that seemed both stoically elegant and impenetrably vulnerable.

A fragile fortress.

But it was greater now.

Age had shaved off some of her vulnerability.

Exposing an underlying strength invisible before.

Like she couldn't help herself, she looked back.

Back at me.

Into me.

It felt like with just that look she could reach in and touch all the places that had only ever belonged to her.

Hers.

I'd been hers for so fucking long.

Did she get it yet? Did she know she was always going to belong to me?

And I was damned sure going to use everything in my power to make her remember it.

Rapidly she blinked, the girl doing her best to block me out. She fumbled over an exposed root. Shocked out of her trance, she quickly jerked away and moved faster. She fled up the hill.

She slid open the patio door, her body just a silhouette in the distance before it shut behind her.

Chatter rose up around the bonfire. Voices lifted and totally at ease. Celebrating Deak's day.

An upheaval rose around me. Strong and fierce and unrelenting.

A building storm.

Minutes moved like a punishment.

Jed met my eye. His chin lifted. Challenging. Brimming with a warning.

Fuck it.

I was on my feet.

Going after what I never should have let go in the first place.

I moved through the darkness.

Called toward the light.

One target on my mind.

One outcome in my heart.

I had no idea if Jed would follow me or not.

If he was wise?

He would.

Or maybe he'd already accepted this inevitability.

I hiked up the worn path and stepped into the quiet of the house. A bright light glowed in the kitchen, making the rest of the house appear dark and dim. Turning to the right, I edged down the dusky hall that led to the bedrooms, passed by mine that sat on the right as I headed for my destination.

On the left side was the guest bathroom. The door was closed. A thin wedge of light bled out from the bottom.

My heart beat out of control. A million miles ahead. Desperate for a chance to make it right.

To take away the pain I'd so carelessly inflicted.

To go back to the way it'd been.

When it'd been so easy yet so fucking complicated.

Both of us had been broken.

Pieces scattered.

But it was our shaky bond that had somehow held those pieces together.

I paced the hall outside the door.

Waiting.

Metal screeched as the lock turned.

That was right about the time my heart caught in my throat.

The memory of just how fucking hung-up I'd been on this girl.

A love-sick kid with butterflies in his stomach and hope in his heart for the first time in his life since the day he'd destroyed it.

Seventeen.

By then, I'd already racked up a whole lifetime of mistakes. All the while being painfully aware I still had the rest of my life to live through the guilt of them.

Yet somehow…somehow Edie had managed to ease them.

Just the same way as she'd let me ease hers.

The door slowly opened. A yelp flew from her when she found me there in the shadows. She reared back in surprise. Just as quick, she tried to duck out and away.

Escape.

Too scared to face what was right in front of us.

"Edie, wait." My voice was raw. Low and desperate.

She choked on a strangled sound, hesitating for a flash, before she surged forward.

I reached out and grabbed her by the wrist.

With just that touch, fire spread up my arm, jolting me all the way through.

God damn.

I'd almost forgotten. Had almost forgotten she had the power to make me feel this way. Like when we connected, those dead parts of my spirit sparked to life.

She gasped and fumbled to a stop. Her body was still turned the opposite direction, her head angled toward the ground. Her back lifted and expanded with each heaved breath.

No question, she wasn't immune.

"Wait," I said again, this time softer.

I gave a gentle squeeze to her wrist.

Wait.

I could feel her surrender. Her tense body gave, and relief

came bounding in when she warily turned to look at me. As she did, our hands slipped together for the briefest second, that connection lost when she took a staggered step back.

She stood there.

So clearly confused.

Torn.

A hundred different emotions played out on her unforgettable face like the raging wind.

Whipping and lashing and inciting.

I wanted to reach out and calm it.

"Wait," I whispered again. I ducked down to bring us level. Coming closer. Because there wasn't anything on earth that could keep me away.

Her eyes pinched closed, her voice a rasp. "Don't."

"Don't what?" I asked, edging even closer, backing her toward the wall. Leaning in, I let myself get lost in the suggestion of sun and warmth. In orange and light and something so fucking sweet and intoxicating I wanted to bury my nose in her hair.

In her skin.

To fall in and disappear.

Forever.

Tears pooled in her eyes. She blinked them open. "Don't do this."

"I don't know what you're talking about." The words came out a rough murmur.

She managed a scoff and a slight shake of her head. "Yes, you do. You've always known the way you affect me. The control you have. Don't play games with me, Austin."

"Seems to me, that's the only thing we've ever done. You're the one who ran, Edie, and you took what was left of my heart with you when you did."

"Don't say that."

Don't. Don't. Don't.

That had been like our fucking mantra.

Don't get too close.

Don't say it out loud.

Don't touch.

"You did this." Her whispered accusation hung between us, a violent shot to the simmering air.

Guilt climbed my throat, tongue going dry. "You didn't stay long enough to let me say I was sorry."

She turned her face away, chin trembling, before she seemed to gather strength, the courage to look back at me. "You know it wouldn't have mattered anyway. I *had* to go. You knew I couldn't stay. *Not when he knew.*"

Anger pulsed, and I gritted my teeth, forcing down my rage for that bastard.

Focused on what mattered and not what I couldn't control. *Her.*

I edged closer and she inched back. She plastered herself up against the wall like she were hoping it might open up and swallow her whole.

My fingertips grazed her cheek, so soft, my body a wisp from hers. Sweet tension throbbed in the air, so dense I swore it slowed our movements. "I never wanted to hurt you."

She caught her bottom lip between her teeth. A disorder of emotions spun around us. "But you did." Pain echoed through her watery confession. "You hurt me so much."

"Edie."

Regret.

Longing.

Sorrow.

They twisted through her name like the whirlwind she incited.

She shook her head. "Why are you here, Austin? In my town. Have you been looking for me?" Dismay laced the last.

I almost wished I could say yes.

Pretty damned sure that would be the correct answer.

God knew my heart had been.

I cleared my throat. "No, Edie. I left L.A. three years ago. I've been traveling up and down the coast since."

Guarded, her gaze wandered, taking me in. Searching. It took me only a second to realize what she was searching for.

Like she was doing her best to see beneath my skin to what was polluting my veins. To discover my demons.

It wasn't a subject I liked returning to.

But it was a part of me.

Who I was.

A piece I was always going to battle.

The words were tight. "I've been clean for more than three years, Edie."

Emotion raced across her features. Quick surprise and sweeping relief.

And then I saw it. Glimpsed the flickers of young love this gorgeous girl had once felt for me.

Her tongue darted out and swiped along her plush bottom lip.

Fuck.

I wanted to kiss her.

"I worried about you so much." Her words were wispy and hushed. Like the admission was her greatest secret. Her biggest pitfall.

Need clawed at my senses. I was fighting desperately not to reach out and take her. Struggling not to give in and tug her body against mine.

To wrap her up and take her whole.

She released a throaty sigh, breath basking me in warmth.

In unrelenting light.

My voice came gruff, and I got closer, my mouth a breath from hers. "I worried about you, too. Too much. Every day. Every night. I missed you so fucking bad it nearly killed me, wondering what happened to you. Where you went. If you were okay."

Sorrow creased the corners of her eyes.

We swam in it. Black, dangerous waters lapped at our chins. Threatening to pull us under. Her light battled against my dark. That dark, dark storm that was gaining speed.

She seemed to shake herself from its grips, both relieved and pained to redirect our conversation. Her voice took on a new edge of desperation. "Do you...do you talk to my brother?"

On a heavy sigh, I gave a reluctant nod.

Shit. Did she think this topic would be any easier?

"Yeah."

"How is he?"

"I think he's good, Edie. But honestly? I don't really know. Told you I left home three years ago. Only keep up through texts and letters, mostly with my brother. But I do know so much has changed. Things with the band have gotten...crazy big."

Her nod was sad. "He has to hate me."

My brow pinched, words nothing less than a growl. "He doesn't hate you, Edie. How can you say that?"

A bitter sound seeped from that pretty mouth, the sound such a contradiction to the softness of her face. "How could he not? I just...left."

This time I did grab her, both hands on her face, forcing her to look at me.

Her heat was nothing less than a shock directly to my heart.

Energy and light.

I wheezed.

Her expression froze in surprise.

I forced the words through gritted teeth. "No one hated you, Edie. Sure. He was fuckin' terrified when you took off, not knowing what went down."

"Did you—"

"Tell him?" I shook my head, exasperated. Trying not to be offended. It wasn't like I didn't deserve her distrust. "Of course I didn't tell him, Edie. Pretended like I didn't know a thing when he demanded answers. Clearly he knew something bad happened for you to run like that, but he didn't blame you."

Maybe Ash didn't know it, but it was me who was to blame.

Her mom, too, for acting like she understood when she didn't have a fucking clue.

But the real blame?

That trophy went to Paul.

Motherfucking bastard.

Anger flashed.

Should've just ended him.

Sacrificed it all to wipe that stain from Edie.

To finally cleanse her of the lingering fear.

Now the only thing I could do was hope the asshole was still rotting in prison like the scum he was.

Her mouth quivered at the corner. "I hate that I left him with so many questions. I can't even imagine what he thinks."

She laughed, but it was in her own disbelief. "I wrote him one letter. Gave him a bunch of flimsy excuses for leaving without a trace, told him I was out finding *myself*."

"Did you, Edie? Find yourself?"

She sucked in a breath, mouth parted as she stared at me through the haze, that sweet, good honesty seeping free. "I just got more lost."

This. Girl.

I wanted to crawl inside her safety. Fill her up with mine.

Silence stretched between us, the stillness riddled with everything left unsaid.

With everything left undone.

Energy lifted and swelled. Trembled through the chaotic air. Tugging and pulling and pushing at us from all sides.

Consuming.

That connection I'd only ever felt with her.

Fear snaked across her features. I was sure it was then she realized nothing had changed.

We were still bound.

Tied in an inexplicable way.

"You ran." It was a gruff murmur, my fingertips moving to flutter along the sharp angle of her jaw.

Because God. I just needed to touch.

Her brow pulled with uncertainty, words soft and sad. "It sounds to me like you've been running, too."

"Yeah. I've been running." I squeezed her a little harder. "And I don't believe for a minute it's a coincidence I found you, either."

She winced. "You know it's too late for us."

I closed in. Refusing to give up. Edged up against my girl until she was caged, her sweet, sweet body plastered to the wall while I was dying to plaster myself against her.

To draw a full breath into my water-logged lungs. A full breath I hadn't had since she'd disappeared from my life.

A breath full of something good. Something pure.

And this time I'd do my damned best not to dirty it.

Pressing both hands above her head, I fenced her in. Just needing to know if I had a fight worth fighting for. Because I wasn't about to harm this girl any more than I already had. Wouldn't ruin what she'd found if what she'd found had put a smile on her face and ease in her heart.

"You love him?"

Confusion lined her face, and she squinted up at me.

I jerked my head in the direction of the door.

My meaning dawned on her expression. The shake of her head was quick.

"Jed? We're just friends," she said.

"Doesn't look that way to me."

So maybe it came across sounding all pissy and surly.

Couldn't help it. Possessiveness expanded against my ribs, making them feel like they might bust open wide. Pressing with the crazy need to claim her.

"You don't have the right to demand answers from me, Austin."

The hall felt so damned small. Like the walls and ceiling were closing in.

And Edie and I?

We were just getting closer and closer and closer.

No matter how damned hard she tried to push me away.

It was acute.

Something fierce and alive.

Something that compelled and urged and impelled.

"You're right, Edie. I fucking don't. But I need to know…need to know what he means to you."

Hesitation slowed her, before she averted her telling gaze.

"We're friends, Austin. Nothing more."

Urges slammed my senses. An assault of frantic darts that pierced me everywhere, each pumping me full of need and overwhelming desire.

My mouth watered. My tongue darted out to swipe against my bottom lip.

I wanted to kiss her.

Claim her.

But somehow I understood now was not the time to push. Those boundaries had never been higher, the walls she hid behind built with the bricks of my betrayal.

Could I ever be good enough?

Brave enough?

Wise enough to stand for this girl?

I wanted to be. I wanted to be so damned badly I could taste it.

I wanted nothing more than to be the man I'd walked out of my brother's house to become.

I'd told him someday I wanted a girl to look at me the way Shea looked at him.

But I hadn't been talking about just any girl.

I'd been talking about *this* girl.

Could I be that man?

A spiral of doubt wound through me, and a thick knot of uncertainty grew at the base of my throat.

The truth of it was, I didn't know.

Swallowing hard, I came to the decision.

To settle.

Just like I'd always done before.

Just like I'd always do.

Because any part of Edie Evans was better than none.

"I could use a friend," I said.

Both of us knew that wasn't close to what I really meant.

Not close to what either of us wanted.

But Edie and I were old pros at taking what we could get.

Crinkles dented her brow, her voice rough. "It looks to me like you have plenty of them. The blonde hanging all over you down by the fire was especially cute."

Jealousy.

It was there.

Blatant and bold.

And I fucking liked it, fed off it, and there wasn't anything in the world I could do to stop myself. My finger was suddenly twirling through a lock of soft waves that framed her stunning face, those silky threads inciting a war of lust and greed and an age-old devotion inside of me.

"I always did like blondes," I murmured low.

"Austin..." she warned.

She didn't need to say it.

I already heard.

Don't.

"Friends," I reiterated, forcing myself to keep it cool. To give her time when I wanted to demand she give me all of hers.

Blinking, she swallowed hard. "How do you always manage to do this to me?"

"Do what?"

"Make me feel like I'm where I'm supposed to be."

"Because you are."

Her eyes darted down the hall, like she didn't trust herself to be standing there with me.

My mouth pressed against the top of her head, and I fucking begged as I breathed the words into her hair. "Don't run, Edie. You've always been my best friend. Time and distance hasn't changed that. Nothing ever will."

Her reluctance swirled between us, her hesitation palpable, her breaths a pant. Filling up the air and space and my heart. She pressed her mouth to it, to the thunder and the roar ricocheting in my chest. Her words were a mumble of hope and dread. "How could you ever expect me to trust you again?"

I enclosed her in my arms. Rocking her slow. Comforting her.

It felt so natural.

So goddamned right.

Like holding her was what I'd been created to do. "I don't, Edie. I don't. But I'm asking you to try."

"I don't know if anything's changed, Austin. If I'm any different than that girl in the dark room."

She said it like a pleading warning.

But that girl in the room was the one I'd fallen in love with.

"I *know* you, Edie. Think I've figured that out by now. You don't scare me."

That was an outright lie.

This girl terrified me.

The things she made me want.

Who she made me want to be.

The fear of losing it all again if I fucked it up the way I always did.

We stayed like that for the longest time. Swaying soft and slow.

Took about all I had not to protest when she finally untangled herself from my hold. "I need to get back outside."

For now, I knew I had to let her go. "Okay."

Slowly, she moved down the hall. Fingertips just grazed the wall as she passed, as if they kept her on her wavering feet.

"Edie," I called.

She paused at the end, shifted to look at me with that gaze from over her shoulder.

"I'll wait. I've been waiting for you forever," I told her.

Aqua eyes stared back at me. The depth of them was staggering.

Swimming in sadness.

Brimming in hope.

She smiled. Slow and cautious. Then she turned and slipped out the door.

Sucking in a shaky breath, I lifted my face to the low ceiling, like maybe in the rutted, pitted surface I could find the cool that remained just out of reach. Grappling for the patience that felt fleeting and fake.

But I'd told her the truth.

I'd wait.

For however long it took.

I headed back down the hall toward the kitchen, dug into the fridge, and pulled out a beer. I wasn't sure I could handle any more of the cozy little party taking place on the beach.

Wasn't sure I could keep my head from spinning or my heart from hammering with the possibilities I couldn't help but hope for.

I spun back around and sucked in a surprised breath, caught off guard by the shadow of a lone figure standing in the middle of the darkened living room. The air gushed out when I realized it was Deak, staring back.

I raked a flustered hand through my hair. "Shit. Dude. You scared the hell out of me."

"Yeah? Better me than Jed."

I both scoffed and sighed. "What's that supposed to mean?"

"You know exactly what that's supposed to mean. You're new around here, and Jed's been around for a long, long time. He's good people, and from what I've gathered, she's a real good girl. Sweet. Neither of them need someone like you swooping in here and mucking up their lives. Seen you in action, mate. She deserves better than that."

"We're just friends, man."

Motherfucking lie.

But what the hell else was I going to say? That I'd already grilled Edie and she promised me there was nothing going on there?

Snorting, he lifted a knowing brow. "I might be getting old, but I'm far from blind."

I pushed out a breath, glanced at the floor, gathering up the courage to look back at him. "There's a lot of history there you don't know about, Deak. And you're right. She's a good girl. And I have no intention of hurting her."

Not ever again.

But what I did intend was to win her back.

Mine.

seven

AUSTIN
AGE SEVENTEEN

"Are you crazy? We're going to get caught." But her smile proclaimed this was the only place she wanted me to be. I tiptoed the rest of the way into her room, quietly latched the door shut behind me.

A rush of something good propelled me forward as I climbed into her bed.

I breathed out in relief when she set those tiny hands on me.

Because this girl…she ushered in the good. Something that felt so right.

Didn't matter that I'd been sneaking in here for the better part of the last three weeks, both of us doing our best during the day to play it cool, to pretend like *this* wasn't transpiring night after night.

It wasn't as if anything salacious was going down between us, anyway, but I doubted Ash would take all too kindly to my sleeping in her bed.

She nestled her head on my shoulder, her sigh so easy when she fisted a hand in my shirt. "Sing to me."

A self-conscious smile wobbled on my mouth, my words lost in the strands of her hair. "What do you want me to sing?"

"Something soft and sweet."

Just like her.

I pressed a kiss to her temple, her heart going thud, thud, thud where it was flush against my chest. "I don't know anything sweet."

Chaotic, heavy beats were what I knew. *Sunder's* sound and vibe were so much a part of my soul, the songs running through my veins like they were essential to sustaining this half-life.

In the shadows, she peeked up at me, trust shining back. "I think you are all things sweet, Austin Stone."

This time it was affection running through my veins. Something foreign and right. A missing link.

Pushing out a sigh, I wrapped my arm around her head, pulling her closer, this girl who somehow managed to make me feel whole when I was so goddamned broken.

I cleared my throat. Began to sing *Broken by Lifehouse*. Softly. My voice was a mere scrape from the back of my throat. The lyrics hit me hard as I held this girl in my arms. Wishing she could truly belong there.

As quiet as they were, the words seemed to impale the air. The meaning of them was dense. Intense and absolute.

I'm falling apart, I'm barely breathing
With a broken heart that's still beating

The words were so true for both of us.

And it struck me as I sang the song to bring her comfort while her touch brought the same to me.

The two of us were barely hanging on.

And in her name…in her name…I'd found meaning.

I trailed off as the song came to an end, my throat nearly closing up with the emotion suddenly locked there.

Edie clung to me, her face buried in the material of my tee, before she inched back and gazed at me as if she were the one who was looking at the light. Moisture swam in her eyes. "You have the most beautiful voice."

Everything went tight, those stupid hopes igniting in her belief. "No."

Wasn't close to being as talented as my brother. As the rest of the guys.

Wasn't even worthy to be in their space.

I fuck it all up. Ruin it all.

Slightly, she shook her head, disagreement and exasperation and adoration so damned clear. "Don't you see it, Austin? How amazing you are? How talented? Do you have any idea what your voice does to me?"

Somehow I managed to get her closer. God, it made me feel insane that I both wanted to tug my damned hoodie over my head so I could curl up and hide and lie back so this girl could completely strip me bare.

"When you're here it doesn't hurt so bad," she whispered. Soft, soft fingers fluttered up the column of my neck and brushed across my lips.

I suppressed a groan, my voice going rough as the two of us dug deeper into the other than we'd ever gone. As if every single layer separating us was slowly being exposed. "What doesn't hurt so bad?"

Would she finally tell me? Trust me enough to fully let me in?

Reservation and fear held her tongue. I could feel it right there, lodged at the base of her throat, begging to be expelled.

"Everything," she whispered into the hush of the room. "I…I don't feel so alone. And the dreams, they don't come, knowing you'll be coming soon."

I cleared my throat, the rasp of words raw. "Mine either."

Maybe that was the scariest part. The fact she filled up all those vacant, hollow places within me. Soothing them with her touch. When she was near, the nagging need to fill up my veins, to distort the pain, to cover the loss, to clot out his voice—it was muted.

Subdued.

Like she was doing all the covering herself.

"What do you dream of?" Her question was almost guarded with the plea.

Those empty places throbbed. "Him. About his laugh." I blinked toward the ceiling, visions so clear. "Mostly his eyes. Every night, it's like he's looking back at me."

Her smile was soft. Filled with understanding when she propped herself up on an elbow, her gaze intent. She touched my face. "Maybe he is...looking back at you. Would that be such a bad thing?"

Sadness tugged at my mouth, the hatred I felt locked up tight, condemned to the well of my toiling spirit. Because she didn't know. Had no clue it was my fault. "Feels like it is...when I wake up and realize it's not real. That he's really gone."

Sympathy pinched her brow. "Were you there?"

A phantom of a memory slithered through me, the feel of his body twitching in my hands. "Yeah. I was there."

She buried her face in my neck. "I'm so sorry."

After a few moments, she pulled back to look at me, aqua eyes sincere and so damned sweet.

Diamonds.

Light. Light. Light.

This girl who somehow managed to pull me from the overwhelming waves that held me under.

The urge struck me with the force of a two-ton truck.

Crashing as it careened.

I wanted her.

I wanted to kiss her and touch her.

Bury myself inside her.

Lose myself in her body and her heart and her mind.

Hold her.

Love her.

That crazy energy blistered, the one that stirred through every time this girl stepped in the room.

But tonight it'd twisted into something different.

Something more.

Fuck. I wanted more.

My mouth watered and my hand was on her face. Her lips parted, and I was inching forward.

Those eyes widened in fear.

She turned her face.

Breaking the connection.

Rejection slammed me. Too hard. So hard it nearly blew me back two years. Back when I'd been spiraling.

Down to darkest depths.

Veins full of poison.

I clenched my jaw, needing to escape. But she was grabbing my hand that'd been on her face, pushing it back to her heated skin, holding it tight. She whispered, "Don't leave me, don't leave me," again and again.

Moisture glistened in her eyes, shimmery pools of sea, her expression so fucking raw. Real and honest. "I just…can't do this, Austin. Not again. It hurts too much. But if I could, it'd be you. I promise, it'd be you."

eight

EDIE

I hiked the sweet little girl up onto the short wall that divided the beach and the road, giving her a soft smile as I helped tame her wild mane of dark brown hair. Gathering it at one side, I twisted the three big sections I'd made into a fat braid.

A breeze rushed around us, ushered in by the waves, the sun breaching the cool air to kiss our skin.

I tapped her nose. "There you go, sunshine. All finished."

She lifted her face up at me and offered me a grin so wide it touched me somewhere deep. In that achy place I tried so desperately to pretend didn't exist. Two of her adult teeth were already working their way in and two baby ones were missing from the bottom. "Do I look so pretty? My daddy told me I'm the prettiest girl in the whole wide world."

A roll of affectionate laughter rippled from me, and I picked her up from under her arms, steadied her on the ground. "You certainly are."

"Billy doesn't say so. He said I'm gross."

"Who's Billy?" I asked.

"From school. Daddy says Billy's a bully. Bully Billy. That's what I call him. He's so, so mean all the time. Always cheating and pullin' hair."

With a frown, I took her hand and began to wander down the lane toward the crosswalk. "Well, that doesn't sound very nice."

She skipped along at my side. "Nope. Not nice. But Ms. Montez says we hav'ta be nice, so I'm always nice even when he's not."

"That's good. You just let me know if he bothers you too much, okay?"

I knew well enough there was a fine line between teasing and abuse.

"Yep...but I hav'ta tell my daddy first. He promised he'd pay *a little visit* to my class if Billy keeps buggin' me. And I really like when my daddy visits my class!"

I stifled a chuckle.

I bet he would.

Heidi belonged to Kane, the head surf instructor down at the shop. Her mom had disappeared with nothing more than a note scrawled on a piece of scrap paper left under a heart magnet on the fridge, saying she couldn't handle being a mom for a second more. It had been two weeks before Heidi had turned two.

It'd left Kane a single dad with a huge chip on his shoulder and an intense love of a little girl the guy didn't always know how to handle.

Old grief spun through my spirit.

It was something I just couldn't understand.

Couldn't fathom or comprehend.

The thought of willingly leaving this precious girl behind.

Maybe that's what bonded Heidi and me so tightly.

From the moment I started working at the shop, anytime she was there, she'd constantly follow me around, chatting nonstop as she scurried around at my heels and tugged at my shirt, desperate for a woman's attention.

There was something about her guileless smile that filled

the boundless void inside me. At the same time, it expanded and throbbed within the confines of the hollow cavern carved out at the center of me. The child was six, going on seven, full of life and excitement and innocent hope.

It hadn't taken Kane all that much to convince me to keep her Saturday afternoons. He had several classes to teach, and Blaire worked the store on Saturdays so I could have a day off.

Funny, since they were typically spent like this.

"So what do you want to do today?" I asked as we waited for the crosswalk light to change.

Heidi danced on her toes. "I want to go to the park and to the restaurant that has those funny fries with the faces and I want to get ice cream. Oh, and I wanna go to the store because my daddy gave me ten dollars. Let's go there first!"

Um, wow.

She was a tiny whirlwind.

But of course I grinned, because I loved every second of it.

After the chaos that had ripped into my safe haven, leveling all the walls, I needed a day like this.

A distraction.

A *purpose*.

"All right, then. We'll see what we can fit in before your daddy gets off work."

Hand in hand, we strolled down the street lined with palm trees interspersed with bushy shade trees, the tourist shops and quaint restaurants painted a rainbow of colors, big plate-glass windows framed in white.

That same calming breeze rode in on the tide, chasing us close behind.

"How's this?" I paused in front of a small specialty toy store.

Heidi released my hand and moved forward, pressed her palms and forehead to the glass, peering inside.

Leaving her little girl mark.

A few fingerprints never hurt anyone.

She looked up at me with that grin, excitement blazing in her gaze. "Oh yes, oh yes! They have dolls, Edie! They have dolls!"

I smiled down at her, touched her chin. "Well, then, we'd better get inside."

I opened the door, and Heidi raced in ahead of me, bee-lining straight to the dolls spotlighted on an end cap.

I cringed. With just a glance, I knew there was no chance she could afford one.

"Edie…look! Look! This one looks just like me." Heidi jumped around at my side and yanked at my hand, pointing at a ridiculously expensive doll with her same hair and eye color that I would lay down bets any six-year-old girl would salivate over.

"Um…I'm sorry, sweetie, but you definitely don't have enough money for that."

And I would totally buy it for her.

Of course, if her dad wouldn't kill me because I did.

She pouted, but even that had something sweet about it. "Oh man. What do I have 'nough money for?"

Soft affection played through my heart. A feeling that was always shaded with sadness. I squeezed her hand. "Well, how about you save it and next time you'll have more money to spend?"

You know…nothing wrong with throwing in a few life lessons whenever you got the chance.

"But my daddy said it was for me to get a treat."

Okay then.

"Well…maybe you could get a pretty dress for the doll you already have?"

There we go.

A diversion.

Compromise.

She bounced on her cute little pink painted toes. "Then can we go get ice cream?"

"After lunch." I gave a small tug to the end of her braid. "Sound like a good plan?"

"Yes!"

That was easy enough.

We rounded the aisle in search of the doll accessories. The whole way I sent up a silent prayer they weren't as pricey as the dolls exhibited out front, because her dad would just have to get over me spoiling her a little bit, because I didn't have the heart to tell her no twice.

And I froze.

The world dropped out from underneath me.

I stumbled to a stop. It was instant. The way I was captivated by the beautiful boy who stood at the far end of the aisle. That ominous, threatening man who rocked my quickly crumbling foundation. As if his stance carried a shock wave of power that rippled along the floor, creating gaping, fissuring cracks.

It slammed into me.

Stealing my breath and my mind and my sanity.

My fingers twitched, itching to weave through that mess of brown hair that was all mussed on top of his head, his face in profile, the angle of his jaw so strong, shadowed by the beard he obviously hadn't the time to shave this morning. His tight gray tee exposed the vast canvas of ink that swirled and twisted down his arms. Ink I wanted nothing more than to explore.

A piece of this boy I didn't recognize.

A mystery.

A riddle.

I was staggered.

So torn.

I'll wait for you forever.

He was the only one I'd wished it was the truth.

Heidi tugged at my hand, her voice full of impatience. "Come on, Edie. We have to hurry or my daddy is going to get home and be all, all alone and then we won't have time to go to the park."

With her tinkling, sweet voice, Austin looked our way.

His own shock vivid, that grey gaze wild and unsettled when it locked on me.

I could feel it, the way his entire body tilted my direction.

Drawn.

He blinked, those earthy eyes so dark and deep.

Heidi hauled me forward. The little girl was completely oblivious to the way my axis had shifted. All direction altered and centered on one man.

The two of us magnets. Spinning. Churning. Attracting and repelling.

Austin moved, each step calculated. His own surprise that had been evident on his face faded away and those delicious lips tipped into an even more delicious smile.

Satisfaction and desire.

A shiver slicked down my spine.

Cold as ice and sharp as a dagger.

God, I had to get it together. Maintain *control*.

He raked a casual hand through his hair as he approached, head cocked to the side with a gleam in his eye.

I would accuse him of following me. Except tucked beneath one arm was a huge golden-brown teddy bear, and a little girl's fashion design set was wedged beside it.

Confusion swirled.

What in the world was he doing?

"Edie," he breathed. Warm eyes traced me as if seeing me was relief, head to toe and right back up again.

I fidgeted, my fingertips fluttering up to fiddle with the strand of hair that had freed itself from my own loose braid.

"Hi," I whispered.

After what had transpired two nights ago, I wasn't sure how to handle his presence. My weakness for him so clear.

Trust.

It was no secret I didn't often grant it.

But right then, who I didn't trust was myself.

He glanced down to the little girl grinning up from at my side. A curious frown pulled at his brow and a small smile worked itself onto his mouth.

"Who's this?" He slanted his attention to her.

She swayed at my side, tucking her head to the side as if she was suddenly struck with a rush of self-consciousness, clearly not immune to the charm that was this boy.

Poor girl.

I could hardly blame her.

"I'm Heidi."

He glanced at me for clarification.

"Heidi's dad...Kane...he works down at the surf shop. I help him out with her on Saturdays since school is out and the summer program is closed weekends."

The smile he gave was slow and cautious. Searching. As if this boy knew and he was silently asking me if this was okay.

If *I* was okay.

I wished with all of me that the place I harbored for him, the place I'd kept like a safe haven, didn't pulse with old affection.

I wished I didn't want to edge forward and bury my nose in his skin, breathe him in the way I used to and confess to him that sometimes it still hurt so bad I wanted to fall to my knees.

I wished most I didn't know he would chase some of it away when he pulled me into the harbor of his arms.

Instead, I forced a brittle smile and squeezed Heidi's hand.

Not exactly sure who I was trying to reassure.

He directed the full power of his presence on her and dropped to a knee. "Hey there, beautiful. It's nice to meet you. I'm Austin."

My insides quaked. The easygoing, confident side of this gorgeous, mysterious boy was completely unrecognizable. Here was a man who'd shed his shy, wary skin.

Heidi giggled and swayed some more, all coy and cute. "Nice to meet you, too," she said, peeking up at me as if seeking approval.

When I didn't pull her away, Heidi reached out and ran her little fingers through the stuffed bear's fur. "Who's that for?" she asked. "It's really big. Is it for someone's birthday? I like birthdays."

A soft smile danced on his full lips. Though something about it felt sad, hinting at sorrow. "This right here?"

Her nod was emphatic.

"This bear is for my niece. Her name's Kallie. You actually

remind me of her a little bit, back when she was your age. I haven't gotten to see her in a real long time, so I wanted to send her something to let her know I'm thinking about her."

Niece?

My brain tried to process the fact of what he was saying, and the question was slipping out, making itself known before I could stop it, the words raw. "You have a niece?"

My head shouted a thousand questions. How? When? Was it even possible?

Austin straightened. Discomfort slithered through him as he met the confusion I knew was so clearly written on my face, as if maybe he understood he was broaching a topic so incredibly difficult for me.

As if he knew how hard it was to stand here and face my past that I'd tried to run so far from, too weak to stand or stay. Now I stood in the dark, a stranger to my family and friends who had become nothing more than a distant, foggy dream.

Wistfully, he shook his head. "How much back home did you keep up with, Edie?"

My laughter was fragile. "You know I didn't."

After I'd left, I'd sent one pathetic, excuse of a letter to Ash. Purposefully leaving off a return address with the hopes it would sever the last connection to the past I could no longer cope with.

In effect, I'd cut off my brother.

My parents.

My home.

My Austin.

But I had to, because severing my connection with them meant I was snipping that last tie to *him*. Being in the same city had been something I could no longer entertain. Hatred fisted in my belly, and I pushed it down, aside, because the last thing I wanted was to give *him* more air time in my thoughts.

He'd already stolen so much.

Because of him I'd completely left behind those I loved.

I hadn't dared keep in touch. It'd hurt too much to look back and know I was no longer a part of their world that had grown to unfathomable heights.

The success of *Sunder* had exploded while I'd hid out in this safe, quiet, secluded town in Northern California.

It was easiest just to leave it all in the past and pretend as if I didn't miss it. *Them.* As if there wasn't this gaping hole in my soul reminding me of everything I'd lost.

Regret tweaked at just one side of Austin's mouth, carrying his own loss. Yet somehow it was still awed and filled with love. Just the longing in his expression was enough to weaken my knees and my resolve and the fortress I tried so desperately to keep erected around my heart.

God.

This shaky feeling took me over. I wanted to run and to stay. I wanted to hold on to the hurt and betrayal Austin had scored into my spirit and drop to my knees to offer him all the fragments that remained splintered inside.

They'd always belonged to him anyway.

He shook his head. "Baz is married."

"You're kidding me." It came out on a breath, and I tried so hard to play it off as casual. As if there weren't tears pricking at my eyes. Tried to stand there in front of the boy who knew me best and pretend it didn't matter that these people who'd been a huge part of my life had moved on and grown and changed.

While I'd stayed the same.

Stuck.

Stagnant.

Stale.

His potent gaze absorbed it all, and there was no missing his own sorrow or the way he did his best to play it off, too.

"Can you believe that? It was right before I left L.A. Met an ex-country star who already had a little girl."

Reverent disbelief seemed to subtly shake his head. "Swooped the two of them up faster than any of us could make sense of it. They have a little boy now, too. Connor. Getting ready to turn two."

My throat suddenly felt tight, the weight pressing down on

my chest almost too much to bear. I squeezed Heidi's hand and forced a bright smile. "That's wonderful. I'm so happy for him."

"Yeah. Me, too. Deserves it more than anyone I know."

My own eyes traced and learned, taking in the way his Adam's apple bobbed heavily against his thick throat.

"Haven't even met him yet," Austin admitted quietly.

I tried to keep my voice from trembling as I drifted in Austin's unease. Knowing I was prying. Diving into deep waters where I wasn't certain I could swim. "Why haven't you met him, Austin?"

He'd told me he'd been gone for three years. I guess I hadn't really calculated what that meant or what it might have cost.

His own demons flickered across his face, a mask of fury and shame, that bright, beautiful boy sinking into the depths of his misery I was certain had cast him out of that world, too.

Where Austin would forever drown.

This boy who'd allowed me to dip my toes into the frigid waters of his torment. Never allowing me all the way in.

His own secrets and shame so profound.

"Don't know, Edie. It's…hard."

My mouth curved, a wistful tug at the corner of my bottom lip. "I get it. You don't have to explain."

Time danced around us. Threatening to pull us into the past or thrust us into the future.

Because in the end, Austin and I had always been so much the same.

I shook myself off, blinked away the tears. "Tell me about everyone else."

Incredulous laughter rolled from him, and he widened his eyes, clearly getting ready to spill on the best kind of gossip, like maybe this topic was a reprieve. "So get this…Lyrik? Dude's married. Has a baby on the way."

My mouth dropped open. "No way."

Lyrik West was the biggest, baddest player I knew. With the exception of maybe my brother.

Austin nodded. "Yeah way. Can you believe that?"

"No. I really can't." I forced the most joking grin onto my mouth, pretending as if I was only playing along, as if he told me otherwise it wouldn't just about be the final straw that wrecked me. "Tell me Ash isn't married, too."

Grey eyes flashed. Knowing and kind and so onto me.

As if I could ever keep a secret from him.

"Nah...as far as I know, your brother is still tearing up the countryside, laying siege to every city he visits. Poor girls don't know what hit them. The boy just loves to spread the love around, doesn't he?"

Playfully, I pressed my hand over my heart. "Some things never change."

Those eyes washed over me. Soft, seductive, and sweet. God. He was going to be my ruin. "Yeah, you're right, Edie. Some things never change."

Heidi giggled, dragging me from the spell Austin Stone had me under. "I need to find a dress for my doll...remember?"

I squeezed her hand, my voice a raspy whisper. "Yeah, baby, I remember." I looked back to Austin. "So...we...ah...better go. We're going to find something fun for Heidi and then grab lunch and ice cream...maybe even hit the park if we have time, aren't we, Heidi?"

I struggled to inject some excitement into my tone.

"Yep, yep! Ice cream is my favorite, and chocolate is my favorite, favorite. I can have chocolate, right?"

"Of course you can," I whispered.

Austin's expression shifted. Waffling on what to say. I could see it, the way his jaw worked and he looked to the ground.

Tension grew thick. Filling up the space.

This magnetic boy blindfolding me with all his dark.

He took a slow step forward. "Go to dinner with me, Edie."

Apprehension slicked through my veins, and my tongue darted out to wet my dry lips. "That's a really bad idea."

Just a week ago, I was running from him like I'd seen a

phantom. A dark, dark obsession.

And here he was…pushing a step closer. Encroaching and enclosing.

And I was letting him.

Damn. Damn. Damn. How could he do this to me?

"And why's that?" he countered.

I almost scoffed.

I could give him a thousand reasons, but he already knew every single one of them.

"You know why, Austin. I'm not…"

Ready enough.

Strong enough.

Brave enough.

I want to trust you. I just don't know if I can.

Those eyes dimmed, and his voice deepened. "I just want to know you again. I miss you."

"I miss you, too." The words left me on a tremor.

God. Had I just admitted that aloud? But was I really that surprised, that this enigmatic man could pluck the truth from me without my permission?

"Come on, Edie. It's just dinner between friends."

Right.

Something sly worked its way into his expression, the confident side of this boy I didn't know, and he turned his regard to Heidi who was hopping from foot to foot at my side. "Heidi, tell Edie here that she has to go to dinner with me. Tell her she's going to break my heart if she turns me down. My fragile ego can't handle it."

Heidi looked up at me with wide, horrified eyes. "Don't break his heart, Edie. That's not very nice. We're always s'posed to be nice. Remember?"

I pressed my palm to my forehead, feeling the heat, this steady burn that lit up in my veins, tugging and tugging and tugging.

Pulling me toward the boy who had been my biggest downfall.

Austin slanted his gaze my way, all the heaviness from the

moment before gone. Vanished. In its place was an expression that was every kind of manipulative and the most dangerous combination of cocky and cute. "She's right, Edie. We're always supposed to be nice."

Why did he make me this way?

Giddy and hopeful and excited.

And completely, profoundly terrified.

The same conflict he'd always incited in me roared.

"I shouldn't."

He took another step forward, so close I breathed him in.

Something masculine.

Spicy and a little bit sweet.

Intoxicating.

I had the urge to bury my nose in his neck. Or maybe in the collar of his shirt.

Memories assaulted me.

The smell of fresh laundry stretched across his hard body.

Warmth.

Security.

A rush of dizziness spun through my head.

His rough voice covered me whole. "You most definitely should."

I shook my head again. But this time it was in surrender.

Austin knew it too.

He knelt down to Heidi's level and pushed his fist out her direction. "Score. We make a great team, little one."

She bumped him back, making a little exploding noise as he did the same. "Score!" she squealed.

Oh God.

What had I agreed to?

And why?

Austin straightened to his full towering height.

Dominating comfort.

"I'll pick you up at seven," he said.

"Austin."

It was a final plea.

One he totally ignored with the arrogant, self-assured smirk that lit on his face. "Seven."

He walked backward, the big bear tucked to his side, his grin so wide while my heart completely thundered out of control.

What was I doing? What was I doing?

This had to be one of the most reckless things I'd ever done.

This, and trusting him in the first place.

He gave Heidi a little salute, before he spun on his heel and began to walk away. He rounded the end of the aisle then paused just before he disappeared from sight. He leaned back to catch my gaze.

"Oh, and Edie?"

"Yeah?"

"Gonna make sure you don't regret this. Not again. Not this time."

I swallowed around the knot in my throat. I could only pray he was right.

nine

"Walk with me?" I asked.

Nervously she raked her teeth over her bottom lip, contemplating, before she peeked up at me and gave me a timid nod. "I'd like that."

We both turned, heading down the boardwalk from the restaurant where we'd shared dinner. We'd eaten in this strange, awkward comfort. Like we were giving time to catch up to the fact that we were here.

Together.

Our conversation had seemed both easy and guarded. Our laughter only ringing with the safe stories we told. Ones that weren't hard and didn't point out our failures or fears.

Now we walked in silence, both of us caught up in that strange intensity.

Neither of us quite sure where we stood.

No doubt, both of us were traversing uneven ground.

Didn't mean my entire body didn't itch with her gliding along at my side, her arm just brushing mine.

My fingers twitched.

Fuck it.

I reached out and took Edie's hand.

In surprise, she jumped, before she peeked up at me again then looked down to watch like she was a little bit in awe as I threaded her trembling fingers through mine.

Shivers rolled through her. Head to toe.

The breath I was holding left me on a gush of relief while my heart flipped with an erratic beat.

A goddamned stampede in my chest.

I had no idea what her reaction to me touching her would be. If she'd push me away. Or maybe run.

Because the girl had every right to tell me to go straight to hell. Right where I belonged.

Instead she seemed to contemplate, chewed at that lip before she gave in and nestled into my side.

God, she felt so damned good.

We strolled along the boardwalk like we were just another couple lost in the mix. Strands of twinkling lights were strung up around us. Tonight, the old worn wooden planks were packed with people, the night air perpetually cool as it rode in on the waves, the hint of a storm just making itself known in the distance.

Edie snuggled even closer and released a deep, deep breath. Like maybe she'd been holding it in forever. It swirled around me, filling up my senses with all that sweet and warmth.

Unable to resist, I released her hand and wound my arm around her shoulders. Pulled her tight against my body that was about five seconds from coming completely unhinged.

And Edie...Edie just curled into me, her opposite hand coming to rest on my abdomen.

"This feels so nice." Her confession was tentative. Maybe insecure.

I pressed my lips to the top of her head. "It feels like the best thing in the world."

"It feels crazy. Impossible," she whispered, almost as if to herself, like she couldn't believe she was here.

"Perfect," I said in return.

And then those arms were winding around my waist. Hugging me tight from the side. Clinging and holding and tugging at everything inside of me.

In silence, we wandered off the boardwalk, wound down and around, veering for the beach.

Like we were both completely in sync.

Drawn.

And I wished upon every damned star in the sky for a second chance.

For something I could do to truly make it right when I'd done her so fucking wrong.

To be good enough for this girl who was obviously created for me.

Inhaling, she lifted that stunning face to the sky I'd just been wishing on.

It took about all I had not to bury my face in the slender column of her delicious neck, to feel the beat and thrum of the pulse I knew raced underneath all that snowy flesh.

Desire belted me right in the gut, lust hitting me hard and fast.

I wanted her so damned bad.

And that was the problem.

I always had.

Wait.

It seemed patience hadn't always been my strong suit.

When we hit the beach, our feet sank into the soft sand. We both slipped off our shoes, carrying them as we trudged across the shore. Further and farther until we were alone in a secluded cove, darkness pressing down and the sky opening up where it went on forever.

Waves crashed where they toiled, an inciting calm, a crazy sense of solitude riding in on the breeze.

A tremor of *his* presence rolled over me.

The way it always did when I got this close.

Dangerous, murky waters calling me to the same depths where I'd condemned him.

Edie unwound herself from me, turned to look out over the sea, crossed her arms over her chest. Her loose-fitted, thin sweater draped around her tight little body just right, caressing every curve, one delicate shoulder exposed, and those long, slender legs were on display in the short frayed jean shorts she wore.

I sank onto the damp sand, toes dug in deep, arms wrapped around my knees as I watched my girl from behind.

"It's gorgeous out here," Edie said reverently, that striking face lifted toward the heavens.

In the distance, a flicker of lightning flashed with the building clouds, and a gust of wind blew through the basin, a misty fog gathering low.

"Sometimes I can't believe how peaceful it is out here. Makes you feel so damned small."

Peace and torment.

Peace and torment.

I fought the tightening of my chest.

She edged forward until her feet were consumed by the slow crawl of the tide.

Taking one step deeper, she turned to look at me from over her shoulder. "Do you want to wade with me?"

She'd laced caution into the question, her head tipped to the side as she searched me.

I could barely croak it out, throat tight and mouth dry. "No, Edie. I don't."

Pain lashed across her distinct features. White, white hair whipped around her, striking in the glow of the full moon shining down.

Firelight.

She looked away, gathering herself, before she was staring back at me in compassion, in this overwhelming affection as she leaned down and let her fingertips travel across the crest of a small wave that rose to brush the middle of her calves. "Is this where you feel closest to him?"

I glanced to the ground, to the glittering pebbles of white sand, forcing out the words. "Yeah. The sea always makes me feel close to him."

She said nothing, solemn as she waited for me to continue.

I roughed an agitated hand through my windblown hair. "It's like I can't get too close…but he never lets me get too far away."

Understanding flickered through her expression. "Which is why you've been traveling the coast."

It wasn't a question.

She was just reading me.

Getting to know me again after the years that had passed between us.

The girl wondering if I'd changed. If I'd healed or was still lost to the grief that would haunt all my days.

I hugged my knees a little tighter. "Crazy…because it doesn't matter what ocean I land up against. He's always there. I felt just as tied to him on the Atlantic when I was staying back in Savannah where Sebastian met his wife. Second I get landlocked? Feel like I'm gonna crawl out of my skin if I don't get back to the sea."

Low laughter rocked from me. Completely lacking humor or amusement. "Then I just fucking freeze at the edge of it. Never able to touch because I can't ever really touch what's always going to be missing."

Right then, I wanted to confess everything. Lay it all out. Let her hold my secret the way she'd allowed me to hold hers.

I knew Edie wouldn't waste it.

Wouldn't toss it aside like it meant nothing the way I had.

Instead, I shook my head in disgust. "I'm not sure I'm any different than the kid from that room back in L.A."

I repeated her affirmation.

A warning.

A plea.

My eyes traced the long stretch of her legs. Cut and toned. Her shoulders firm.

Her exterior had grown so strong. Kinda like me. Youth scraped away by the years.

Yet I knew the inside still harbored all those broken pieces.

wait

My mirror.

Edie began to edge back out of the water.

She watched me carefully as she slowly moved up the beach in my direction.

Hair a halo of ripping flames.

Like a white witch who'd cast her spell.

Mesmerizing.

Entrancing.

I gulped around the heaviness. Around the hold she had over me. My heart went wild with the need to bury myself in all the comfort she gave.

She stopped two feet away.

Looking down like she could see straight inside of me, the way I swore I could see inside of her.

And I was again regressing back to that helpless kid.

Wishing for my damned hoodie so I could rock in the shadows.

I knew she knew it.

Knew she *felt* it.

Edie didn't even know all the details and she was still the only one who really *got* it.

She dropped to her knees in front of me. That sweet, pouty mouth twisted in stark compassion, in her own vivid confusion. "How do you both break my heart and heal it at the same time?"

I reached up and cupped her cheek.

"I don't want to break you."

She blinked at me through misty, aqua eyes, the words thick with emotion. "You broke me a long time ago."

"I'm so fucking sorry, Edie. I know I wrecked it. That I wrecked us. For the last four years, I've woken up every single day regretting it. I went to sleep wishing I could take it back. But right here…with me…this is where you're supposed to be. Where you've always belonged."

Fate.

I felt us spinning around it like it was the sun and we were in orbit.

Sadness climbed into her expression. "I used to think that...from the first night you crawled into my bed, I believed wherever you were, that was where I was supposed to be. Something about it just felt...right. You made me feel like no one else in the world could understand me the way you did. Like you saw me."

Wetness gathered in her eyes. A glimmer of diamond in the night. Priceless and precious. Her voice dipped in sorrow. "I believed it right up until the night you threw me to the wolves."

And those wolves had jumped right in with the intent to destroy.

Regret shimmered in my consciousness. Suffocating. Doing its all to squeeze out the glimmers of hope.

"And now?" I asked, because I was a masochist like that.

I watched the trembling roll of her throat as she swallowed. "And now...I feel more confused...more conflicted...than I've ever felt in all my life."

She averted her gaze, before she turned her admission back on me. "When I first saw you on that stage? I knew I had to run. To get as far away from you as possible."

Her tongue darted out to wet her lips, and a harsh gust of wind barreled down upon us.

Whipping.

Stirring.

Inciting.

"And here I just turned around and ran right back to you."

Her words struck me like an arrow to the chest. One of those lovesick kinds. The kind where my pulse pounded through my body like the vibration of a drum and I had zero thoughts except to make her mine.

It was unavoidable.

Inevitable.

Because Edie and me? We were always gonna be.

I weaved my fingers through the length of her hair.

So damned soft.

I tugged her closer.

Her mouth parted on a sigh.

I inhaled it.

The subtle hint of orange.

Sunshine and innocence and something so deliciously sweet.

Light. Light. Light.

Intoxicating.

She blinked as if she were trying to make sense of it all. "How is it possible you have this hold over me?" she murmured quietly.

"We never even…" She trailed off, leaving the idea of it hanging in the air like a tease.

But Edie had it all wrong.

It was her who had me enchanted.

Bewitched by the best kind of spell.

I dipped my mouth close to her ear. "Just because we've never actually had sex doesn't mean we weren't lovers."

She gasped and pulled back a fraction, her gaze heated and hot.

God. I couldn't take it a second longer, and I leaned in closer.

Closer.

Edie did the same.

My heart damned near beat out of my chest.

At the last second, fear took her over and her eyes grew wide. She tipped down her chin while still falling forward.

My lips landed on her forehead.

I lingered there.

Breathing in the girl.

The sweet and the pure.

Refusing to count it a disappointment.

She collapsed against me and let me wrap her in my arms.

We stayed that way for what could have been minutes or hours.

Finally, I whispered into her hair, "Do you feel that, Edie Evans?"

"What?" she mumbled, her face tucked against my chest,

like she was speaking directly to my heart.

"Me."

ten

We wrestled around. The girl bit back her laughter, giggles a slight tinkle in the easy air.

Tickling at my ear.

I pinned her down, her wrists above her head, sweet, sweet smile so free. "Let me go," she demanded quietly.

Playfully.

My heart thrashed and the room spun.

Light touched me everywhere.

Warming all those cold, dead places.

Life.

It was there.

For the first time since I was eight.

I felt alive.

Like I could finally take a full breath.

"Never."

eleven

AUSTIN

*D*ropping her at home just damned near killed me. But she'd told me she needed some space. Time to think. We'd said little the rest of the way home. Neither of us seemed exactly sure of where we stood.

It felt like we were rushing, all the while knowing we'd taken a thousand steps back. No doubt, we'd be in an entirely different place right now if it wasn't for one fucked-up night.

It was the night that had sent me spiraling, right back down that slippery slope.

The night that'd stolen her from her family. From her brother. From her home.

Now she was returning to that makeshift comfort. Finding it in people she'd found along the way.

I didn't blame her or them.

All the blame fell on me.

Of course, that didn't come close to meaning it didn't twist through like the dull edge of a blunt knife when she unlocked the front door to the house she now called home.

Pausing, she allowed herself a single second to glance back at me from the stoop, her body all a perfect shadow in the night, before she pushed it the rest of the way open and disappeared inside.

On a sigh, I forced myself to put the car I'd borrowed from Deak into drive and do exactly that.

Drive away.

Home.

Straight to the confines of my own makeshift comfort where I still remained utterly alone.

But tonight?

Tonight I felt compelled.

The remnants of the sea still calling for me.

Lost and found.

I was quick to run to my room and dig through the nightstand drawer, slowed when I edged out the back and down the worn path. At its edge, I kicked off my shoes and let my feet sink into the soft, cool, wet sand.

In the distance, the storm gathered. Encroaching. A bustle of clouds flickered with flashes of light.

Wind gusted.

Low and deep.

A howl.

I pushed toward the ocean then sank down onto the sand six feet away.

Just like I'd told Edie.

Not close enough to touch.

Never so far that I'd ever get away.

Lights burned from the house behind me on the hill, darkness swallowing me whole, the foamy white caps of the waves rolling onto the beach barely visible.

I gripped the tattered, worn green monkey to my chest. Pressed the dingy stuffed animal to my nose.

I brushed a hand through the longer pieces of my hair that thrashed around my head, just as hard as my heart thrashed in my chest.

Only the sound of the sea and the damned monkey was

there to keep me company, every part of me completely and utterly alone.

All except for *him*.

"Did you know she'd come back to me?" I whispered into the driving wind.

Grief gripped me by the throat. "Is it wrong, man, to love someone when *you* won't ever get the chance? When I was the one who stole *that* chance from you?"

The sea thundered back. A mournful cry, and my spirit throbbed and ached and spun.

Reaching out for him.

"Can't mess this up again, Julian. I can't. Wouldn't make it if I ruined it all again. Tell me it's gonna be okay."

I closed my eyes. Behind my lids, I saw him running along the edge of the sea like a tightrope. Sunlight streaking down, striking against the white of his hair we'd had when we were kids, forever marked as an eight-year-old boy who'd never had the opportunity for time to age him. To deepen and darken and scar.

I bore all the scars myself.

I could almost see him turn and smile my way.

So free.

Pain gripped and pulled and somehow comforted.

Like a lifeline to the afterlife.

That…that was where I was bound.

Maybe it made me a little sick.

Twisted in the head.

Maybe that's why I'd fed everything and anything into my veins to cover it.

My phone buzzed. I flicked into the message.

Sebastian.

Come home, man. This is where you belong.

My breaths became choppy as I read my older brother's words.

I looked to the endless sky.

Fuck. Wasn't sure I belonged anywhere. If I'd ever be worthy enough to return and become a part of their lives without making it worse.

Did I have something more to offer than my constant bullshit that only served to bring them down?

Baz had always worried I'd finally go tumbling over the edge. Harm myself in some way because I was missing this piece of myself.

A piece I wasn't ever going to get back.

An unknown feeling gripped me. As light as it was heavy.

Maybe I'd always known there was a reason. A reason I was here.

Tied and bound in an entirely different way.

And I knew...I knew.

The reason was her.

twelve

EDIE

Walking away was always the hardest.

I paused at the door to our townhouse and peered back at the boy who sat in the car, his big body a mere outline in the dark. But I knew it. The way his hands were fisted on the steering wheel as he stared back at me across the space.

Restraint.

I could feel it like a force as he sat and watched.

Containing himself to keep from tearing out of his car and coming after me.

A thrill I couldn't stop slithered slow beneath the surface of my skin, my breaths short and ragged.

I'd asked him not to follow.

I needed time.

Space.

Clarity.

My insides felt like a jumbled mess, my emotions an avalanche of disorder.

wait

So I asked him to stop.

To *wait*.

To give me a moment for my head to catch up with the direction my wayward heart was stampeding.

I just needed to make sure that rebellious organ knew what it was getting itself into.

That it was strong enough to brave the storm that was Austin Stone.

That my cracked, brittle shell was sturdy enough to take on water and not sink.

Because when it came to him, my decisions were always skewed.

A shiver slipped free when those potent eyes gleamed in a spray of passing headlights.

Trained on me like I was the target.

The goal.

Maybe even the purpose.

An overheated current ran between us. A short circuit one degree away from combusting.

He was anchored to me so deeply I could feel him pulling at me from every angle.

We were magnets in opposition.

Trembling lures.

A fierce tug of war raged around us, unseen but profound. As if the tether that bound us was being stretched too thin. Tugging and tugging and tugging. It was only a matter of time before it snapped and we collided. So tangled we couldn't tell where one's spirit ended and the other's began.

That was a hazardous place to be.

Your next breath sustained by another.

Your next heartbeat reliant upon the one who held it in their hands.

So difficult to mend yet so easily crushed.

I forced myself to break the connection and stole into the quiet of the darkened house, the hour late as I padded down the hall and into my room that was softly illuminated by the attached bathroom light.

A smile played across my face and a new sense of joy teased at the fringes of my consciousness.

I set my phone and my small bag on my nightstand, slipped off my sweater so I was just wearing a tank, crawled onto my bed.

I was too amped up to sleep. Too torn to make any decisions.

So instead I stared out my window at the emerging storm.

Beckoning it.

Welcoming it.

The chaos and mayhem and disorder.

A flash of lightning lit up the sky. Energy prickled across my skin like a clash of fear and desire.

God, I knew I was so dangerously close to falling over the edge. My body angled so I could peer down into the unknown depths.

Worst part was knowing the *darkness* below would welcome me. Embrace me in its arms.

I stayed that way for the longest time before my phone chimed.

The befuddled smile I'd worn grew.

Austin.

Excited, I scrambled to grab it from the nightstand.

Pushing to my feet, I ran my thumb across the screen.

Sender unknown.

Not Austin.

A nudge of unease prodded me, but I shoved it down and clicked into the message.

My eyes flicked across the words.

Processing what I read.

Confusion.

Dread.

Horror.

It took me all of a second for those stages to process.

Then a wave of nausea hit me so hard I dropped to my knees on the floor.

Tears blurred my eyes as I read the message again and

again.

Head shaking.

No.

How did he find me?

No.

Finally figured it out. You did this. Did you really think you'd get away with it? That I'd never find out? That I wouldn't find you?

I clutched my phone to my chest, as if it might keep my heart from breaking free of its confines and bleeding out on the floor. Fear mixed with a hatred so intense it boiled inside. Bubbling up and spilling over. Saturating every cell.

No.

How did he find me?

It seemed crazy that question seemed more important than the other that swirled around me.

What was he talking about?

I did this?

What did he find out?

Oh God.

What did he want? Hadn't he done enough?

I tried to stop them. But I couldn't. The memories were so vivid as they impaled my mind, another stake to my spirit.

Excruciating.

I squeezed my eyes closed. Trying to block them out. They only played out in a greater intensity.

Heavy metal blasted on the other side of the door, voices shouting and laughter carrying through the thin walls of the house she'd never been to before.

She'd begged her oldest brother Ash to bring her with him. Gave him her most pleading smile as she'd told him how much she was going to miss him when she and the rest of their family moved to Ohio the next month. She'd told him she didn't get to see him nearly enough as it was. Eight years and two brothers separated them, and Ash had long since left home while she was just set to begin high school that year. Now almost clear across the country since their father had accepted a job in Cleveland.

When Ash had first refused, she'd begged, insisting she hardly knew him anymore.

It was the truth.

But now she wondered if she even knew herself.

Fear clouded at the corners of her eyes, and she pressed closer against the wall, wishing she could somehow disappear as she curled into the tightest ball.

Naked.

Hair tangled and matted, thick pieces stuck to her snot- and tear-stained face.

A dull, throbbing pain ached between her thighs and bile burned in her throat, climbing up and stinging her tongue.

"What do you say we keep this little party to ourselves, yeah?" he said casually, bouncing a little to tug his ripped up jeans over his hips, the fly open wide as he pulled a ratty old band tee over his head.

"Not so sure your brother would take too kindly to the two of us hooking up." He chuckled as if he hadn't just shredded her innocence. "Of course, the asshole is probably balls deep in that Casey chick as we speak. But you know how it goes, do as I say and not as I do."

He raked his hand through his dingy brown hair, ran a hand over his chin that was coated in a coarse five o'clock shadow, his dull brown eyes somehow glinting as he smirked down at her where she tried to withdraw deeper into herself.

She felt so dirty.

Used.

Shame consumed her, and she choked over a sob as she quickly nodded her head. "Okay."

His snort was spiteful. "You gonna sit there and act like it was all that bad? Twenty minutes ago you were begging for my attention, now you're over there sniveling like it was terrible or something. Way to boost a guy's ego. Fuck him then cry."

It was true.

She'd been begging for attention.

Flirting.

Wanting to fit in among all the girls who were clearly so much older than she. The guys throwing back beers and playing music in the rundown house were really men.

But she'd wanted to feel what it was like to be wanted.

Pretty.

Mature.

She'd just never intended for it to go this far. Too stupid and naïve to recognize when he led her back to his room where it'd lead. What he intended. Too ignorant and scared to force out the word that had remained locked in her throat.

No.

She could have said it.

But instead she'd lain there shaking and shaking and shaking while he undressed her then fumbled carelessly out of his clothes. She hadn't even realized what was happening when he'd quickly flipped her onto her belly and grabbed her by the hips, dragging her up onto her hands and knees.

He'd pushed into her from behind.

She'd cried out, and that's when the tears had come.

Could she blame him? She'd asked for it, after all. Put herself in this position. Granted him control.

Her momma had warned her. Told her to be careful and not give herself away so easily.

Because there were always consequences to every action.

Cause and effect.

And tonight the ramifications were greater than her fourteen-year-old mind could ever have expected.

Foolish.

When she didn't answer him, he shook his head, tossed a smirk over his shoulder as he left her in the grubby room.

She staggered to her feet. Winced as she pulled on her clothes. Slipped out as quietly as she could.

She found herself alone on a dark, desolate, rundown neighborhood street, her fingers trembling so bad she could barely type out a text to her brother.

Headed home. Don't worry about me.

Because Edie couldn't bear her big brother's worry.

Not after what she'd done.

One night.

One mistake.

Cause and effect.

I'd just not known how harsh the consequences would be.

And I hated. Hated. Hated. I just didn't know if I hated him or myself.

I felt disoriented.

Lost.

Fearful.

I gulped for the air I couldn't find.

Pain constricted my lungs.

Drowning.

That's what I had to be.

As if I'd physically been pulled under a black surface of glass.

Where I was alone and scared.

Swimming in a remorse I could never make up for.

Tears pricked my eyes and rain began to pound at my window. Gusts of wind rattled the panes.

Blindly, I reached over to my nightstand and fumbled around for the dream catcher.

My fingers curled around it.

Desperate as the sadness came.

I clutched it to my chest as I rocked myself.

Barely coherent words fumbled from my mouth. "I love you. I love you. I'm so sorry."

And it hurt.

Oh God. It hurt. Fierce and brutal and relentless.

I wasn't even sure I entirely processed staggering to my feet, tears streaking fast and free. Frantic, I tugged on a sweatshirt, shoved socks and shoes on my feet.

Outside, rain had begun to pour. Fog rolled in thick waves across the ground.

I darted to my car, clicking the key fob as I went, shaking as I floundered into the driver's seat. My little red Fiat roared to life as I turned the engine. Windshield wipers sliced streaks of clarity into the glass when all I saw was the consuming haze around me.

Headlights cut into the darkness that surrounded me on all sides. It only added to the suffocation.

All I wanted was breath.

Life.

To feel that peace and ease and understanding.

He was the only one who could give it.

I swiped at my eyes and strained to focus through the bleariness as the wipers swept back and forth. My foot laid into the pedal.

I pushed out into the night, traveling the twisty cliff-side road.

The storm raged around me. Bright bursts of lightning lit up the earth.

A split second of white.

I squinted, choking over my sobs where they erupted at the base of my throat.

And then I was there, parked in front of the sleeping house.

Five minutes.

All these years, and my solace waited five minutes away. My solution for the turmoil I was never going to escape.

I should have known it would always be him.

I killed the engine and cracked open the door. I stumbled out into the storm that pelted down in heavy sheets of freezing rain.

My heart clamored in my chest.

A constant bang, bang, bang that urged me forward.

And again, I felt myself standing on the precipice. Teetering at the edge. The only thing I wanted was to jump.

Lightning flashed.

Uncontrolled, my hand shook as I lifted it to the door. My fist rapped twice.

I knew only seconds could have passed when the overhead light suspended from the front stoop blazed to life.

Lighting me up in a blurry daze.

Metal scraped and the push latch clicked and disengaged.

Then the door swung open to that devastatingly beautiful boy.

My savior.

My knees went weak.

The gorgeous man looked at me in shock, sleep lost from the murky depths of his grey, shadowy gaze, so deep and dark and knowing. His feet were bare, his thick legs covered in soft, faded jeans, the tee clinging to his muscular chest wrinkled and stretched, hair in complete disarray on top of his head.

Mayhem and peace.

Conflict and comfort.

His breath caught, and he issued my name on a whisper. "Edie."

thirteen

AUSTIN

Dread compressed my chest.

Edie.

In my entryway in the middle of the night.

In the middle of a raging storm.

So damned broken.

Haunted.

Lost.

My throat constricted.

In the middle of it all, she came for me.

"Edie." Her name came from my mouth like tortured praise.

The girl was drenched. Sweatshirt soaked. Clumps of white locks stuck to that unforgettable face.

I was quick to widen the door, and my voice cracked with the crushing worry. "Edie, baby, what are you doing out there? You're soaked. Come in out of the rain."

She shivered but didn't move, her shoulders slumped and heaving. "I...I...I'm so sorry. I just...I can't...I can't do this by myself. I don't want to do it by myself."

The onslaught of devotion and relief nearly dropped me to my knees, and I was reaching for my girl, pulling her inside and into my arms. "Edie."

My nose was in her hair, drawing in one of those full breaths I could only get when she was near.

Everything tightened to pinpoints.

Empathy and hurt and regret.

"Shh…" I murmured. I placed a gentle kiss to the top of her head. "Shh…don't apologize. Promised you I'd always be here. This is where you belong."

A tight sob erupted from her throat. She pressed her mouth to my neck. As if she were doing everything to bury the sound.

To hide whatever it was that'd sent her running here.

Grief clenched every cell in my body, and the words were tumbling free as I swept her off her feet and into my arms. "Fuck, Edie. Baby. Don't cry. Kills me to see you cry."

A gasp of her own relief jetted from her mouth, and she wrapped those long, slender arms around my neck, her face still buried in my skin, my mouth still in her hair, whispering reassurances.

"It'll be okay. I've got you. I've got you."

I've got you.

The girl was completely surrendered to my hold.

Her body and her spirit and the torment that wouldn't let her go.

In that moment, everything about this fragile fortress felt so frail.

Vulnerable.

In need.

Needing *me*.

I refused to let her down.

Not ever again.

I carried her down the hall to my bedroom. Only the dim light leaking in from the attached bathroom gave sight to the room.

She made a whimpering sound as I laid her sideways in the

middle of my bed. Tears continued to course down her sweet, innocent face.

Maybe it was because I didn't want to lose touch.

That I wanted to hang on.

I knew she was safe, right there in my bed. Still, I palmed the side of her waist with one hand while I set aside the notebook I'd been jotting lyrics on, propped my guitar on the floor against the wall.

I turned back to her, my body bent so I was hovering over her.

So damned close.

"I'm wet," she mumbled. Shame came bleeding through.

"I know," I told her. I leaned back a fraction, pulled her soaked shoes from her feet.

"What are you doing?" A frantic edge made its way into her voice.

"Taking care of you."

Trembles rolled through her tight little body.

So goddamned tempting.

She squeezed her eyes shut as if she were steeling herself, allowing herself to be brave enough for this moment.

For the moment when she gave me back a little more of her trust.

When she let me watch over her.

Care for her.

The way I used to.

The way I was always supposed to do.

My pure, courageous girl.

I shed her of her socks.

"Don't move," I warned.

I hurried into the attached bathroom and grabbed a big, plush towel. On the way out, I stopped at my dresser for an over-sized tee.

When I returned, she was laying there.

In the middle of my bed.

Chest heaving and eyes so wild.

My pulse spiked, blood speeding through my veins, this

thrumming need barreling free.

I set a single knee on the bed. "Come here," I whispered.

Tension built in the quiet confines of my room.

Intense and deep and severe.

I took her hand to help her sit up right in the middle.

Did my best not to shudder at the contact.

Fire and ice.

Blinding.

Fuck.

A small, uncertain moan parted her full lips, and I knew there was no chance this girl didn't feel it too.

I climbed the rest of the way onto the bed.

On my knees looking down at my light.

I watched her closely as I wrapped the towel around her shoulders, those blue eyes just as cautiously watching me.

"It's okay," I murmured, "I've got you." I gathered the exposed edges, using them to draw her just a little closer. I brushed the fabric tenderly across her face. Dabbing at that striking jaw and making a smooth pass over those full, trembling lips.

They parted when I did, and a panted breath seeped out to penetrate our atmosphere.

God.

My dick pulsed.

Clenching my teeth, I pushed down the surging need.

I could handle this.

This was Edie we were talking about.

I rose a fraction, getting higher, massaged the towel through her hair. Her head tilted back when I did, teeth biting down on her lip as she expelled an uncertain whimper, this girl looking up at me as if she'd found her meaning.

That's what I wanted.

To be her meaning.

Tossing the towel to the floor, I gathered the hem of her sweatshirt in my hands, hesitated, making sure she got it.

That I wasn't ever going to hurt her.

Not ever again.

The words were thick. "I've got you, okay?"

Blinking, she stared, before she tentatively lifted her arms with a slight nod.

Had to hold my damned breath as I slowly pulled the material up, revealing her inch by inch. A fierce lash of that energy blistered around the room as I tugged it over her head.

A torrent of white locks fell all around her, kissing her slender shoulders and dripping down over her sheer, white lace bra.

Something like an earthquake rocked my body.

So fucking gorgeous.

Angel through and through.

Was it wrong to say it?

Wrong for her to know the way I saw her?

Slowly, I worked my big tee over her head, my voice nothing more than a growl. "Stunning, Edie. Most beautiful thing I've ever seen."

Thought so the first time I saw her.

Now I was sure.

At my words, a sharp intake of air wheezed into her lungs.

Carefully, I adjusted the shirt, covering her.

"Lay back," I said, voice raw.

Her aqua gaze shimmered with outright fear and timid trust as she did what I asked. Her chest jutted up and down as I pushed my hands under the shirt.

She trembled and shook.

I freed the button on her jeans, loosed her zipper.

Whole time, my heart was going so damned wild.

And I felt hers too.

Beating loud. A thundered chaos in the silence of my darkened room.

I tugged her damp jeans down, revealing miles of slender, toned legs. An endless expanse of soft, alabaster skin.

I gritted my damned teeth, averted my gaze.

Dying to touch.

To taste.

Explore.

Claim her in ways I knew I shouldn't.

Couldn't.

Her tears had subsided.

They'd been replaced by a suffocating intensity.

It climbed the walls and pressed down from the ceiling.

Anxious want. Unchecked need.

Her jeans joined the pile on the ground. I slid off the bed and dragged the covers down. I stopped where they were pinned by her body. "Get in."

Edie got to her hands and knees and crawled up, not even questioning what I was asking.

I gulped around the magnitude.

Trust.

That's what she was giving me.

I climbed in next to her.

She searched my face. "You're getting in wearing your clothes?"

I almost laughed.

Almost.

"Think it's best if I leave my clothes on right now, yeah?"

A self-conscious rush of redness flushed her cheeks.

"Oh right…yeah," she rambled as if she didn't have the first clue what she did to me, casting her gaze aside.

Shy. Sweet. *Enchanting.*

"Goddamn it, Edie." I pulled the covers over us and guided her head to my chest.

Just like I used to do.

My arm wrapped around her shoulders and I hugged her close, leaning up so I could scatter a bunch of kisses to her temple. I released a rumble of words at the delicate skin that drummed with the erratic beat of her pulse, "You think you don't still affect me the same? That I don't look at you and just about come undone? I get your boundaries, Edie. Respect them. But you gotta know I've never wanted anything…anyone…the way I want you."

Hoped my saying it wouldn't scare her away.

She curled her tiny fist in my shirt and held on for dear life.

Like I might have the strength to support her. Protect her.

Silence swelled around us, and all those ugly, vacant spaces inside ached and moaned with the need to be filled.

Because this girl touched me in a way no one *ever* could.

"What happened?" I finally asked, softer. Just because I was thanking all those stars I'd wished upon that she'd come running to me didn't negate her pain. Her breath caught at the question.

"Paul texted me."

Rage.

It was instant.

Darkness threatened to be my own demise. The desire to destroy.

Eliminate.

I squeezed her. Probably too tight. Just as tight as the words I gritted out. "What?" Sickening fear was in an outright war with the hot hatred burning inside of me. "That bastard...he's supposed to be rotting in prison."

Edie pulled back, those aqua eyes a toil of torment and confusion. "Prison?"

Motherfuck.

She didn't even know that.

I forced the words around the bile. "He's been in prison for a few years."

Four years.

Her hand tightened in my shirt. "For what?"

"He got picked up for the usual shit that takes down guys like us."

That fucking wannabe rocker, always trying to be a part of the scene. My brother had more talent in the tip of his pinky finger than the entire being of that asshole. But that didn't mean he wasn't always there. Lurking. Thinking he was going to take a bite of the fame.

Of course he and Ash were pals, though I wouldn't exactly call them friends. Wondered just what Ash would *call* the prick if he knew.

Her voice trembled as she blinked, trying to make sense of

what she didn't know. "Drugs?"

"Yeah."

Guilt gripped me by the throat. Omission was nothing less than a lie.

But what was I supposed to do?

Because telling her sure as hell wouldn't win me any points. It wouldn't help her. Would only harm her. And I couldn't protect her if she pushed me away.

My stomach soured, but I forced it down. "What'd he say?"

Bewildered, her brow pinched, and she chewed at her lip. "That he knows what I did. Asked me if I thought he wouldn't find out." Everything began to leave her on a desperate rush. "I don't know what he was talking about. How he found me."

Her face was suddenly back in my neck, the words mumbled at my skin. "But I'm terrified that he does."

Knows what she did?

That thought spun around me before it sunk in like toxic waste.

He thought it was her.

Shit.

He thought Edie was responsible.

How did I always manage to fuck everything up?

Every good intention gone bad.

I wouldn't let it.

Not again.

My mouth was at her ear, my own desperation falling from my lips while I made a million silent promises.

I won't let him hurt you.

I'll protect you.

Keep you safe.

"What did you tell him, baby?"

Her head shook against my chest. "Nothing. I didn't reply." I wanted to scream. Tear out my hair.

Instead I let the bitterness free. "I'll kill him, Edie. I'll kill him before I ever let him touch you again."

I felt her shake under my promise. I was quick to corral the fury. She was here for me to support her, not watch me come unglued.

Same as I'd done that night.

"I just want it to be over. For him to leave me alone. I don't understand what he wants from me."

All the bullshit that marked our lives seemed piled around us. Promising to snuff out life and light.

"I won't let anyone hurt you, Edie. I won't."

She turned her head, her mouth pressed to my side. "I believe you."

Silence stretched between us. Baited and bottled with all the questions left unanswered.

"Do your dreams still come?" she finally whispered.

Opening up.

Taking us back to where it all began.

I ran my hand over the top of her head, cupping her neck.

How was it possible that after that asshole contacted her tonight, she was turning her concern back to me?

"Think they'll always haunt me," I admitted. "Do yours?"

I already knew the answer. But I wanted to climb into the center of that fragile heart. The strength holding it together.

Fingertips tapped across my chest like a tentative tune.

"Almost every night. I wake up and feel so alone. Empty."

I edged back so I could read her face. She sucked her bottom lip into her mouth, fighting the moisture glistening in her eyes. I brushed my thumb along her jaw, encouraging her to continue.

Her admission quieted like a secret. "I wake up floundering. Lost. Feeling so desperate to fill the void. To cover the ache. And absolutely terrified to take the chance ever again."

She swallowed around the tight emotion. "They say it's better to have loved and lost than to never have loved at all. I want to agree, Austin. I want to believe. I'm just not sure I know how."

Old insecurities wound me up like an antique clock. "Do you…"

God. Seemed I'd lost the capacity to even speak. To go back to that time. Seventeen. Stupid and naïve. Still knowing with all of me I'd finally found what I'd been missing. The question was raw. "Do you still have it?"

A sad smile graced her sweet mouth, and she gave me the softest nod.

I swallowed hard. "Did you think of me?"

Her reply was so quiet, so timid, I felt it rather than heard it. "Always. How could I ever forget you?"

Affection pushed at my ribs, and I held her a little closer as I offered my own confession. "Won't ever forget the day Ash brought you to the house…saying you were going to be staying with us for the summer while *Sunder* was on break from touring."

Sunder had just made it big, and my brother and the boys had gone and bought a mansion in Hollywood Hills, moving us from that shithole house into a luxury none of us had been accustomed to.

My fingertips played through strands of her hair as I mused. "I remembered seeing you as a kid…but you'd been gone for so long. And there you were, the most gorgeous girl I'd ever seen. Looking so shy and unsure."

Wistful laughter rumbled in my chest. "And me? I could barely look your way, I was so lost. But then that night, I heard you crying. I was terrified, really. Looking around my dark room and wondering what the fuck to do. Had no idea how to deal with whatever you were going through. But still, I knew I was supposed to be there. That you *needed* me."

I blinked into the shadowy darkness of my room, the girl's heart beating with mine. For a few moments calmed in this never-ending frenzy. "Crazy…I grabbed that catcher, not really thinking it through. But it was like instinct. The first thing that popped into my head."

Edie caressed those soft fingers up the hollow of my throat. Making me tremble. Soothing and provoking.

I squeezed her tighter. "My grandma gave that to me, Edie. When I was eight. Couple of months after we lost Julian."

Lost.

What bullshit.

Grief balled at the center of my chest. "Other than Baz, she was the only one who'd recognized I was dyin' inside."

Exactly like I'd deserved.

"She'd stayed with us for a while, and the day before she had to go home, she'd come to me in the middle of the night. She'd heard me crying. She'd pressed it into my palm, whispering it like it was the greatest secret, telling me to always keep it close. She told me it was *peace and safety*."

My lips pressed into her hair, praying she'd understand. "And that's what I wanted *it* to be for you."

Of course, the truth was, that's what *I'd* wanted to be for her.

Peace and safety.

Not her demise.

Her tongue darted out to lick her dry lips, gaze darting down to where she fiddled with the collar of my tee, as if she needed a distraction. "That's the way it's always made me feel, Austin. Every time I hold it. When I'm missing and hurting and alone. I hold it and I think of you. The comfort you gave me. The hope."

Fuck. I had the impulse to weep.

I was the one responsible for ripping it away.

For taking that good thing and crushing it in my hands.

"I should have been there all along, Edie. Making you feel safe. But I never forgot. Never stopped missing what we had."

"I missed you so much." She muffled a sob in my shirt.

I hugged her closer, making promises I really hoped I had the strength to keep. "It's going to be okay. I promise you, it's going to be okay."

"How?" she whispered.

"Together. We'll be okay if we do it together."

"When I got here…were you still awake?"

I hiked a shoulder. "Couldn't sleep."

She ran her fingers across my chest. Tenderly. "Why?"

A quiet chuckle left me. Humorless. "Because I felt a lot of stuff tonight, Edie. Being with you. Thinking about my brother. I…" I hesitated, hating this part of myself, the part I didn't know if I could ever snub out.

The worthless.

The fucked up.

The one who destroyed every damned good thing he was given.

"I…was having urges."

Edie stilled, then set her palm right in the middle of my chest. Filling me up with that unending belief.

You are good. You are good. I feel it here.

That's what she used to tell me on those nights years ago when I thought I'd succumb to the darkness, the girl breathing her light into my black soul, her hand always so steady where it was pressed over my erratic heart.

That spot would always belong to her.

I drew in a shaky breath. "I didn't give in, Edie. Can't. Won't. But I figured picking out a song on my guitar was a better way to exert that energy than anything else."

A tiny smile that was almost awed pulled at one side of her mouth. "I always wondered if you'd start to perform." She set back to tracing her fingers across my chest. Lighting me up. The way she did.

"God, I was so shocked when I first saw you on the stage at *The Lighthouse*. But I can't say I was surprised. It just seemed…right."

"It's weird…playing. The kind of songs I write and where I do it. Used to have this crazy fantasy that one day I'd be up on a stage at my brother's side. Playing with him."

But that was nothing other than a fool's game.

"Maybe that's where you're supposed to be. Do you think you'll ever go back?"

"Back to L.A.? Maybe. Make things right with my brother for good. Let him know I'm okay so he can stop worrying about me once and for all. Otherwise? No. You know as well as I do I don't belong there."

That kind of world wasn't for me. The money and the fame

and the lifestyle. People looking at you like you were *something* when you knew with everything you had you were *nothing*.

Pretty sure the only thing I'd do was turn around and let Baz down all over again.

Wasn't about to let that happen.

Not ever.

"But I can't escape the music either. For so long I felt like an outsider in *Sunder's* world. I fought the need to play for a longed damned time. But music…I guess it's a part of my soul."

"So you play in small, quiet places." She said it as a statement. With understanding. With no judgement.

"Sometimes we settle, Edie."

Sadness wove into her tone. "Yeah, sometimes we do."

My confession seemed to mix a whole new brand of confusion into our mess.

"What about you, Edie? You ever going back?"

The shake of her head was vehement. "No. Never. L.A.'s the last place I want to be. Not with Paul there. Especially now."

Remnants of her loss burned like a fiery storm in the middle of my darkened room.

She inched closer, her admission murmured dangerously low.

Ripe with shame.

Loaded with disgrace.

"I miss my brother. So much. Does…does he talk about me?"

Felt like a landslide of jagged rocks gathered at the base of my throat. I swallowed around the razor-sharp edges. "Told you I haven't been home in a long, long time. And when I was there, a ton of shit was going down, so I wasn't exactly a part of easy conversation. Think you leaving like that hurt him. Confused him. The few times you were mentioned, it was him wondering how you could just take off."

Wasn't going to lie to her.

Hadn't heard him mention her name all that much. And it

was always offhanded and quick to be dropped.

He was either the world's most self-centered asshole, which I'm sure just about every chick he'd ever crossed paths with would attest to, or thinking about her just hurt him too damned bad.

My stake was on the last.

"I didn't mean to hurt him," she whispered in defeat.

I blinked hard. "If he knew, Edie...he'd understand. I promise he'd understand."

But that was the biggest obstacle of all.

Edie didn't want anyone to know.

She'd been shamed and convinced into thinking it was better that way.

So instead, she ran, because it was impossible to keep your past from being brought out into the open.

Her voice fluttered out like soft ribbons that spun me in warmth. "Thank you, Austin. You make everything better. You always have."

Soft and true.

Blameless and pure.

This angel girl whose only crime had been giving into one night of bad.

I just didn't know how to rid her of the shame.

Convince her she was nothing less than a victim.

She burrowed into me. Each breath I felt against my heart, and each innocent touch burned my skin in want.

God I wanted her.

But for now...

For now...

I'd simply hold her where she knew she'd be safe.

"Sleep, beautiful girl, sleep."

fourteen

AUSTIN
AGE SEVENTEEN

*M*uted cries echoed through the walls.

But tonight...tonight they were different.

Fear clenched my spirit, my entire being consumed with the compulsive need to go to her and wipe away whatever it was that hurt her this way. What haunted those aqua eyes.

Quickly sneaking out, I stole into the confines of her room.

There she was, facing me, lying curled around a pillow in the middle of her bed with tears seeping free.

But this time I knew she hadn't woken from a dream.

I climbed up behind her, wrapped her in my arms, wishing desperately I could do something to take away her pain.

Erase it from her spirit and ease it in her soul.

But this sorrow?

It was bone deep. Written in her marrow.

I knew firsthand that type of pain couldn't so easily be scraped away.

My nose nuzzled beneath her hair, my mouth at her ear, whispering ease. "You can trust me, Edie. Trust me. Whatever it is, I get it. I get it." My voice dipped deeper as I pulled her closer. "Talk to me."

Hesitation tensed her body, before she clung to me tighter, her voice the quietest plea. "Promise me, Austin…promise if I tell you, you'll keep my secret safe. Because I need you to know."

"I will never tell." The oath fell without hesitation.

What I wasn't expecting was that secret to tear me into a million pieces as I listened to her confide it in me.

Anger.

I wasn't sure I'd ever truly felt it before.

Not before then.

Protectiveness rose up in me like the darkest storm.

A consuming destruction that billowed and built.

Hate.

That piece of shit Paul.

I hadn't seen him in a year or so. Not since we moved to the new house in the Hills. But I knew him. The slimy bastard who was always hanging around backstage like he belonged. Trying to take what didn't belong to him. Wanting to be a part of *Sunder's* world while having absolutely zero to offer it.

But this time?

This time he'd taken *too* much.

I hugged a trembling Edie as close as I could, whispering ease. "I've got you. I've got you."

In the middle of all those words I made a silent promise in my head. Paul Nagle was going to pay.

fifteen

AUSTIN

My eyes popped open to the fading darkness. Dawn was nothing but a suggestion preparing to break.

My heart raced like a thoroughbred horse, and every single muscle in my body was hard.

Rigid and straining.

A needy growl fought to burst free when I realized what'd drawn me from sleep. I tempered it, gritted my teeth in restraint.

Problem?

I was lying flat on my back, and her sweet, delicate body was tucked to my side, the girl too fucking close for comfort. She had one leg hooked around my waist and a fist tightly wound in my shirt.

Heat burned hot, and the satiny underwear she wore did nothing to conceal the fact her pussy was pretty much grinding against my hip.

Yeah.

Perfect. Problem.

I groaned, hating myself a little bit. Leave it to me for my thoughts to go straight to the depraved and corrupt.

But the truth of the matter was my cock was harder than fucking stone.

I had the intense urge to bang my head against the wall.

Instead, I banged it against my pillow.

Shit. Shit. Shit.

Fuck.

When that didn't work, I crushed the heel of my palm into my eye. Hoping the pressure might quell the overpowering lust. The all-consuming need to bury myself in all that sweet and soft.

To get lost in the warmth tucked into my side.

A tiny, breathy moan.

This from that pouty mouth.

And I was sure I just might die.

No chance could I just lay there like some kind of saint.

Because I was nothing more than a man.

Begging for some kind of mercy that I didn't disturb her, I unwound her gorgeous body from mine and slipped out from under the covers, sucked in a cleansing breath I hoped would rein it in, and tiptoed into the bathroom where I quietly latched the door shut behind me.

Needing space.

Distance.

Or maybe a fucking brick wall with padlocks and chains.

I scrubbed both hands down my face, before I pushed some of the tension out with a heavy sigh.

What the hell was I supposed to do?

God, this girl had me in knots.

Wanted her so bad. But I knew better than to push her. Knew she deserved time and respect.

My gaze traveled right.

Shower.

Yes.

Shower.

Hidden away in this tiny room with her on the other side, a

cold one might be the only solution.

I turned the faucet on high, all too quick to strip out of my clothes. I stepped right into the driving cold.

"Shit," I hissed, bracing myself against the spray of icy shards pelting from the shower head.

I sucked in a breath, released it between clenched teeth, and forced myself fully under it.

Head dropped and chest heaving as rivers of ice-cold water slicked down my shoulders and back.

But it did nothing to lessen the need. Gave me no sanity or pacification.

Because all I could think about was the girl on the other side of the door.

My girl.

In my bed.

Wearing just her panties and *my* shirt.

An angel I wanted to dirty.

I always had.

Love was messy like that.

All of my restraint scattered. I gripped my cock. Squeezed the base. My mouth dropped open at the pressure of my hand against my rigid length.

I was a fool to think it might be enough.

Shit.

God, I was a bastard, but there was nothing I could do before I was giving in, leaning forward and bracketing my forearm above my head to hold my weight.

Water pounded down on my head and back while I pounded my fist against my dick.

Trying to keep silent when all I wanted was to moan, teeth digging into my bottom lip as I pictured the girl spread out for me.

My breaths were coming short.

Panted and hard.

I gave into imagining the sounds she would make when I finally got to bury myself in her body.

A soft, soft gasp.

I slowed, trying to convince myself that throaty sound was all in my mind.

Just another part of this fantasy.

Until I heard the small thump against the wall.

Shit. Shit. Shit.

I mashed my eyes closed, like it might hide me.

Conceal the depravity of my actions after I'd just been comforting her hours before.

Heart thrashing, I turned and moved far enough to peek out the small section where the fabric shower curtain hadn't been drawn fully closed.

It was just a little sliver that left me exposed.

But it was enough. When I peered out, I was looking right at my girl pressed up against the wall.

She stared right back at me.

And I wanted to be horrified, my mind scrambling to conjure every weak apology I could summon. Ready to fucking grovel to keep her from turning and running once again.

Because that's exactly what I expected her to do.

But her expression…her expression clutched me in the center of the chest and sent what little brain function I had left stampeding south.

Red, lush lips were parted, her hand pressed to the hollow of her throat, pupils dilated so big that her hooded, cerulean eyes appeared black. Needy breaths were coming at me from that sweet mouth like a goddamned freight train.

Desire swelled in the confines of the too-tight room.

Alive.

She pressed deeper into the wall as if it might support her weakened knees. Head rocked back. Thighs squeezing together.

Motherfuck.

My hand shot to the shower wall to steady myself. "Warning you, Edie, you need to get out of here. Right now."

"I…I…" The words caught, and a tremor rode on her exhale. "I heard you."

"Edie." Another warning from between gritted teeth.

"Austin...I..." It was a plea.

If I were a wise man, I would jerk the curtain shut tight. Shout at her to go before we both did something so stupid we'd end up driving a wedge so deep between us we'd never be able to cross it.

But no.

Like a fool, I pushed it aside. Metal rings screeched against the rod. The part of me that'd wanted this girl for what seemed like forever convinced me it was okay to return to pumping my cock.

Body soaked, water streaking from my shoulders and chest in thin rivulets.

Words raw. Rough. "This what you heard?"

She gave me no answer.

Instead those eyes roamed.

Hungry.

Desperate.

Tracing the parts of me she'd never before seen.

"Edie," I groaned, not looking away when I reached over to kill the faucet, turning back to face her in the emerging light.

"You're so beautiful." She whispered it like it caused her pain.

"No...Edie...it's you. You who did this to me. You've always done this to me."

A needy gasp and she was pressing harder against the wall.

Begging.

I stepped out of the shower.

Closing in.

I *felt* it the second she saw it, when the design etched into my skin became clear in the faint rays of morning light.

A tremble rolled through her like thunder and everything went from intense to severe.

Escalating.

The power that bound us surged.

Magnified.

I took another step closer, completely exposed until I was standing right in front of her.

Standing in the storm.

Firelight.

With a trembling hand, she reached out and traced her fingertips across what had been marked over my heart. Reverent and awed, she touched the spot that was always going to belong to her.

It was the first tattoo I ever got.

My chest was covered in ink. Like the demons inside me had been captured on my skin.

Hidden in the middle of it all was a dream catcher.

It blew in the wind, bright feathers ripping and wild as they were pummeled, in flight where they lashed down across my abdomen. The entire thing was threatened to be ripped apart by the raging storm that ruled our lives, the leather strands clung to the webbed foundation that held it all together.

That endless ring stamped right over my heart.

A diamond sat right in the middle.

My forever.

My hand cupped the side of her neck, thumb brushing along her jaw. "You get it now, baby? What you mean to me?"

The words grated as they were expelled, me standing there naked in front of her.

Physically.

Emotionally.

"I was never supposed to mean anything."

I pressed her hand flat over the web. "Doesn't matter. You were right here, all along."

Her chin trembled as she lifted it, gaze catching mine. "You make me want things I can't have."

I wanted to tell her I could give it all.

That all her boundaries were safe with me. That I'd protect them. Wouldn't cross them until she was ready.

Until she was sure.

Instead I leaned in and barely brushed my lips at the corner of hers.

The softest promise.

I've got you.

She rocked with a full-body quake.

This time I uttered it aloud, voice soft. "I've got you. I won't ever hurt you."

That storm raged and warred. "Austin."

We were held back by all those reservations, pushed forward by need and want.

"*I know you,*" I told her so quietly, placing feather-light kisses along the curve of her jaw. Eliciting chills.

And I knew she got my meaning.

She recognized I still clearly saw the limitations.

I wasn't going to push. I wouldn't chase her until she was trapped.

She'd always maintain control until she was ready to surrender it to me.

She lifted her chin and whimpered, "*Don't.*"

"Don't what?" It oozed on a growl.

"*Don't* hurt me. *Don't* leave me."

Don't.

Don't.

Don't.

This time it was surrender.

The word sent tension bounding through the room.

Winding us up higher.

Tighter.

Until neither of us had a choice but to snap.

She threw her arms around my neck and my mouth came crashing down.

Taking that mouth I'd been dying to take. So fucking soft and sweet. And I was pretty sure I still had to be lost somewhere in that fantasy when I sucked at the plush softness of her bottom lip, rolling it between mine.

I turned and did the same to the top.

Savoring.

Tasting.

Taking.

She tilted her head back and her tongue peeked out.

Tentative.

That was until the second mine brushed hers.

Fire.

We were gone.

Absent but to us.

Hot hands pressed against my chest and she pushed up on her toes, the girl shocking me by being the one to deepen the kiss.

Demanding more.

A low growl rumbled deep in my throat, and I drove my hands into the long locks of her hair.

So damned soft.

I yanked a little to grant me better access.

And I kissed her and kissed her.

Dancing tongues and nipping teeth and soaring spirits.

My bare cock pressed into her belly.

She whimpered, the girl sagging into my hold when her knees went weak.

I pinned her to the wall, keeping her from falling. Her body felt so fragile beneath mine.

"I've got you," I murmured as I lifted her into my arms and carried her back into the sanctuary of my room.

The barest light slipped in and washed the white walls in warmth.

It bathed the bed in shimmery light.

I laid her in the center of it. Looked down at the one who'd changed everything. My heart and my focus and all the fucked-up thoughts that ruled my head.

Standing there with my hands fisted at my sides and her trusting eyes taking in every inch of me, I yearned to be someone better.

I'd walked from my brother's house hoping to find that man. To find the strength inside of me to be the person I wanted to be.

I'd left knowing with every part of me I had someone out there who needed my strength. A girl who needed someone to stand for her.

The same way as she'd stood for me.

Breathing belief.

Imparting faith.

Could I become him now?

Could I handle something so delicate without again squashing it in my hands?

Edie writhed. "Austin… Please."

I was damned sure going to try.

My movements were cautious and controlled when I climbed up onto the bed. Her feet were planted on the mattress, and I crawled into the well of her legs.

Hovered and gazed.

So beautiful.

I palmed her cheek.

"You steal my breath."

"And you make me weak," she returned.

I dropped to my elbows, and she arched.

Our bodies met in the middle.

That energy pulsed.

She stuttered out an exhale as I settled over her, careful not to crush her.

Never.

I sifted my fingers through her hair. "No…Edie. I'm gonna be your strength. Your courage. Stand behind you when you need the support. Hold you up when you're failing. And when you're soaring, I'm going to be the one watching you fly. I will never drag you down or hold you back. Tell me you trust me."

Tears gathered at the creases of her eyes, and her tongue swept along her lips. Her heated gaze darted to my lips before it flashed back to my eyes. Transparent and clear. "You know I wouldn't be here if I didn't."

Relief stole my exhale, and that hope was no longer just a glimmer. Now it was blinding light. Blazing and burning and consuming. My chest felt so damned tight, and I leaned down to kiss my girl.

Slowly at first.

Relishing what it felt like to stand in the sun.

She clung to my bare shoulders and wrapped her slender

thighs around my hips.

I rocked against her.

All my hard against the softest soft.

She whimpered a sigh.

And I did it again.

And again.

And it was too much.

And not close to being enough.

Edie started panting as I increased the pace. Increased the pressure. Kissed her harder and deeper.

Losing her grip.

She looked up at me as if she was begging me to rescue her.

"I feel you," fumbled like desperation from her mouth.

My spirit lit in a frenzy.

I shifted my weight to my knees and set a single hand next to her head. The pads of my fingers crawled over the material of my shirt, my heartrate kicking an extra beat when I brushed over the swell of her breasts, nipples tight and straining against the fabric, before I went skimming down.

A shiver racked her when I moved over her belly.

I caressed over the satin of her underwear.

She panted.

I pushed the satin aside, caressing soft. She moaned encouragement, and I pushed two fingers into the deep well of her hot body.

Oh fuck. So warm and tight.

Edie gasped and her back bowed.

"Please."

God.

She was so fucking sweet.

Hot and wet.

I brushed my thumb across her clit.

So damned light.

Back and forth as I slowly began to fuck her with my fingers.

Still, that's all it took for her to be crying out, my name on her lips as her walls clamped down, riding the sharp edge of her orgasm.

My chest tightened at her expression, her sweet, sweet face lost to the bliss I was bringing her.

She lifted her hips from the bed as she gasped. Fingertips sank into my shoulders. Clinging as she broke.

Beauty.

Fucking beauty, watching her come undone, my spirit going wild with the need to get closer to her.

The girl whimpered and writhed as aftershocks sent tremors through her body.

My hand that had been exploring her body was back on my cock. I gripped tightly in hesitation, wondering just how much this girl could take before she spooked, then I gave in because she was looking at me like I could possibly be the light in her darkness, too.

I jacked myself with brutal, savage strokes. Our faces were so close, my nose was brushing hers.

Staring down at eternity.

Into those bottomless depths that led directly into her soul.

My mouth dropped open and every muscle coiled, this girl my complete ruin.

White hot streaks of ecstasy ripped through my body, shudders ripping far and wide, my body going rigid above her as I came.

Her hands flew to my cheeks, holding fast to my jaw, her emotions laid bare when she mouthed again and again, *I feel you, I feel you, I feel you.*

Pleasure gripped me everywhere, and I slumped forward as I struggled for air, my arm wrapped tightly around her head as I pressed her face into my neck.

Because Edie Evans was my *first.*

The first girl who'd managed to touch something within me when I'd been completely dead inside.

A strike of light in the darkness.

The one to evoke. The one to inspire. The one to instill this burning hope that flickered and flamed at my insides.

Spurring me to *stand.*

Since the dark day I killed him, she was the first to make me *feel*.

sixteen

AUSTIN
AGE SEVENTEEN

She kissed me. Her mouth timid. Her tongue slow.
    I let her lead.
    Let her fingertips explore tentatively across my face.
    Let her breath become one with my spirit.
    Let her release a soft shudder.
    Let her sigh.
    Let her moan.
    Let her slowly but surely sink into me.

seventeen

EDIE

"Good morning." The deep, gravelly voice roused me from sleep.

My eyes blinked open.

My heart rate kicked.

My gorgeous boy hovered two inches above me. When I met his intense gaze, his sensual lips twisted into a smirk that somehow verged on adoring.

Like sleight of hand. Impossible. Yet completely, totally captivating.

Rods of golden light streaked into his room. The morning's warmth stretched out to touch everything in its path. Kissing his face and lighting up the boundless darkness that welcomed me.

I wanted to drown in it.

Poetic eyes traced my face, the fierce grey somehow softened and swimming with songs and mystery. Steeped in intrigue.

My insides quivered and my overloaded heart fumbled on

an erratic beat.

"Morning," I whispered back.

Oh, how we fall.

But I should have known the harder I fought him, the faster that fall would come.

Just like quicksand.

The more I struggled, the deeper I sank.

And I didn't ever want to climb out.

I let loose what had to be the sappiest smile when one fluttered at the edge of his full, red lips.

God.

He made me happy.

"How'd you sleep?" he asked.

Giddiness escaped in a giggle I couldn't contain.

Better than I had in years. Did he need to know that?

"Did Edie Evans just giggle?" He leaned in closer, washing me in a surge of that energy that lived around us. His grin was a little on the predatory side. "Now that's a sound I haven't heard in a long damned time. Where do I sign up to hear it every single day for the rest of my life?"

My grin was out of control.

Hope.

Joy.

This boy once again awakened it anew.

I quirked a teasing brow. "The rest of your life, huh? You're getting awfully ahead of yourself there, Stone."

Sly, he shook his head. He pushed up onto his hands and knees on either side of me.

Caging me in as if he had no intention of ever letting me go.

And God.

I liked it.

Being surrounded by him on every side.

He dipped his head lower. Coming closer. "I've been ahead all along. I was just waitin' on you to finally catch up."

Redness flushed. A sizzle of heat consumed my skin. Just like flames consuming paper.

I squirmed and my body lit up in remembrance of last night.

Last night.

Shivers rolled and I bit at my bottom lip, trying to contain the reaction.

Austin caught it.

Clearly he knew exactly what direction my thoughts had gone traveling.

The heat increased.

Amplified.

Tenfold.

Maybe a thousand.

God, I burned.

Here I was, pinned beneath this beautiful man. Thirsting for things I wasn't sure I knew how to give. Itching to cup my hands in the well of those murky waters to take a quenching sip.

That was the thing about Austin. Both my spirit and heart recognized it was always supposed to be him. It was the old traumas that held me back from reaching out and taking what I wanted.

A flicker of unease wound through me, and my thoughts traveled to the text I'd received last night.

What could he possibly want?

What good could it possibly do?

I swallowed down the glimmer of anxiety. The last thing I wanted was to dim this moment. To allow Paul to steal more from me—more from us—than he already had.

More than that? I couldn't shake the severity of Austin's reaction when I'd mentioned Paul's name last night. I wasn't sure he could handle the unnecessary worry about a man he'd ultimately only wanted to protect me from.

Fingertips tapped softly across my collarbone, slower still as they trailed up the hollow of my neck. My chin lifted with his exploration. Everything trembled beneath his tender touch.

On a sigh, my mouth parted.

The quietest plea for more.

"Gorgeous," he murmured. He brushed his fingers higher, shivers racing as he traced the line of my jaw. "So damned gorgeous. Can't see straight when I look at you. Or maybe I'm finally seeing everything right."

A tiny moan slipped free when he patted his fingertips across my lips.

Testing, his attention flicked between my eyes and my mouth, the action measured as he dipped them just inside.

My tongue licked out for the barest taste.

This boy was breaking me piece by piece.

His head tilted as he peered down at me. "Do you have any idea how good it feels to wake up next to you?"

Awe filled my tone. "It couldn't have possibly felt as good as it felt waking up next to you."

"That's where you're wrong, Edie, because there's no place in the world I'd rather be than right here with you. So I'd say that ranks it up there somewhere in the range of magical and miraculous."

My throat swelled with affection.

"What's above miraculous?" I questioned, eyes flitting, searching that striking face.

Slowly, he shook his head. "There's no such thing."

Oh God.

That potent stare flashed with something significant.

Bold and strong.

Everything rushed and surged.

Anticipation.

Need.

Hope.

There was zero hesitation when he pressed his lips against mine.

This...

This was a caress I felt right at the center of my soul.

He lingered there, before he delved deeper, the sweet kiss taking on an edge of hunger as he moved against my mouth.

With me.

For me.

His tongue was wet. Both hot and sweet.

Quick, firm lashes.

Slow, soft strokes.

Possessive and claiming.

Hypnotizing.

The world spun, and I felt lightheaded.

Elevated from the agony of the girl I didn't want to be.

Lifted to the plane where I was the woman I wanted to be for him.

For me.

My palms pressed flat against his heart. Just needing to feel the thundering pound, pound, pound. The strong beat that pumped life back into the diamond at the center.

Austin was one-hundred percent right.

Waking up next to him verged somewhere between magical and miraculous.

Impossible and perfect.

He made a growly sound against my mouth, both frustrated and playful, before he forced himself back onto the weight of his hands. "For the record, can we let it be known I can't believe you're here. In my bed. Never would have dared to imagine it a week ago. And let the record also know *I like it.* A lot."

I reached up, shaky fingers stroking the contours of his bold, striking face. "I'm not sure I'd ever choose to leave."

His red lips wound up at the side as if he wanted to play, a smirk taking hold. "Then don't."

Don't.

My own smile flirted at my mouth. "I do believe that might be the proper use of that word."

He nipped at my fingers as I brushed them across his perfect pout. "I do believe you're onto something, Edie Evans."

Another giggle escaped, before my grin slid into the softest smile, affection pulling far and wide. "You don't know how amazing that sounds. But I have to go. I have work."

His brow pulled with a frown. "When will I see you again?"

"When do you want to see me?"

He chuckled, light and carefree while he mindlessly played with a strand of my hair. "Well…considering I don't want to *stop* seeing you, I would say as soon as humanly possible. What do you say you come down to *The Lighthouse* tonight? Watch me play?"

Something about his expression turned hopeful. As if he couldn't stop his own vulnerabilities from weaving through. It seemed a stark reminder of the broken boy I used to know.

My gaze caressed the uncertain hope in his expression.

The man was so very different yet so much the same.

I hesitated, searching for the right words. "Are… we…"

He took my hand and threaded his big fingers through mine, held them against the dream catcher etched on his chest.

A permanent mark that had somehow *marked* me.

"Are we an *us*, Edie? Is that what you're trying to ask?"

Shyness seeped in, carrying all the promises I'd made myself to remain alone.

But I didn't want to be.

Not when what I wanted was right in front of me.

Uncertain and somehow brave, I chewed at my lip. "Are we…?"

Gravity stole his expression. It was something so genuine and sincere. Unrelentingly fierce. "We've always been an *us*, Edie. Now we've just gotta figure out how to keep that *us* together."

"Together?"

"Yeah. What do you say?"

Maybe I should be ridden with old fear. Clinging to the past that would never let me go.

Instead, I was washed in faith.

Faith in him.

He understood me. The lines and the boundaries and the fears.

Respected me.

I swallowed hard. "Just…be careful with me."

I yelped in surprise when he quickly flipped us, the action

so fast I couldn't make sense of it until I was suddenly straddling his waist.

Then I was gazing down on the breathtaking boy who held my heart.

He smiled, so beautiful and bold.

Shivers rushed, lifting a rash of goosebumps on my skin.

I placed my hands on his strong, strong chest. Trying to keep myself steady.

On uneven ground when I knew without the shadow of a doubt there was really no ground beneath.

I'd fallen.

Now I was swimming through waves of the blackest black.

The darkness waiting below had taken me whole.

It should be cold.

Terrifying.

Instead I felt safe in the security of his arms. In the surety of his heart and his intentions.

My hair flowed down around my shoulders. He lifted both hands, sifting his fingers through the long strands. He spread them out, cradled my head. "I think it's you who's going to have to be careful with me."

I gripped his wrists. Feeling so free.

Free in his touch.

Free in his belief.

"Austin."

Eyes roamed, making me feel adored as he stared up at me. "Edie."

His expression shifted into something playful. Joyful. Slanting a little on the frisky side. He tugged me closer and whispered close to my mouth. "Kiss me before you go."

"That's funny…because I was just hoping you'd kiss me."

He smiled, and my tongue darted out, wetting my lips. I dipped down, eager for his kiss.

He wound his arms around my head. Enclosing me. Making me feel safe.

Adored.

His kiss was long and slow and rimmed with the sharp edge

of desperation.

It was the same as I always felt when I was with him.

What I felt for him.

Desperate.

It'd almost killed me when I'd let it go.

When I'd let him go.

Another piece torn away.

A tiny shiver of fear rolled through me. The thought of losing him again was almost too much to bear.

I wasn't such a fool that I didn't realize the two of us were messed up. Nothing but a mess of shattered, broken pieces that had been scattered and mixed together.

I could only pray together, somehow, *this* time, we could make them fit.

Reluctantly, I pulled away. My lips had to be swollen and red, my hair a mess from his fingers.

I didn't care.

I felt no shame or remorse for what I was giving this boy.

This part of myself that had always belonged to him.

"I really need to go."

His nod was reluctant. "Okay."

I eased out from beneath him.

After last night, it seemed silly I had the urge to tug the hem of his shirt down over my thighs when I stood, to cover myself in modesty.

Apparently, old habits really do die young, because I did, and I peeked over at him, feeling the rush of redness as he grinned my way. His mind so clearly set on rewind, to those moments we'd shared so early this morning.

I hurried to the bathroom, my body still flushed as I was taken back to what had incited the fire that'd roared between us last night.

Quickly, I freshened up and headed back out, flashed him a shy, knowing smile as I glanced at him where he grinned at me where he lay on his back in the middle of his bed with the sheet pushed aside.

His beautiful body on display.

Too beautiful.

I was doing my best not to stare.

Goodness, he had me spun up.

Twisted and tied.

I pulled on my jeans that were a little stiff where they'd dried in a pile on the floor. "I'm totally keeping this shirt, by the way," I told him as I slipped into my shoes.

He chuckled slow and climbed out. He was wearing just his boxer briefs, and I was doing my best not to look when he just looked so ridiculously *good*.

One hand attempted to tame his hair. "Believe me, Edie, that shirt belongs on you."

Another flush of redness crawled hot, and I dipped my head and tucked my hair behind my ears, finding my keys where they'd been discarded on the floor.

Austin followed me down the hall and out through the living area and kitchen.

He kissed me one more time at the door. "I'll see you tonight, beautiful."

And I knew I was in so much trouble.

Because I couldn't wait.

eighteen

AUSTIN
AGE EIGHTEEN

Soft fingers brushed the length of my spine.

Flinching, I curled into a tighter ball and kept rocking.

I needed to block it out.

To make the excruciating hurt go away.

Stop it.

Fuck, I needed something. A hit. A line or a pill. Just about any fucking thing would do.

"Austin...what's happening?" Her voice was so tentative. Unsure. Scared.

I yanked fistfuls of my hair, rocking more as I buried my head between my knees. "Go away, Edie."

How the fuck did she even know I was here? Hidden on the rooftop, only illuminated by the faint crescent moon. My body was angled toward the sea that I could almost hear, could almost taste, even though it was fifteen miles away.

"Austin...please. Let me in."

It seemed so messed up. Upside down. The way I'd

burrowed into her. Into her heart and her mind and her secrets.

And I didn't know how to let her into mine. They were too intense. Too private. Too fucked up.

I was too fucked up.

That was the problem.

I couldn't stand for her to see the depravity.

"Please," she said again.

Tried to fight it, but I gave. Just a little. "It's his birthday."

My birthday.

Only we didn't celebrate it, me and Sebastian. The day was too fucking brutal for either of us to acknowledge.

And here I'd gone and done it.

Said it aloud.

Because this girl...this girl. She kept getting closer. Digging deeper.

I was supposed to be there for her.

Not the other way around. And here she was, looking back at me. My mirror. Making me face all things I didn't want to see.

"Oh." Understanding filtered out on her breath. She pressed her sweet, sweet face into the back of my neck, wrapping me in those tender arms from behind.

"Tell me what I can do. Anything." The girl was all too eager to offer me the comfort I didn't deserve.

Only she didn't really understand. Didn't really know.

She wouldn't be here if she did.

If she knew just how disgusting I was.

You'd think I'd have learned by now. Figured out how to stop being a selfish asshole.

But here I was, taking a little more of what I had no right to take.

"Just...please. Don't leave me." I gritted over the words. Over the need. Over the desperation.

Don't leave.

Not ever.

Because it was in her that I found all my strength.

nineteen

AUSTIN

I watched her drive away.

Grinning like a damned fool.

Heart pressing full and pulse pumping wild.

When she disappeared from sight, I roughed a hand down my face like it could rid me of the haze of lust and need, that sweet, sweet spell she had me under, and pulled the door shut behind me as I turned back into the house.

Shock punched the air from my lungs, and I froze, before I was harshly shaking my head.

"Goddamn it, Deak. What the hell is wrong with you? Always slinking around like you're some kind of peeping Tom. Scared the shit outta me."

He was sitting at the small round table just on the other side of the bar that separated the living area from the kitchen, his ankle crossed over his knee, rocking back in the chair with a cup of coffee lifted halfway to his mouth. Chest bare and the mess of his wavy, dark blond hair ratted on his head.

"What? A man's not allowed to enjoy his coffee early in the morning? In his own damned house?"

He said it like he was doing nothing more than flitting the morning away. Relaxing. But the way he was eyeing me was far from casual. The jolt he'd given me quickly morphed into a rustle of disquiet.

One brow quirked just as he cocked his head. "Though seems to me you were enjoying a sample from a different kind of menu this morning."

Yeah.

Guess I should have expected that. Didn't mean it didn't piss me right the fuck off.

"Not any of your business, man."

"No? Because I could have sworn you and I had a conversation right in this very room just a few nights ago. Seem to recall somethin' about you promising you had no intention of hurtin' that girl."

"That's exactly what I said and that's exactly what I meant."

"So what's she doin' sneaking out the door with the sun just coming up?"

I exhaled, hoping it might quell some of the annoyance churning in my gut.

Deak didn't have the first clue about my intentions. As far as he saw, she was just another chick skating out at dawn, never thought of again.

I raked a hand over my head, moved across the floor toward the kitchen. "I also told you there was all kinds of history between us that you don't know about."

"Yeah, mate? And what kind of history is that?"

Felt like a lifetime of history.

Forever.

I grabbed a mug from the cabinet, poured a cup of coffee, hiked a shoulder in a nonchalant shrug. "She's my girl."

Simple as that.

And so fucking complicated it made my head spin.

He needn't know any of that.

A disbelieving chuckle fell from him and he sat forward. "Is that so?"

"Yeah, man, that's so."

Damian was suddenly lumbering down the hall, scrubbing a hand over his face, looking about as irritated as I felt. "What the hell, assholes? Anyone ever heard of a little thing called 'respect your roommate'? Because there I was, having about the best damned dream I think I've ever head, and all of a sudden *we're* interrupted by two voices that did nothing but *kill* the mood. So not cool. Not cool at all."

I stirred a shot of creamer into my coffee, smirked his direction. "Glad you're at least getting some in your dreams, my friend."

"Hey…I'll take what I can get. And believe me, this was a *lot.*"

He held both hands up, palms out and stretched like they were mitts.

Dirty paws, no doubt.

Taking a sip, I stifled a laugh. "You're hopeless, Dam."

"Nah, man. This boy here doesn't have anything if he doesn't have hope. I'm just practicing."

You'd think he was twelve and not twenty-four. But there wasn't an ounce of disgrace in his admission, his grin all kinds of wide. Just as fast as it'd come, that grumbling displeasure had vanished, and he was pouring his own coffee and clapping me on the back. "What's on the agenda today?"

Deak pointed at me. "Our boy here was just telling me about his girl, weren't you, Austin?"

Damian frowned, slanting me an eye. "Which girl?"

Asshole *so* knew which girl.

The one that made me crazy with want. The one who'd had me so tightly wound I couldn't see straight. Last night she'd finally let me *spin.*

"Edie."

"So *the* girl."

See, Damian had it right.

Deak?

Not so much.

Because he was looking at me like he was imagining the two of us in a ring, going a few rounds.

"Worked with her for the last couple years, mate," he said. "Told you before, she's a good girl. Doesn't need you mucking her up the way you like to do. And I'm pretty sure Jed-boy called dibs a long time ago. He's been waiting for her for a long damned time."

Well, I'd been *waiting* longer.

Deak continued, "From where I'm sittin', seems to me you're asking for trouble."

Trouble.

Yeah.

That girl was disorder and the perfect kind of chaos.

Sweet as sin.

Soft as snow.

Firelight.

Sighing, I forced myself to keep my cool and not let loose on my friend. "Pretty sure *dibs* weren't Jed's to call. She's a woman, not a fuckin' toy."

Deak cracked a smile. "Well, well, well…someone's getting all riled up over a *girl*. Never thought the sun would rise on this kind of day." He sat back like it was settled. "Get you, man. Better on you than me. Just watch your back, because I consider her a friend, and I won't hesitate to kick your arse if you do her wrong. Bettin' Jed won't for that matter, either."

"Won't be necessary."

That was a promise I'd damned well keep.

twenty

EDIE

*T*onight, *The Lighthouse* was packed. A din of voices vied for attention above the canned music pumping from the speakers, the music filler between the band who had played before, one we had missed, and Austin who was supposed to play in fifteen minutes.

I blamed Blaire for us being late.

Anxious excitement wound me tight.

I couldn't wait to see him with his guitar again.

Out in the light.

Where he belonged.

Blaire hiked up on her toes and craned her head around the crush of people gathered in the bar. "Ugh," she groaned. "I don't think we're going to find a spot to sit."

I shifted around, searching for a straight shot of what, or rather who, I wanted to see. "Let's just...get as close as we can to the stage."

"Fine. But let's order drinks first."

She grabbed my hand and hauled me behind her. She

pushed through groups huddled tight, no remorse at all as she clung to my hand and cut us a path toward the bar.

I yelped when a hand suddenly clamped down on my elbow.

Firm enough to tug me back.

My head flew around. I was still on edge from the text I'd received last night, and I was struggling with all of me not to allow Paul to ever again have any hold over me.

The harsh breath I'd sucked in eased out on what I was certain was nothing less than a pathetic, dreamy sigh. Like a school girl with a hardcore crush she just couldn't shake.

Who could blame me?

Poetic eyes glinted in the shimmer of the strung-up lights. It felt like we'd been set to pause, the two of us staring at each other while the bar buzzed round us.

God. His face was so mesmerizing it twisted right through the middle of me.

Ever so softly, the hand that'd clamped down on my elbow trailed down until he was weaving his fingers through mine. Tugging me closer. Brushing his mouth against my knuckles.

Oh God.

My heart.

It was all mushy and soft and just…swoon.

It was so strange, being this girl. Giddy and light.

But that's the way this boy had always made me feel.

A little needy and so much stronger.

Twisting me inside out.

Revealing to me what was waiting to be exposed within.

Reminding me that despite my mistakes, there was hope.

I guess the problem was I'd never figured out where that hope left me. What it could offer and what it meant, before Austin and I had run out of time.

It'd left me unsure if I could find that hope on my own.

The truth was, I'd always been aware it was there. Lurking behind the shadows that kept me frightened of the dark. Now, I felt as if I were standing out in front of it. Opening my arms and welcoming possibility. All the while I was on my knees praying I wasn't a fool to give in so easily.

I wondered if every single one of those emotions had played out in my expression, because Austin smiled a soft, almost somber smile and dragged me up against that delicious body that was so big and warm.

"Don't," he murmured low, his mouth inclined close to my ear.

And I would have laughed if I hadn't been burying my face in his neck, where his pulse was steady and strong.

"Don't what?" Should I have been surprised when my mumbled response came out like a tease?

"Don't freak out," he said. I could feel the hint of his grin emerging at the top of my head.

"Ahem."

We both jerked to find Blaire standing there with her hands on her hips.

"Hello." She waved her hand in a flourish around her face. "Best friend? Sound familiar. No ditching me for a boy, Edie."

Austin tucked me under his shoulder, turning so we both were facing her. "Sorry, Blaire, but you're gonna have to share. Edie and I? We've been *best friends* for a long, long time."

Blaire shook her head. "Ha. That's *totally different*, right?"

His head tilted to the side. "Well, I'd certainly hope so."

Eyelashes fluttering, her lips curved as if she were going in for the kill. "Are you sure about that, music man? Because most boys I know would think that a bonus. I'm totally game if you're up for it."

Shock shot from my mouth. "Blaire." I smacked at her. "You're so gross. What is wrong with you?"

She shrugged. "What? Just testing him out. That's my job as *best friend*. You know, make sure new super-hot boyfriend isn't just another scumbag."

Austin chuckled and raked a hand through his hair, gaze slanting my way. "Remind me to watch out for her," he said. He glanced between us with his eyes full of a tease. "Pretty sure this one's going to be setting all kinds of traps."

So maybe I was surprising myself again, because I popped

up on my toes and swept a quick kiss to that soft mouth.

It struck me that was the first time I'd ever initiated a kiss. Reached out and taken what *I* wanted, confident in that decision.

Change.

Change was good.

"Just don't fall in one and you'll be fine."

He ran his fingers from my temple all the way down to my chin, lifting it slow. "Wouldn't dream of it."

"Okay, okay, you two. Break it up. There's plenty of time for that later." Blaire shooed him with her hands. "We have to grab drinks and hopefully find a place to stand before you go on in…oh…like two minutes."

"That's actually why I came to find you. Saved a seat for you. Deak and Damian are down close to the stage."

There she went, Blaire's mouth as big as the Cheshire Cat as she looked my way. Obviously her words were meant for me even though she was speaking to him. "Oh, Austin Stone, I believe you're a keeper."

I couldn't agree more.

Austin led us to a round table close to the stage, secluded beneath the high-topped tables where I'd initially seen him just the week before.

Crazy, because that seemed a lifetime ago.

Damian was already standing. Antsy. Searching the crowd as we approached. Relief flooded him with he caught sight of us. "Austin, man, there you are. You gotta move. You've got like thirty seconds until you need to go on, and you are already so high on Craig's shit list I'm pretty sure you're gonna get pushed right *off* the top of it if you mess this one up, if you know what I mean."

I smiled, getting ready to push him off, to tell him to go, when my cell I was holding in my hand vibrated. On instinct, I lifted it, the screen bright against the dimmed-out lights of the bar.

I gasped in a sharp, horrified breath, stuffed my phone in my back pocket as if it would hide the cruelty of the notification that had scrolled across the top. Short enough to be read. Clear enough to be understood. Even though it'd again come from that unknown number.

Fucking bitch. You owe me. You owe me big. Gonna collect.

Austin tensed at my side. Anger fierce. A brutal hostility and a raging fear. All of it mixed with mine.

Flooding fast.

Rising higher and higher.

Pulling me deeper and deeper.

"Edie." Austin said my name as if it caused him pain.

My words shook just as violently as my hands. "Go. You can't be late."

"Can't...Edie...can't."

Torment wrenched his expression. The dichotomy of the way he'd wanted to protect me when in turn he'd only harmed me. His hands tied too tight and his tongue set too loose.

The secret he'd unwittingly exposed that had sent me running.

I gripped his tortured face. "I'm right here. I'll be right here."

Distress left him on a moan, and his voice lowered, only meant for me. "How can I leave you? I want to be the one taking care of you, Edie. Standing up for you."

Confusion lined Damian's face, but he was tugging at Austin's arm. "Now, man. You can't fuck up another show. You're too good for that."

"He can't touch me here, Austin. Go. Up there is where you belong," I said. If only he believed it. If only he realized he deserved so much more. If only he recognized the talent I saw when I looked at him.

"I'll be right here."

He hesitated.

"I promise."

His words were muffled where he uttered them into my

hair. "We're going to make it, Edie. The two of us together. Won't let that bastard change that this time."

Reluctantly, he jerked away, gaze commanding when he peered at me from over his shoulder as Damian led him to the side of the stage.

I sank into a chair. Overwhelmed. Ripples of fear slid through my veins while Austin's promise saturated me everywhere else.

Every cell.

Every fiber.

Belief and hope.

Blaire's voice was in my ear. "What the hell was that?"

My head shook. "Nothing."

Her glare was worried, calling me on the lie without saying anything, but she sat back when the crowd rustled. Austin climbed three steps onto the small stage. Deak sat on the other side of her, and Damian settled in the open chair next to him.

Austin moved across the stage. So big and dark, everything about him so complex.

A riddle.

He settled onto the stool close to the mic, pulled his guitar onto his lap as whoever was working the spotlight angled the beam just right. Lighting him up in his ethereal glow.

Beautiful.

Devastating.

Captivating.

"Seems you've met my boy Austin?" Deak took a sip of his beer, eyeing me over it.

I didn't look toward the voice. I just absently nodded and stared ahead.

Enamored.

"I've known him. All my life."

Deak gave a slight nod. Processing. Adding up. "You look different, Edie."

Austin strummed and my heart went mad within the confines of my chest.

Like he had a direct connection and he'd zapped me with a

lash of that energy that roared between us.

Deafening.

And his voice…that gorgeous, mesmerizing voice…Austin set it free.

That haunted harmony wrapped around me.

Tonight it was even more intense than it'd been the night when I'd first stumbled upon him here.

As if through his music he was trying to speak to me.

Tendrils of solace and joy and despair reaching out.

Conflict and comfort.

Beneath it, even with everything, I didn't feel afraid.

"I feel different." It was a murmur I wasn't even sure was intended for Deak or for myself.

But I did.

I felt different.

I felt courageous.

As if I wanted to reach out and grab life.

The life I hadn't been brave enough to live. Too afraid to lose.

Austin played his songs.

Each of them seemed at one with the sea. The sea that gently rolled right outside *The Lighthouse* doors. Those doors were open wide to welcome the cool night air that trickled in with the breeze.

Meshing with the lyrics that were so dark. So deep.

Packed with a kind of meaning I doubted anyone could understand but Austin himself.

But I heard them.

Felt them.

Understood.

That broken boy hiding beneath that brilliant, intimidating man was so transparent to me.

And I hurt for him.

Hurt for us.

Wanted to hold him and soothe it away, just as strong as I knew he wanted to keep it at bay.

To pretend as if it no longer had a hold over him.

But I saw it in those flickers of vulnerability. His truth so clear to me in the depths of those stormy eyes.

Austin drifted in and out of songs seamlessly. Expertly. With enough talent to fill a thousand rooms and give peace to a million hearts.

Affection and longing pierced through me. God. How much I wanted him to recognize it.

The gift he'd been given? So clearly he viewed it as some kind of curse.

But I guess we always run from the things that scare us most.

Austin wrapped another song. He didn't launch into another the way he had during his entire set, this seamless transition that sewed his songs together like a quilt of comfort.

Instead, he paused, his hesitation thick. I thought maybe he was going to call it, utter a thank you for coming out, and stand.

In discomfort and indecision, he rubbed a big hand over his defined, strong chin.

He seemed to make a decision, and he exhaled, spoke into the mic. "Wrote this song a long time ago. It was during one of the toughest times in my whole life. I never played it for anyone other than for myself, because it was private. Between me and a girl I'd done completely wrong. I didn't have any other way to reach her but through that song. Praying somehow she'd understand it, *feel* it across time and space, even when there was no chance for her to hear the words."

His gazed roamed over the crowd until it locked on me.

I gasped a tiny breath under his stony stare. Both bare and restrained.

A perfect, unsettled contradiction.

Impenetrably hard and excruciatingly soft.

Broken and bold.

"And tonight...I want her to know."

I sucked in a breath, and I could sense everyone sitting at the table peering my direction, searching for my reaction, questions darting through their minds and passing in their eyes.

But the only thing I could see was him.
Tied.
Bound.

Don't say a word
Come inside
Lie down while I hold you up
Don't get too close
I know nothing but
Broken promises and broken bones
Pieces that just don't fit

His voice shifted, and the chords became more intense as he drove into the chorus. While I stared up at that striking face, his lips so full and his voice so smooth.

Its pitch perfect.

A match to my soul.

Standing on a mountain
Swept beneath the sea
Lost somewhere in between
Condemned to the darkness
My whole world in black and white
Until I was staring at it
Through the eyes of Firelight

I felt as if I were floating in the middle. The two of us drifting through the floor of the darkest sea.

Lost.

Found.

That husky voice once again veered and dipped into the raspy lilt of another verse.

Aimed to be better
Would've given my life
This statue nothing but rubble
Good intentions gone bad

Just when they started
Baby, you were the best secret
I never got to keep

Standing on a mountain
Swept beneath the sea
Lost somewhere in between
Condemned to the darkness
My whole world in black and white
Until I was staring at it
Through the eyes of Firelight

With his eyes closed, Austin's hand moved over the frets, quick and precise as he bled his beauty across that stage. Pouring it out over us. Filling up all the vacant places of my heart.

Can I keep staring at it
Through the eyes of Firelight
Say I can keep on staring at it
Let me see it
Let me see it
Through the eyes of Firelight
Through the eyes of Firelight

Blaire dragged me to standing when Austin suddenly stood and left the stage.

"Oh my God. That was incredible. Seriously, maybe the hottest thing I've ever seen in my entire life. For real, Edie. That boy. If I thought you had no chance before...you're a goner, girl."

Blaire raved as I struggled to find my footing.

A rush of lightheadedness swept through my head, and I blinked.

Stunned.

Staggered.

Completely overcome.

Those who played at *The Lighthouse* were typically there as a side note. A complement to the setting of the sea. Entertainment while people ate, chatted, and drank from their glasses while they drank in the breathtaking view.

Breathtaking.

That's exactly what this had been.

And mine hadn't been the only breath that had been stolen by this hypnotic boy. The entire room had been entranced, arrested by his voice and song that weaved through slow and sank in sure.

A quiet devastation.

A soundless, raging storm never expected until the moment it touched down.

Ravaging everything in its path. Stripping you bare.

I'd never felt so exposed.

Now, people vied to get closer. Austin exited to the right of the stage, and they circled him as if he were some kind of celebrity. As if they wanted to brush up against fame.

A profound urge throbbed. Urging me to go to him.

I knew the people surrounding him would be unwanted attention.

I could *feel* his distress.

The remnants from the stress of another text before he'd taken to the stage mixed with his need to remain in the shadows when his talent forced him into the light.

This boy who'd always believed he had so little to offer, his talent nothing more than a penalty.

Yet still he'd somehow managed to offer everything to me.

I fought my way toward him, elbowing through like some kind of fangirl who couldn't get close enough.

Damian stood beside him, angled so he was almost in front, smiling and talking to the handful of girls who competed for Austin's attention. Clearly, Damian was acting as interference.

It wasn't a large crowd.

Not in a place like this.

But there was no missing the torment etched on Austin's face.

Because his songs weren't for them.

Especially the last.

It was for *me*.

Just like this boy was meant for *me*.

I shouldered past a brunette.

She shot me a glare.

I couldn't find it in myself to care.

Because I knew...felt how badly this boy needed me. Through a break in the crowd, those flinty eyes caught mine. Impenetrable and translucent.

I moved toward him.

Drawn.

Energy pulsed.

Almost suffocating it was so profound.

Swelling and swelling until both of us were taken under by the wave.

The second I got close enough, he reached for me and dragged me through the ring of admirers.

He looked at me as if I was the only person in the room. Big, strong hands cradled my face as he lifted me toward him.

He kissed me in the midst of it all.

As if I was the center of his world.

And I knew without a doubt, this boy was the eye of the storm.

The eye of *my* storm.

Relief gusted from him on a wheeze. He barely pulled back enough to whisper his plea. "Edie...don't know how to do this without you. Don't want to. Don't leave. Don't leave. *Don't ever leave.*"

twenty-one

My hands wandered. Wanting more.

"You're killing me," I murmured at the back of her head, my nose in her hair, palms pressing at her belly.

I drew her deeper into the well of my chest.

My dick strained.

So hard it was close to blinding.

This pent-up need close to driving me insane.

She pressed back, rubbing her sweet ass against my cock, easing some of the ache.

"Austin," she whispered in confusion and need, all messed up with outright fear.

"I won't hurt you. Ever," I promise at her ear.

I rolled her onto her back and crawled over her, caging her in.

Her face was a silhouette in the shadows of her darkened room, the night so deep and dark we could hardly see.

I took her hand, pressed it to my cheek. My voice scraped

with need. "Do you feel that, Edie?"

"What?" The word left her on a pant.

I released it against her lips. "Me."

She sucked in a razor-sharp breath, the girl driving me wild when she grew near frantic as she searched me in the night.

Hands, tongue, and mouth.

It was an exploration I wasn't sure either of us would survive.

Both of us needing more.

So damned much more.

The two of us were tied by the boundaries looming in front of us.

A clear line never to be crossed.

Hot hands spread out across my chest.

Strayed and searched.

Groaning, I joined in, my palms wandering and my fingers pressing.

Edie gasped.

Her head rocked back on her pillow, her hand a fist on my cock as my fingers plunged into the warmth of her body.

This girl was the brightest flame within my blackened soul.

Her trusting gaze latched onto mine, and I pumped my fingers faster.

Harder.

Edie came.

She bit down on her bottom lip to still her cries. "You. I feel you."

And my body was manic, my underwear too tight, her hand not enough. "I want to be inside you. Please...Edie...please."

She froze. All except for her fingernails that dug into my shoulders while I rubbed against her like a sick, twisted fuck.

"*Wait*," she pled so quietly. Tears were suddenly streaming from the corners of her eyes and into her hair.

Hate for the bastard who'd touched her flamed, a torch to my skin.

It only stoked the hate I would always harbor for myself.

Life bleeding out.

I forced myself off her and flopped onto my back. I fisted the base of my dick, like it might soothe the ache. I flung my other forearm over my eyes.

"I'm so sorry." It was a whimper from her sweet, sweet mouth.

And fuck, that right there?

That right there made me want to break.

Quickly, I rolled back toward her so both of us were facing the other on our sides. Strangers except in the shadows. I brushed my fingers through her hair. "No. Don't say that. Not ever. It's not your fault. I didn't mean to push you. I'm the one who's sorry."

I saw her blink, the blue glinting diamond, aqua, and night.

"I love you, Austin."

Everything shivered.

The energy tight.

Too fucking tight.

My chest squeezed.

My mind reeled with the magnitude of what I felt for this girl and what should be the impossibility of what she felt for me.

I palmed her face. Beauty in my hands. My thumbs caressed the moisture gathered in the hollow of her eyes. "You are my light."

twenty-two

AUSTIN

"*Don't ever leave.*"

I probably was squeezing Edie too damned tight as I begged it into those silky strands of white, my hands fisting them tight.

I was struggling.

I had struggled through the whole damned set.

Usually I lost myself to the lyrics. The words I bled out for Julian. Offering him more of the penance I would forever live.

I hadn't planned on *singing* her song.

But I'd felt overcome. Overcome with the rage that blistered through my veins. Rage directed at that bastard who had the audacity to text her and demand more of her than he'd already taken. That violent need had gotten bound up with the undying devotion I had for my girl.

So I played her the song. It was a song I'd written and played only for her during the years she was gone. Usually I played it within the quiet confines of my room. Sometimes on the rooftop of the *Sunder* house as I looked over the sprawling city below. Wondering where she was and if she was okay.

Those lonely nights had been spent praying she could somehow sense it...feel it...gain some kind of comfort from it even in our separation.

Playing it tonight?

I knew what it'd been. It'd been an obscured plea for her to *hear* me. For her to understand why I'd done what I'd done after she'd gone. All the while praying I could figure out how to *fix* it without her ever finding out.

I was so tired of always ruining the good I was given. This time I was going to make it right. Wipe away the horror that had seized her features when she'd looked down to find that text. Of course because she was Edie, she'd tried to hide it just as quickly, the girl trying to protect *me*.

"I'm right here. I'm not going anywhere." Her breath was at my ear. Whispering ease. I hugged her again. I allowed myself one more second of pretending it was only the two of us and there wasn't anyone surrounding us.

Finally, I pulled away and threaded her fingers through mine. I turned and talked to a few of the people who'd come forward. Most of them were just there to tell me how much they'd enjoyed the show. Saying they were moved. Curious if I'd signed a deal or if I was waiting for my big break.

None of them had a clue that I was just an outsider in a world that was so much bigger than me.

That I was *almost* a part of greatness. A stranger to it all the same.

But I forced smiles and pleasantries, focused on my girl.

My strength.

A few of the chicks who always hung around hoping to take a bite out of any guy who had a mic or a guitar or a lick of talent circled like wolves. Like some kind of pathetic groupies. Waiting for the perfect moment to strike.

Not a fucking chance.

"Show was awesome, man," Damian said once everyone had finally moved out of my space. He gave a clap to my back. "Craig will be pleased. Want me to grab you a beer?"

"Sure. That'd be cool."

Blaire was right there. Grinning with a flirty cock of her head. "What about me?"

Damian's head swiveled her direction. Like the guy was surprised she was talking to him. "Oh...sorry...can I get you something?"

She sidled up to him, linked her arm with his. "I'll come with."

I chuckled.

Dude never picked up on the scent right under his nose.

He lifted his chin to Edie. "How about you?"

"Um...a beer would be nice." She said it almost like a question.

So fucking cute.

"Got it." Damian and Blaire disappeared into the crowd.

I turned to Edie. Kissed her softly. "Thank you for being here."

"Where else would I be?"

I edged closer, lining us up in an embrace, my body just about eclipsing hers. "Nowhere but with me," I reaffirmed.

She fiddled with the top button on my shirt, peeked up at me. "You were amazing, Austin. Truly amazing. I hope you realize that. How you affected everyone here. The songs...they're brilliant."

I gulped around the thickness evoked by her praise. Wanting to accept it. All the while my spirit rejected it. "I sing because I have to, Edie. Nothing more."

She nodded like my statement made her sad.

Damian and Blaire broke back through the crowd. Damian lifted the beers he carried in the air. "Time to celebrate, suckers."

"Oh, yeah? And what is it we're celebrating?"

"Um...me being the most kickass manager you could ever have. I'd think that'd be obvious."

I laughed. "All right then. Wouldn't want the talent to go unrecognized, now would we?"

"Hell, no. That would be a damned travesty," he said,

widening his eyes like he couldn't even fathom it.

Edie cast me a sweet, sweet glance, one that streaked through me like warm rays of bright summer sun, just as warm as the fingers she wound through mine. "Are you ready?"

Yeah.

I was ready.

Three hours later, we stepped out into the late Santa Cruz night. *The Lighthouse* lights clicked off behind us. A slight chill hung in the air, and a misty fog crawled through the streets. The sound of the sea crashed in the distance.

I hiked my duffle bag higher up on my shoulder and carried my guitar case in my other hand.

I glanced over at the girl walking at my side.

It felt like a miracle she was there.

She lifted her face to the thick clouds sagging from the sky. "It's gorgeous tonight."

I grinned. "It's gloomy."

She shot me a wry smile. "You don't always need sunshine for the weather to be beautiful."

My hungry gaze raked the girl.

I had to disagree.

Wholeheartedly.

This fucking gorgeous girl dressed up in a flowy white skirt and a fitted blue blouse, little heeled boots rising up to her ankles, wavy locks flying around her.

My sun.

"No?" I asked.

"No." She lifted her hands out to her sides. "There's beauty in all things. In the deepest night and in the brightest day. In the snow and in the sun." Her voice dropped. "Sometimes the greatest beauty is in the darkest storms."

I breathed out, leaned in close enough I could press a kiss to her head. "Edie."

It was a statement.

This girl who got me the way no one else ever could.

Our footsteps echoed as we walked the deserted streets to where my truck was parked along the curb. Considering the late hour, it sat by itself. "This is me."

Last night I'd had Deak's car. Figured since I had a *hot* date, she might want an AC that actually worked.

A smile lit up Edie's face, a question in her teasing tone. "This is you?"

"What? You don't like Bessie?"

She ran her fingertips along the outside panel of the bed. "Oh I like Bessie. I think she's perfect for you."

Bessie was an old girl, dinged up body and rusted from the sea. I'd scrounged together enough money when I'd first left L.A., knowing if I wanted to roam, I needed a ride. I'd figured she wouldn't get me far. Yet somehow she'd taken me exactly where I needed to be.

I hoisted my guitar case up and over the side, setting it in the bed. "She's been damned good to me, that's for sure."

I moved and pressed Edie up against the metal, my mouth coming in close, lips brushing her jaw. "She doesn't look like much, but she brought me to you."

Edie was all smiles as she gazed up at me. "Then I'd say Bessie is my new best friend."

I groaned, lust clutching my guts, because *this girl*. She had me in knots. "Let's get out of here," I said.

"Where are we going?"

"Ice cream?" Seemed safe enough.

She feigned a gasp. "You want to get ice cream on such a gloomy night?"

Laughter rolled from my chest. "Well…I guess it is a beautiful night, after all."

On the passenger side, I wedged the key into the old lock, opened the creaking door, and helped Edie into the cab, before I rounded the front. She leaned over and unlocked my side just as I got there, and I was slanting her a wide grin as I climbed up and tossed my bag in the middle of the bench.

There was something so completely normal about the act. Like we were an ordinary couple who didn't have the need to hide or pretend.

Two people who weren't ashamed.

It felt…good.

Right.

I turned over the ignition, and the big engine rumbled to life. Ten minutes later, we were pulling into the drive-thru of the 24-hour ice cream shop.

"Plain vanilla cone for me," Edie said, while I ordered a vanilla dipped in chocolate.

"Here you go, baby."

Redness flushed her cheeks at the affection, but she didn't do anything but give me one of those smiles that twisted through me when she accepted it.

She licked up the side, moaned a little.

Good God.

I cocked my head, shot her a smirk and lifted a brow, accelerating as I did.

So maybe I had some ulterior motives when I suggested we get ice cream. But damn. I remembered the one time we'd shared it before, me sneaking downstairs in the middle of the night and grabbing a tub from the freezer and two spoons, two of us sharing it in bed.

The little noises she'd made.

The taste it'd left on her tongue.

Who could blame me that I wanted to experience it again?

I drove the short distance back to her place. Little droplets of rain pelted the windshield as we drove in comfortable silence. Both of us relaxed and enjoyed the ice cream. The company. The *change* and the *chance*.

One I didn't think I'd ever get.

I parked under a big shade tree in the front of her yard, cut the engine. Silence descended, the little house Edie shared with Blaire and Jed sleeping. A foggy mist hugged the truck and the sky. The subdued glow of the moon peeking out in a break in the gray, heavy clouds was the only illumination.

Peace.

We both sat there, licking at our ice creams, me watching

her and her watching me.

She giggled.

A grin took hold of my mouth. "What?"

"You've got a little something…" She reached out and wiped a fleck of chocolate from my chin, lifted it out between us. "…right here."

I leaned forward and sucked her finger into my mouth.

Chocolate and girl.

Fucking delicious.

"Mmm."

The freest laughter rang from her, and she jerked her hand back. "Watch yourself, Stone. I might get the impression your intentions were more than just to please me with the most awesome ice cream in the whole wide world."

Oh yeah.

I had all kinds of *intentions*.

She sat there grinning at me in the big cab of the truck, not even noticing the glob of her ice cream going for a slippery slide. It dropped onto her shirt. "Oh crap."

She cupped her hand under the vanilla that began to melt faster than she'd expected, quick to lap up the rest, laughing the whole time. "Oh my God, look at me, I'm a total mess."

Did she think I'd ever stop looking at her?

I popped the rest of my cone into my mouth, unzipped my bag. "Hang on a sec…has to be something in here you can clean up with."

I rooted around in the bag, finding a clean, folded up tee at the bottom. I yanked it out.

My breath locked with what I dragged out when I did.

The green monkey flipped up and landed in a heap on its side, body tattered and dirty, one of the arms hanging on by barely a thread, the forever grinning white face peeping out.

The damned stuffed animal my twin had carried with him everywhere. The one thing that'd set us apart. His security blanket.

Now I took it with me wherever I went. Still wasn't sure if I thought it was comfort for me or for him.

Edie frowned when she saw it, before she slowed in awareness, glancing up at me for my reaction.

She'd never seen it before.

Of course she hadn't.

Baz had had it all those years. That was until the day I left L.A. last, when I'd gone hunting for it and found it in his room.

Edie picked up the shirt, her movements slowed as she dabbed the goop of ice cream from her shirt and wiped her hands clean.

Every so often she glanced at me.

Gauging.

Calculating.

Understanding.

Setting the shirt aside, her fingertips crawled out, moving just far enough to stroke the plush fabric, as if she were petting it. "Was this Julian's?"

Hearing his name come from her mouth the way it did? With some kind of adoration?

Brutal, searing pain cut me right down the middle.

I squeezed my eyes closed, just as tightly as I squeezed my fist against my leg, trying to keep it contained.

"I can't imagine how hard it is for you." She released it on a murmur as she continued to pet the monkey while she stole quick glimpses at me. "Can't imagine how much you must miss him."

Could almost feel my Adam's apple getting caught in the web that'd grown thick in my throat. Trapped in the memories. In the misery. For once in my life, I wanted to climb free of it.

Fuck. I just didn't know how.

My teeth ground, and I stared out the windshield that was now clouded with fog and condensation.

Closing us in.

Like we were back in the sanctuary of her room back in L.A.

I found myself speaking before I even realized what I was going to say. "It's not as simple as me missing him, Edie. It's

181

that he's a missing *part* of me. And being without that piece makes me feel like I'm forever drowning. Like I can never get a full breath. Like my heart doesn't beat all the way."

She kept petting the monkey.

Giving me time.

Silent encouragement.

My voice turned wistful as my mind drifted back in time. "I remember hating being a twin."

I laughed, but the sound was pure torture.

"Hated that everyone confused us, always switching up our names. Hated that we wore the same clothes and the same eyes and the same fucking everything. Hated we were compared at every turn. Hated that he was always *better*. Hated most that I felt like I couldn't do a damned thing without him. When I wasn't with him? I always felt antsy. Like I'd forgotten something. Like I was *empty*."

The last broke.

Because that was an emptiness that was going to go on forever.

Vast and wide.

I looked over at her. Moisture had gathered in those aqua eyes. The clearest ocean and the deepest sea. She shook her head. "Maybe the emptiness is meant as a reminder. Maybe it's a gift so we don't ever forget. So we don't really have to live without them."

Pain crushed my chest. Pain for her. Pain for me. It squeezed so tight I thought it might crack my ribs.

Because her voice had gone so soft. Filled with longing. I knew she'd gone missing to her own emptiness.

Clinging to the loss like it might be a good thing.

Refusing to let go.

I reached out and cupped her cheek. "You're so brave."

She shook her head against my hand. "No. I was so weak."

I tried to keep my voice even, because every part of me wanted to lash out and cut down that bastard who'd made her feel that way. "It was his fault, Edie. He was the one responsible. Not you."

"You're wrong. I didn't even tell him no."

Anger fired through my nerves. "He was a man, Edie. A fucking *man* and you were fourteen years old. He—"

"Don't say it," she pled, cutting me off. "Please, Austin. Don't say it. I don't want to give him voice."

She'd shifted, one leg twisted under her so she could fully face me. She clutched one of my hands in both of hers and held it against her chest. "I don't want to allow him to steal any more of *this* than he already has."

God. I wanted it to be as simple as that.

Of all the things I'd leave in the past?

It was that asshole.

But there he was. Catching up to us again.

"If he texts you again, you need to tell me, baby. None of this hiding shit. You got me?"

She nodded, moving closer. "I won't let him take you from me again."

Unease gusted. A gale force wind.

I knew with every part of me that was going to be on me.

That if we were going to make it, I was the one who had to *fix* this. I was the one who fucked it up in the first place.

A smile trembled at her mouth, the somber mood shifting as she moved to her knees. The girl's tiny body filled up the big cab with her overpowering presence. She leaned over the bag to get to me, hair falling around her, and I lifted my face, welcomed her tentative kiss.

Her lips so soft.

So warm.

So sweet.

Vanilla and sunlight.

Blindly, I stuffed the monkey back in my bag, pushed it to the floorboards to make more room. I weaved my fingers through her hair and pulled her closer until she was straddling my lap.

Thank God for big ass trucks.

My hands wandered her back, skidding up and down, while I kissed her slow.

Long.

Deep.

She'd begun to sway, and I tucked her closer, her sweet body rubbing on my dick.

"Oh," she whimpered. Like she was surprised. Like she had no clue how my body was going to react to her.

She pulled back. A wistful smile graced her face. "Look at us, fooling around in a truck like a couple of teenagers."

She traced her fingers across my lips, glancing at my eyes, her tease netted in something serious and severe. Her tongue darted out to wet her lips, tentative fingertips fluttering along the hollow of my neck. "But I feel like this...right here...is where we left off. Where our time was stolen."

She glanced up at me, insecure and bashful, teeth tugging at her lip. "And here I am, still fumbling."

My hands framed her trusting face. "You're perfect, Edie. Every girl I ever touched should have been you."

Regret captured her expression, before it was chased away by the desire filling the cab.

Waters rising.

She kept moving over me, looking down as I stared up. Intensity growing and building.

That power that held us profound.

Fogged up windows.

Thrumming hearts.

Panted breaths.

"You're so beautiful, my sweet, sweet girl."

Her sigh was slow, and she clutched my shoulders as she rocked against me. My cock hard and begging.

Be careful with me.

I was always going to be, so I just gently gripped her hips and let her set the pace.

She rose up on her knees, her perfect tits bunched against my chest as she rode me with our clothes separating us.

Still, I didn't think I'd ever felt so close to someone than now.

She kissed me so deep I was sure this girl managed to touch

my soul.

Everything spun.

I shifted so my back rested against the door, and I spread my legs out across the long bench seat, my head against the window.

Knees on either side of me, Edie edged back, her head touching the roof, her hands on my face.

Touching.

Memorizing.

The girl left a trail of fire as she slid them down my neck and across my chest. Pressing over the spot that would forever belong to her. The girl marked on my heart.

You are good.

You are good.

I feel it here.

I felt her whispering her belief as if she'd uttered it aloud, just as sure as I could feel her entire body shaking as she moved to fumble with my fly.

My hand went to her wrist. "Baby...what are you doing?"

"I want to touch you."

My dick jumped.

Totally on board.

I swallowed hard, beating back the lust. "You don't have anything to prove."

Her words were breathy. "You've never made me feel that way. Never. Let me touch you. Taste you."

Oh. Fuck.

I exhaled a shuddered breath, lifting my hips a fraction so this courageous girl could tug them down.

My cock jumped free.

Edie gasped a tiny gasp, furiously chewing at that bottom lip in uncertainty as she stared at me exposed. Hard and ready.

Then she turned her attention to my face. Something bold and brave filled her eyes. Lust and desire.

She wrapped her little hands around my cock, right at the base.

So soft.

So good.

My head rocked back and I groaned her name.

Fuck.

Slowly, she tightened her hold, stroking up, palming my throbbing head like she knew exactly what to do. But she kept glancing up at me for encouragement, so clearly asking if she was doing it right, and I was cupping that sweet, sweet face, brushing my thumb across her lips. "Nothing's ever felt so good."

But then she dipped down. Flattened her tongue across the tip. Swirled it around.

I jumped.

And I was quick to change my mind. Because nothing had ever felt better than that.

Edie stroked me and sucked me in sync. Her hot mouth pulled hard at my head. Pulling pleasure. Pulling belief.

She glanced up. The intensity behind those eyes nearly gutted me.

The unadulterated shock.

The rapture.

The need.

The regret and remorse.

Above it all was the hope that shined around her like a white halo.

That girl taking me under her spell.

My stomach knotted and tingles gathered at the base of my spine.

"Edie, baby, I'm going to come. Fuck, you feel so good. So good," I mumbled as she continued the perfect assault of tongue and mouth and hands.

And this girl...

This girl just took me deeper.

Moaning as she began to writhe.

Her thighs pressing together.

And that was all I could take.

"Edie." It was a moan as I gripped her hair, my hips lifting from the seat as she took me as deep as she could take me, holding me there in the firm clutch of her mouth while I came apart.

Fucking sublime.

She eased off and my chest was heaving, my eyes hooded as I stared back across at this girl who sat back, facing me.

Looking a little stunned.

I sat up. The pad of my thumb brushed across her swollen lips, because I just couldn't help it. "Are you okay?"

A shy smile, and she nodded. "Really, really okay."

And I knew she meant more, that she was feeling proud and brave.

Beyond that?

She was flushed.

Hot.

Wet and wanting.

I slanted her a grin, knowing it was predatory and full of promise.

Because God damn. This girl had just blown my mind.

I tucked myself back into my jeans, shifted to a knee, edged forward. She inched back as I moved over her and pressed her back against the door. Getting her in the same position she'd just had me.

All except for her legs.

I nudged them open.

Spreading her for me.

Her skirt gathered at her waist, her little white panties covering up that tight little body.

Edie moaned, shifted in nervous need.

I edged back, let my hands wander up the soft, soft flesh along the inside of her thighs. "You are so gorgeous, Edie. Do you know that? Did you know every night for the last four years, this is what I've been dreaming about? About touching you the way I never got to. Loving you the way I should have."

An anxious, incoherent murmur mumbled from her mouth.

I hooked my fingers in the edges of her underwear, and she lifted her hips. I slowly pulled them down, the movement a little awkward in the confined space.

But so, so worth it.

Her pussy was bare, and there was nothing I could do but run my fingers through her slit.

My movements slow.

Filled with caution as I parted her.

Watching the whole time.

A groan escaped me when I found her wet and so deliriously warm.

Exquisite.

Her legs dropped open farther.

A needy sigh.

Of course, that sigh was my name.

I placed the softest kiss at her inner thigh, holding her open by the knees as I whispered at the silky flesh, "Can't wait to taste you."

She bucked when I licked through her folds. "Oh...God."

My head spun with an onslaught of dizziness.

Completely consumed by her. By her taste and her trust and her touch.

How long had it been that I'd been desperate for them all? How many fantasies had played out?

But reality was always so much better than fantasy.

Because the girl was fucking spectacular.

Her whimpers filled up my ears and her belief filled up my spirit.

I lapped at the delicate flesh, tongue exploring and memorizing. I changed direction and let my tongue sweep across her clit.

Those soft fingers ripped at my hair.

I sucked and pushed two fingers into her tight body.

Her walls clenched down.

I fucked her with my fingers, my tongue stroking soft and sure against that sweet spot, my other hand burrowed into the lush skin of her ass.

Her body bowed. Tightening. The energy rising higher and higher.

And she was making all these little noises that shot straight through me, all her pleasure dependent on the hands I'd come to hate.

The ones that'd caused so much destruction.

And fuck…all I wanted…all I wanted was to hold on to something good. To be responsible for it.

And then this girl…this girl broke as I held her in the palm of my hands.

Shattered.

Her hands fisted in my hair. And she was trying to hide the scream that erupted from her throat as pleasure took her hostage.

The severity roared and raced. Bounding around the confined space. She clamped around my fingers that were touching her deep.

She was panting, her body still bowed when I pulled her back onto my lap. My mouth demanding as I kissed this girl.

The girl.

The girl I'd once thought another penalty. The loss of her had almost been more than I could bear. It'd sent me spiraling to a depth I never could have anticipated.

Rock bottom.

She moaned my name, kissed me back. My mouth moved, this time a breath from her lips. And the words were so fucking low, like grit as I sang them quietly into the confines of the cab.

"My whole world in black and white…Until I was staring at it through the eyes of Firelight. Let me see it through the eyes of Firelight."

Edie pressed against me. Clinging.

I wrapped my arms around her waist, buried my face against the beat hammering in her chest. "You change everything, Edie. Everything."

We stayed that way for the longest time. Holding each other the way we always should have done. She leaned down, her lips gentle at the top of my head, at my temple, at my mouth. "Together," she said.

I breathed out relieved laughter, giving her another squeeze.

Helped her back into her underwear. Touched her face.

The windows were fogged and the cab steamy.

"We'd better get you inside."

"Yeah," she agreed, and I hopped down from the cab, silently moved around the truck and helped her down. We held hands as I walked her to her door.

She hesitated, glancing back at me, and I kissed her slow. "I'll see you tomorrow."

"Promise?" She smiled a shy smile. "This almost feels...like a dream."

I tugged her close, murmured at her mouth. "You are my dream." I pecked her lips before I nipped at them to lighten the mood. "I'll see you tomorrow. I promise."

"Okay." She let herself into her house, and I shoved my hands into my pockets, rocked back on my heels while I waited to hear the lock engage, then waited a little longer because I couldn't seem to be able to pull myself away.

With a smile pulling at the edge of my mouth, I finally spun around and headed back to my truck, swung open the door.

Then I fucking froze.

I could feel it.

The freezing cold chill that slid down my spine. The presence encroaching on me from behind was definitely not the pleasant kind.

Slowly I turned.

That big, burly motherfucker stood there with his fists clenched, looking like an irate bull who was getting ready to charge.

And apparently I was wearing red.

I stood up taller.

Knew I could take him simply because I *knew* exactly what I was fighting for.

His face pinched, and he gave his head a harsh, disbelieving shake. "You think she doesn't deserve better than that? A quick fuck in some piece of shit truck?"

This guy didn't have the first clue what Edie deserved.

Had no idea she deserved absolutely everything.

All things good.

And I was going to be the one to give them to her.

I tipped my voice into something I hoped was placating, knowing full well it was edged in spite. Just couldn't curb it. "You don't know what you're talking about, man. Maybe the better question would be what the hell are you doing, lurking out here like some kind of perv?"

He flinched.

Yeah, asshole. Not cool.

He shook it off. "You know that's not what I was doing. Heard that pile pulling in here close to forty minutes ago. You think I didn't know what was going down?"

"I know you don't know what was going down. But even if you did, it isn't any of your business, so I suggest you take a step back and cool the fuck down. Edie doesn't answer to you."

And I sure as hell didn't.

He tore at his hair. "I waited for her. Fucking waited for *years* for her to be ready. And you waltz in here and rip her right out from under me."

My brow twisted, and I took a step forward as I cocked my head. "Did she ever tell you once to *wait* for her? Did she ever give you any indication there was more to the two of you than what you made up in your head?"

His rebuttal flew out fast. "I'd treat her right."

"That's not what I asked."

Silence. No words said as he stared at me through the hazy glow of silvery moonlight. Because we both knew she hadn't.

I roughed a hand over my face. Because fuck. This was Edie's friend and I wanted to tear into him. Beat him if only for the fact I knew where his thoughts had been.

In her body and in her head.

But I knew well enough you couldn't help what the heart claimed. "I'm sorry, Jed. Sorry if you're hurting. Sorry if it hurts you to see her with me. But I'm not going anywhere. As long as Edie wants me...this is where I'm gonna be."

He seethed the words. "Hurt her, asshole...hurt her...and

I'll be coming for you."

A snort shot from my nose and I hopped into my truck. I leaned out to grab the interior handle, attention turned on Jed. "I sincerely hope you do."

Because the thought of hurting Edie again?

I'd rather be dead.

twenty-three

EDIE

*H*eidi swung her feet where she sat on the counter beside me. I pushed the old-school cash register drawer closed with a clink. "There," I said. "All done."

"All done!" She offered me one of those crooked smiles showcasing her two missing teeth.

Affection pulsed my heart an extra beat.

"Thank you so much for helping me." I ruffled her hair.

"Workin' at the shop is my fav'rite," she said with her cute lisp.

"Well, that's a good thing, because you working here at the shop with me is my favorite, too."

Her entire face lit up, and I picked her up from under her arms and set her safely on the ground. I glanced at the clock.

"Your daddy should be finished with work really soon. Why don't you run into the back office and gather up your things?"

This morning, she'd come rushing in at the crack of dawn with her backpack bouncing on her back, the bag stuffed full of coloring books and paper dolls. She'd somehow convinced her dad it was much more important for her to help me in the shop today than a day of summer school could ever be.

So here she was.

Keeping me company.

Helping me keep my thoughts focused on the here and now instead of drifting back to last night. Back to that miraculous boy who made me feel so free.

Considering she kept having to snap me out of my daydreams, apparently my concentration was shot.

The door banged behind her as she disappeared into the back, just as the front door chime jingled. All the guys plus Blaire piled in, lugging the equipment after today's lessons.

Clay shot me one of his overabundant grins. "Hey there, gorgeous. See you managed to hold the fort down for the entire day. Still standing. I'd say today was a success."

Clay was probably one of the most positive guys you could run across. He wasn't even a cup half full kind of guy. His was just always overflowing.

"Yep. No major disasters other than a bottle of spilt milk, so I'd call that a win."

Kane roughed a hand through his dark brown hair, fighting a grin. "And I'm gonna step out and guess that spilt milk might have to do with one little hurricane running around here today."

Before I had the time to answer, Heidi came barreling back into the shop, her arms raised over her head as she flew across the floor. "Daddy!"

He swooped her up, tossed her into the air, hugged her tight. "There's the love of my life," he said.

God. How much he adored that child.

My chest felt a little tight, but I couldn't look away as he peppered her with kisses.

She wiggled. "Eww...Daddy. You're still all wet."

He scoffed playfully. "Well I *am* wearing my wet suit, so you shouldn't be surprised when it gets you all *wet*."

She howled with laughter as he tickled her, the two of them

getting lost in their own little world.

Jed shot me an off-putting, sidelong glance when he passed, following Deak to the back wall where they stored the rental boards.

What was that?

Blaire came behind the sales counter where I stood. She forced out a hard exhale as she started to wiggle out of her wet suit. Totally struggling. "I swear, I'm going to break my neck one of these days trying to get out of this thing."

I giggled. "Need a little help?"

She widened her eyes with the tease, balancing on one foot. "Oh, I need a *lot* of help. But I think I can handle this."

She stumbled as she yanked it free. "Okay, maybe I can't even handle this."

When she finally freed herself, she lifted the rubbery, black body suit like a trophy. "Score. I do believe that earned me a margarita."

"Don't get too proud of yourself, Care Blaire," Clay called. "You think *taking a breath* earns you a margarita."

Clay loved to bait her. The two of them were constantly going round and round.

She popped a hand on her hip. "Says the guy who showed up to work still drunk this morning. On a *Wednesday*."

"Hey, where the hell do you think the name Topsy Turvy Tuesday came from?" He was all unremorseful grins.

"Um...from you?" But Blaire was grinning too, gathering her things and heading out to help Clay and Kane with the life vests.

Deak joined them, and they headed into the back where they were stored, Heidi chattering nonstop as she trailed behind.

Jed hung back, and I knew it was on purpose, because normally he would have been right in the middle of putting everything away.

Tension filled the room.

I tried to keep my attention down, trained on end of the day paperwork, because I wasn't sure I could deal with Jed's judgement right then. But I couldn't keep ignoring him when he was suddenly there, right behind me.

"What are you doing, Edie?"

"Paperwork?" It came out a question because I knew full well that wasn't the answer he was looking for.

He scoffed. "You know that's not what I'm asking you. I want to know what you're *doing*. A week ago, you're jumping up and running from this asshole, looking like you've seen a damned ghost. *Scared.* Next thing I know, I wake up in the morning and you've never even been home, and that very same night you're out in his truck in the middle of the night like some kind of cheap whore."

He might as well have slapped me.

I reeled around, facing him. "What did you say?"

Frustrated, he raked a hand through his hair. "Shit. I'm sorry. Shouldn't have said that. But fuck, Edie... You deserve so much better than that. I'd treat you like a queen."

My head reared back, his implied words so clear.

My entire being rattled with even the idea, the thought of fully giving my body still ushering in a surge of fear.

My accusation was thick, coated with embarrassment. "You were watching us?"

"I wasn't watching you, Edie. I was *worried* about you. There's a fucking difference and you know it. And never in all the time I've known you have you not come home at night. Never dated or flirted. And I...I..."

Harshly he shook his head, looked at the ground. "Shit."

Sadness spread slowly, this man who'd never been anything but kind. And I knew he was hurting. That he'd had illusions that he and I would one day grow into an us.

"I was *waiting* for him."

The truth of that statement slammed me.

Pain sheered across Jed's face, his tone almost pleading. "But he broke your heart."

He didn't know the story. Of course he didn't. But I knew he'd made his own assumptions about my past life. That he had no clue.

I couldn't blame him.

I'd never allowed anyone to get close to me.

Only Austin.

Only Austin.

"He did," I admitted softly. "But I think I broke his, too."

I swallowed around the regret I felt at hurting Jed. Because I loved him. I did. The way I loved a brother.

"I will forever be grateful for everything you've done for me." I lifted my hands out at my sides, offering up the shop as evidence. "For taking me in and giving me a job."

My voice lowered in emphasis. "For your friendship."

I blinked, and my chest squeezed with the admission. "But my heart…it's always belonged to him."

All the broken pieces.

Austin was the one who held them together.

The same way as I held his.

"Not gonna stop fighting for you, Edie. I can't."

My face pinched, and I pressed my hands to my chest. "Jed…you have to stop fighting for something that's not there. You're going to realize it one day…that you're meant for another. She's out there. I promise."

He was shaking his head to refute me when everyone came bustling out from the back.

Deak clapped his hands together. "Let's call it a day, shall we?"

"Day!" Heidi shouted, jumping around.

Blaire rounded the counter. She hopped up to sit on it, facing me. "Day," she mouthed.

I chuckled, trying to let go of the unease rippling through me, hating that I'd unknowingly hurt Jed. Knowing it would take him time to accept I was right.

Twenty minutes later, I locked the front door behind us, and everyone filtered out and into the approaching evening.

"Who wants to grab a beer?" Deak asked, turning to walk backward, grinning back at us.

"I'm in," Clay said.

"Of course you are." Yeah. Blaire was right there with that one.

Clay raised his brows. "And you're not coming?"

"Uh... Margarita, remember?"

"Right."

"I'm game," Jed said.

Kane palmed the top of Heidi's head. "I have a hot date with the prettiest girl in Santa Cruz. Gonna have to pass it up."

Heidi grinned up at him as if she was looking at her hero.

Emotion twisted my insides, and I almost called out that I'd find a ride home since I'd ridden into work with Blaire and Jed, when my gaze drifted to the left.

Drawn.

God.

This boy.

Austin leaned up against the side of his truck. The truck that sent a rush of red up to flush my cheeks, the memories making my knees weak with the way he made me feel.

With him, I felt like I could fly.

Something like a smirk took over that pouty mouth, and I shivered, my voice probably as weak as my knees when I called to Blaire, "Um...I think I got a ride."

"I bet you have a *ride.*" She winked, catching up to Clay, Deak, and her brother, while my footsteps diverted.

I glanced both ways, quick to trot against the road, until I was flush with his chest, pushing up on my toes, stealing another one of those kisses I'd never been brave enough to steal.

Heaven.

That's what it was. His mouth on mine, his hands pulling me close, his breath washing over me.

"See, I promised," he mumbled at my mouth.

A giggle rolled free, and I clutched his shirt. "Promise I'll see you every day for forever."

I tried to keep it playful. To keep out the desperate hope that blossomed within it.

Austin softened, ran his hand over my head, cupping the side. "We're going to have to see if that can be arranged."

Butterflies scattered. I couldn't stop them if I tried.

Austin tilted his head, the boy so beautiful he stole the air from my swelling lungs. "I think I'd like that."

He wound my fingers through his. Without further words, we walked as if we were called. Down to the beach where I kicked off my shoes. Austin released me, held back and watched as I dipped my toes in the cool, cool water. The gentle waves rippled, embracing me up to just above my ankles.

Just like they'd done before.

My invitation the same.

For this boy to touch on what he'd lost.

Wind rustled through, whipping my hair around my face. Hugging my arms across my chest, I watched the sun as it began its descent, the calm so great up against that constant chaos that moved around us.

I glanced over my shoulder at the boy. The intensity stark and severe. Vast and profound. Rays of burning light blazed down on him, the striking, defined lines of his gorgeous face cast in golds and reds.

Edged in twilight.

A storm brewed in his expression, his hands fists at his sides, his breaths harsh, though I knew he tried to keep them controlled.

His demons fought to be brought out into the light that was giving way to dark.

I took one step deeper into the ocean, and turned to face him.

The eye of my storm.

I stared at him as the tide rushed against my calves. Silently, I fed him all the faith I could find inside myself, pouring it into him.

Praying he could *feel* it.

His jaw clenched and he took a step back.

Away.

Refusing my invitation.

Harboring all that hurt and holding on to every regret.
This beautiful, broken boy was lost for one more day.

Three weeks passed this way. Just Austin and me. Renewing the faith that had been damaged. Finding the hope we'd lost. Breathing our belief into one another.

He pushed my boundaries. And I pushed his.

"Wait," I whispered.

I asked for it. More time. Even though we both knew one day our walls would crumble.

twenty-four

AUSTIN

*E*die moaned around the mouthful of lasagna she had in her mouth.

Homemade.

Only the best for my girl.

"Oh my God…it should be a crime for anything to taste this good."

I shot a smirk at her from where she sat across from me at the small table in my house.

Her brow dented and her eyes narrowed. "Are you thinking dirty thoughts, Austin Stone?"

I shrugged. "Possibly."

"More like possibly definitely," she said, nudging the sole of my boot with the toe of her shoe under the table.

She had me there.

"You are sitting three feet away from me…making noises like that. What did you think I would be thinking about?"

The tease was clear, all mixed up with an undertone of seriousness.

Drop-dead seriousness.

Because this was Edie Evans we were talking about. The girl who blew me away every time she stepped into the room. Stealing more and more of my breath. Becoming my air.

A blush flushed her cheeks. But that sweet innocence? It was always there beneath the flirty ease that seemed to show up more and more often with each day that passed.

"I like when you think about me." She said it low.

I groaned and leaned forward. I stared at her striking face through the flicker of candles arranged at the center of the table. "Not *when*, Edie. All the damned time. Every second of every minute of every day. I don't know how to *stop* thinking about you."

Didn't want to, either.

She looked at me the way she'd been looking at me for the last three weeks. Like maybe she saw the man I'd left my brother's house to find. The man I wanted to be.

Kind of the way Shea looked at Baz.

Like I was her meaning.

Her life.

And I wanted to be the one strong enough to stand at her side. Protect her.

Her voice was a wisp. "Don't ever stop."

I set down my fork, pushed back my chair. "Come here."

She slid out. Desire belted me when she stood, the girl so bright amid the shadows, something so pure and good in the dark.

She curled onto my lap, slender arms around my neck, so much joy and contentment in the sigh she released at my throat.

My guts knotted in lust and devotion. I pressed my nose into her hair. "Won't ever stop. I never did. All the years we lost still belonged to you."

She peeked up at me. Her words were breathy and sunk straight into me. "We shouldn't waste any more."

My grin was slow and my heartbeat was fast. "No, baby, we most definitely should not."

wait

We sat there for a while, just enjoying the peace. I'd basically threatened Damian and Deak with their lives if they showed up back home before midnight tonight.

Date night, and all.

Seemed crazy doing such normal, couple things.

Spectacular.

I patted her thigh. "Hop up. I'll do the dishes really quick and then we can head down to the beach. I got us a bottle of wine."

"You know exactly how to woo a girl, don't you, Austin Stone? Make dinner? Do the dishes? Wine? Could I ask for anything more?"

Everything about her had gone coy, from the tease falling from her lips to the perfect curves of her body, her shorts short and her tank tight, legs so damned long.

But it was the soft tenderness in those wells of aqua that captured me.

"I might just have someone really important to impress."

She giggled. God, I loved that sound. Making her that way.

Happy.

"Is that right?"

I tucked a strand of hair behind her ear. "That's right."

She climbed off and helped me to stand. "Come on...I'll help so we can get finished faster."

"Someone's anxious."

"Um...you did say wine, didn't you?"

I laughed toward the ceiling and gathered our plates. "That I did."

We headed into the kitchen, rinsing the dishes and shoving them into the dishwasher. We worked effortlessly side by side.

My phone buzzed where it sat on the counter.

I glanced at the screen.

Dread skidded beneath the surface of my skin, my heart stalling out.

Baz.

He never called.

And I meant never.

Our correspondence over the last three years had been entirely through texts and letters.

My throat grew thick, and I gulped around it as it went to voicemail.

Edie scraped a plate. "Who was that?"

I didn't even have time to answer before it was ringing again.

Her gaze landed on my phone, and she quickly darted her attention up to my face, just barely lifting her chin in that silent, powerful encouragement she always gave. "You should get that."

Should I?

I stepped back. Unsure. Hating the fear that clawed at my senses. Making me feel small and useless. That fucking worthless kid who only ever made things worse for his brother.

I forced it down, my stomach raw as I picked up the phone. I stared at it for a beat before I accepted the call and put it to my ear. I was already walking toward the back sliding door when I said his name. "Baz."

Choked it really.

Because I hadn't heard his voice in so damned long and I had no idea why he was calling me now.

"Austin." It sounded just as thick as mine. Low laughter vibrated through the space, disbelieving and incredulous. "God...you sound different."

Cool air collided with my heated skin when I stepped out onto the wooden porch overlooking the beach spread out below. I closed the door behind me.

Wind gusted through the trees and the sea howled at the night.

Peace and chaos.

"A lot of time has passed," I said. I was crushing the phone to my ear like it could break up the tension when I felt his hesitation and turmoil through the line.

Apprehension clutched my words. "What's going on?"

I aimed for it to come off casual. Like this was just a normal fucking conversation on a normal fucking day.

Wishful fucking thinking.

"Need you to come home, man. To L.A."

Saliva pooled in my mouth. Soured in my stomach when I swallowed it down. I stared out into the obscured horizon. Endless darkness. An abyss of black.

The ocean moaned, forever a prisoner to its unrest.

It stirred through me. Inciting old, unrelenting pain.

"Told you I wasn't ready to do that yet. Is...is everything okay?"

Okay.

That sentiment sounded so goddamned cheap.

"That's what you keep sayin', Austin. That you're not ready. And what that tells me is you're still out there blaming yourself and you haven't figured out the truth of it yet."

Felt like he kicked me. That presence shivered through the atmosphere. "When are you going to let me accept responsibility for what I did? When, Baz? I left because of this. Because you've always taken the blame when it was mine."

"Not your fault."

I scoffed. "Come on, man. I'm not a little kid anymore. You don't have to go around trying to protect me, and you can stop trying to convince me different than what I already know."

"If that's what you want, then fine. Accept it, baby brother. Take it on your own damned shoulders when I know it belongs on mine. Then come home. Where you belong. Need you, Austin. I can't keep going on the way I am. Need you to take the place that belongs to you."

"What the fuck are you saying?"

"You know exactly what I'm saying. Don't lie to me and tell me you haven't always wanted it. That you haven't always *felt* it."

Anxiety skimmed my flesh. "That's not my place. You know I don't sing for them."

Sorrow stretched between us like a brittle, dried out rubber-band. It didn't matter how many miles separated us. It was there, distended between us.

205

"Yeah? Then tell me when you're gonna start singing for you. It's time, Austin. It's time."

The glass door slid open behind me, basking me in light. Slowly, the slider shut. That overwhelming peace surged, spreading ease and comfort. She wrapped her arms around me from behind. Energy buzzed. She buried her face between my shoulder blades.

I gripped her hands where they hugged my stomach. Holding her closer.

"Think about it," Sebastian said.

I rejected the flare of anticipation that flamed in my spirit.

"I'm not what you're looking for."

Wouldn't put myself in that position. The last thing I wanted was to let my brother down again. Let the boys down. I wasn't sure I could ever be what *Sunder* needed me to be.

Someone who could lead. Support and guide.

"Austin…" Baz attempted.

"I'll talk to you later, okay?"

He sighed. "Okay. But soon."

"Yeah."

I knew it was coming. I had to make a decision. I needed to go home and set things straight for good. Prove to Baz I was going to be okay out here on my own so he could move on and live his life right.

For his family.

He clicked off and the line went dead. Silence swooped in with the rushing wind. All except for the sound of the sea and the pant of our breaths. Edie squeezed me tighter, like she was trying to convey she wasn't ever going to let me go.

"Is everything okay?"

She was broaching. Pushing me to let her into those places I'd always refused to give her access to. I'd always offered her bits without burdening her with the brutal reality.

"Yeah."

"He wants you to come home?"

"Yeah."

The breath she released was a shudder, sweeping her in a

fear she tried to contain but was so clear.

"He misses you."

My words were rough. "He's hinting…but I know, Edie. I know my brother so damned well, and when he loves, he loves with everything he's got. And he loves his family, and no doubt, they've become more important than the band. I don't blame him. Not a bit. But I know he sees me there, taking his place."

"Is that where you see yourself?"

"You know it's not."

"Why?" She hugged me closer, her words a caress from behind. "You're so talented, Austin. You are destined for great, great things."

I inhaled, breathing in the chaos churning in the sea.

The chains that bound me to it cinched tighter on my spirit.

"Singing is part of my penalty." A moment passed with a thousand questions.

"I don't understand," she finally whispered.

I clutched both of her hands in mine, balling them over her mark on my heart. The place that would always belong to her. "You're the *only one* who really does understand, Edie."

Slowly I turned to face her. Lights from within the house shined around her, the girl outlined in a white, shimmering glow. She reached out and brushed her fingertips along my jaw, her touch breathing all that belief, eyes searching me in the night.

Getting it all without having a clue. And I couldn't keep it contained for a second longer. Couldn't keep up the walls that shut her out.

"I did it, Edie. It was my fault."

The confession gushed from my lungs. So quiet. Still, they hit with the force of a sonic boom.

She stilled, and there was no missing the confusion that flashed through her gaze. Then that sweet mouth turned down at the corner.

In sympathy.

In love.

This girl who saw right inside of me.

Pain slammed me as memories flooded behind my sight, and everything just poured out.

Rained and flooded.

Right into her hands and into the well of her pure heart where I knew she'd hold it safe.

Julian balanced right at the edge of the sea. As if he were walking a tight rope. Body shifting this way and that as he hopped along the white foam lines left by the receding tide.

"Check this out, Austin," Julian called to him.

Austin clambered two feet behind, skipping along those lines, doing his best to keep up.

"Check out what?" Austin called right back, grinning wide. Austin loved the sun. The ocean. The days just like this one when they were completely free.

"This!"

Julian suddenly darted into the waves, flapping his arms all around like he was flying. He jumped then dove, tumbling headfirst into a wave. He rolled with the tide, jumped back up. His mouth was parted with his laughter, big rivers of water soaking his face.

"You see that?"

Laughter bubbled up from Austin's belly, and he went running, too. He dove in.

Their older brother yelled from where he was farther up on the beach, "Not too deep, Austin and Julian."

"We're not," they both promised in sync.

Always in sync.

Julian gave Austin a sly roll of his eyes. "What's he doin' with that girl?"

Austin pffed. "Baz is always with a girl. Always talkin' to them. Dad says that's what men do."

Julian curled his nose. "I'm glad I'm not a man. Girls are gross."

Austin laughed. "One day we're gonna be. And Baz said one day we're totally gonna change our minds."

Julian shook his head. "No way."

Then he shoved Austin with a grin, and the chase was on. "Bet you can't catch me," he hollered over his shoulder.

"Bet I can."

Austin did. Just barely. And then he was it and Julian was running after him.

"Bet you can't stay under water as long as I can," Austin challenged.

"Bet you five bucks I can."

They shook on it.

The waves were deep enough to come up to their waists where they played. Austin took a step deeper, dunked down, and held up his fingers to count. By the time he got to thirty, he felt the need to take a breath. He started to pop up, but Julian pushed down on his shoulders, keeping him under.

"No fair, Julian," he wanted to shout, but he was still under water, and the two wrestled around the way they always did.

Julian finally released him and Austin shot back up, breaking the surface and gasping for air.

"You jerk." He punched at his arm. "But I think you made me win. Thirty-seven."

"Thirty-seven? I'm totally gonna win."

Julian lifted his feet, sinking his butt to the floor of the ocean. He stayed down there for longer than thirty, then forty, and Austin knew he was beat. Just when Julian started to float up, Austin held him down. Just like he'd done.

His twin kicked and flailed.

Austin was laughing and Julian was struggling.

That's what Julian got for holding him down longer.

Baz looked their way, and Austin grinned at his brother, figuring he'd laugh at him rough-housing with Julian. Maybe come and play with them when he stopped flirting with that dumb girl.

But then Julian wasn't flailing anymore. He twitched, and his body jerked in Austin's hands.

Something cold washed over Austin. And still, he just stood there, Julian held under by his hands.

Julian wasn't moving anymore.

Fear throbbed in Austin's throat, this achy feeling taking him over, like he was missing something. He struggled to lift Julian from *the water. Grappling to hold him from under his arms.*

Baz started running. Screaming. Yelling. "No, no, no."

Baz splashed through the water. He ripped Julian from Austin's arms.

Empty.

That's the way Austin's gut felt, and his head spun as he watched their older brother haul Julian onto the sand.

Austin heard screams somewhere. All around him. Dead silence at the same time.

Like he was watching it from above.

Empty.

He crawled up the beach. Terrified. Wanting to touch Julian. To shake him. To tell him to get up.

Please, please, get up.

Baz pumped his chest, pinched his nose and blew into his mouth, pumped his chest again. Tears streaked down Baz's face, something frantic and shaky in his movements. "Austin...what did you do...what did you do? Oh my God, what did you do?"

Austin scrambled backward on his feet and hands when people circled around Julian.

Pushed his back up against a big rock. Hiding. Rocking.

Empty.

I buried my face in her neck, letting all the wetness seep out there.

Gutted.

Empty.

I hadn't cried in so damned long. God knew I'd shed enough of them, and I hated being that fucking pathetic kid who couldn't stand.

But there was no stopping them now.

Not when she was crying with me. For him. For me. Her tears streaked hot into my hair, and she held on to me like she knew she was my lifeline.

A beacon in the distance.

Calling me from the dark.

Guiding me home.

Even when I didn't have the right to have one.

"They let me go see him in his hospital room. All these tubes and wires...they were everywhere. Keeping him alive. But I knew, Edie...I fucking knew he was already gone. I could *feel* it, could feel the other half of me was missing."

My voice was gravel, sorrow saturating me all the way through. "Baz...he took me aside, shaking me when I kept crying and crying. He kept saying it wasn't my fault. That it was his. He told our parents he wasn't watching us and Julian got caught up in a wave. Took the fall when it was me."

"I'm so sorry, Austin. I'm so, so sorry."

Her soft mouth was at my ear, lips kissing at my temples, her lips almost frantic where they were pressing at my cheeks and my jaw and every inch of my soaking wet face.

She didn't give me any bullshit about it not being my fault. She didn't tell me it was *okay*.

Because she knew it wasn't.

"Think my mom knew the truth the second I walked in."

Hurt gripped my heart. Squeezing so damned hard I was sure it was going to burst. "But she was just as gone as Julian. I stole his life. Her life. My dad...he turned into a monster. Baz was the only thing I had."

Her upper back was pinned up against the wall, my arms around her waist. "Baz saved me, Edie. Kept me alive when I wanted to die. I can't be that person anymore. The one who's always taking from him. Disappointing him. *Hurting* him. But I don't know how to stop failing everyone I care about. Everyone I *love*."

Nudging me back, she set her hand over my heart. Palm flat and firm. Those aqua eyes were wide. Vulnerable. Sharing in my pain.

Understanding the way only she could.

"You are good. You are good. I feel it. Right here." She whispered the words she'd always given me. Her belief.

My arms were back around her. "I didn't mean to, Edie. I swear, I didn't mean to. I'd do anything to take it back. To trade him places."

"I know. I know. I know."

She mumbled it as she kept covering me in those manic kisses, her hands sliding all over my body. Like she'd give anything to be the one to patch it back together.

I pushed her further up against the wall. My mouth captured hers. This kiss...this kiss was filled with all the torment the two of us had shored up. What'd been locked away.

What for the first time I'd released into her hold.

She whimpered, and I held her by the hips, my hands greedy as I tugged and pulled at her body.

Desperate to get her closer.

Desperate to stand in her light.

"Edie."

"I know...I know," she promised.

I shoved the slider open, kissing her the whole time while I edged her back into the house, my hands holding her sweet, trusting face.

She wrapped her hands around my wrists, lifting to me as I backed her down the hall and into the refuge of my room.

Didn't even know how we made it there, but Edie was on the bed, and I was hovering over her, licking into the well of her mouth. Her tongue hot and needy.

She tore at my shirt. Our kiss was only broken for the flash of a second when she ripped it over my head.

Our movements were frantic.

A frenzy of needy hands and hungry mouths.

Our spirits thrashed and tangled. The energy grew intense. Billowing around the room. Demanding to be sated.

Then her shirt was gone, and I was slipping my hands under her back to free the clasp of her bra, her tits small and so goddamned perfect. I grasped them in my palms, brushing my thumbs over pink, pert nipples.

I sucked one into my mouth, teased at the other.

Edie writhed. Her head rocked back on my pillow. Her fingers locked in my hair. My tongue traveled up the valley between her breasts, licking up the delicious slope of her neck and into her mouth.

A shimmer of lust glowed in the air.

Our bodies rocked.

Searching for friction.

For relief.

Both of us desperate to drown in belief.

I pushed up onto my hands to look down at her, and she slowed, staring up at me with trusting eyes. She didn't break her stare as she touched her mark forever imprinted over my heart.

My heart that thundered and rushed.

Every nerve alive.

Right then, all our truths became so damned clear.

I reached out, palmed one side of her jaw, my thumb running across her cheekbone. The words were low.

Emphatic.

"I am so in love with you, Edie Evans. With all I have. With everything I am. I have loved you for as long as I can remember. That will never change."

More tears leaked from her eyes, that precious face aglow with brilliant light. "I love you, Austin. I never stopped. You will always be the next beat of my heart."

A strangled breath left me at her confession, all those empty places so close to being full.

I couldn't tell what I hated more—the flare of guilt for feeling it or the decision to push it aside and let Edie fill me with her comfort. To let her drown me in her relief.

Fingertips fluttered across my eyelashes, my lips, my chin, back to the spot that would always belong to her.

"I don't want to wait. Not anymore."

Shock froze everything, before hesitation crept through her name. "Edie…"

The two of us were right there, teetering on that line, so close to breaking through that barrier.

A soft, wistful smile fluttered across her sweet mouth. "Be careful with me."

twenty-five

EDIE

*H*e stared down at me through the shadows of his room. I thought maybe there was a part of me that had always known his secret. A part that recognized the devastation of a single mistake. A mistake that could never be taken back, no matter how much you had never wanted to make it in the first place. Despite the fact you'd willingly give up everything to go back and make it right.

Those stony eyes watched me. In them was a love so intense it came shining through the storm.

Obliterating darkness. Conquering fear.

I was no longer afraid, and I refused to continue to be chained.

"I trust you."

For two beats, he searched my face, then he swallowed hard. My gaze trailed the thick bob of his throat, his Adams apple pronounced. I knew that was the moment he accepted what I was saying. What I was offering him.

I was giving him the last broken piece of me.

The root of my every fear.

My every regret.

One mistake.

That's all it ever takes.

After tonight, I knew that was something Austin could never be. I'd thought so once. But I knew better now. Knew we were meant and bound, and he would never waste what I was giving him.

I trusted him to cherish it the same way as he cherished me.

I trusted he would be *careful*. Because he knew I could never go back *there*. He knew I could never risk the type of loss I'd spent so many years sure I would never survive.

I couldn't do it again.

He brushed back my hair. The smile he tipped at me was adoring. The need in his expression profound. "You are my world."

He dipped down, his hands still pressed to the bed on either side of my head. He kissed me slow and deep. The power of it was so devastating I wanted to weep.

My fingers dug into the strength of his shoulders, the muscles twitching beneath my touch, his body so beautiful as he eclipsed me in his perfect dark.

His mouth moved over mine, lips sucking and brushing, our tongues lost to our own slow dance.

The room spun and my body lit.

He sat back on his knees, his striking face bold in the shadows. Mesmerizing. Breathtaking.

My back arched, my body instinctively begging for his touch.

Slowly, he tugged at the button of my shorts, watching my reaction. The sound of the zipper rang in the air. A rush of palpitations scattered through my heart.

Oh God.

I felt so nervous.

So alive.

I lifted my hips an inch off his mattress. Every part of me shook as he slowly peeled my shorts and panties down my legs.

His voice was hoarse. Both rough and soft. "I can't wait to be inside of you. To feel this body beneath mine."

That voice dipped, coated with slow seduction. "Can't wait for my cock to be buried so deep neither of us knows where one of us starts and the other begins. To make you mine. I promise you, I won't be giving you back."

It was almost too much when he grazed the tips of his fingers between my legs, barely touching all those places I was dying for him to be.

"Take me." It was all a throaty mumble.

He slid off the bed, shed the rest of his clothes. Energy bounded from the walls. Dense and deep. Dark like this boy.

Every inch of him was smooth, muscled perfection, the ink etched into his skin a work of art, so much like his body.

He moved across the room. The defined curve of his ass made my throat close up and my thighs clench tight. Desire wobbled like a top in the lowest part of my stomach.

His body was flawless.

Exquisite.

Meant for me.

He grabbed a box of condoms from the drawer in his desk. He turned back, affection playing at his mouth when he gazed down at me as he approached.

Be careful with me.

He climbed back between my quaking thighs, his eyes never leaving mine as he covered his thick length.

Trembles rocked me like a landslide.

"You're shaking," he said, smoothing his hands from my knees to my hips, cinching around my waist.

An unsteady smile breached my swollen lips. "Because you make me shake."

He groaned and crawled over me. Caging me in. Shrouding and protecting. My safety. My haven.

He rocked against me. The tip of his cock brushed my belly as his mouth brushed across my lips.

Shivers rushed, free and fast, skating across my skin.

"And we're barely getting started on this journey that's

never gonna end."

He nipped at my chin. At the cap of my shoulder. The top swell of my breast. "I'm going to love you forever. Touch this body every night. Kiss these lips every morning."

I fell a little further.

Every inch afire, my nerves zinging and my heart rate careening out of control.

He would be my ruin.

My utter demise.

My chaotic, blissful end.

This boy who'd finally let me all the way into the deepest part of his soul.

And I was letting him into mine.

"Make love to me. Please."

Austin shifted, and I released another shudder of anxiety, my body wracked with pent-up need and old fears I was so ready to let go. He held onto his cock at the base, aligned himself with *me*.

He ran just the tip through my center.

Testing. Teasing.

I moaned a wispy, "Yes," and bowed from the bed. Begging with my fingers that clawed at his shoulders.

Austin pushed into me. Not even an inch. But deep enough to knock me from my foundation. Deep enough to send a stampede of emotion galloping through my senses, my heart a thunder and my ears a roar.

All singing his name.

Love. Love. Love.

His jaw clenched, ticked in restraint. "Are you okay?" he gritted, and I forced his bare chest to mine.

Our skin tinder.

The contact a match.

I lifted my hips. "Take me."

He sucked in a breath and filled me in a long, hard stroke.

Fire.

I cried out against the stunning intrusion, breath stolen and body full.

So, so full.

It felt like the boy was touching me everywhere, taking me whole.

His.

Austin wrapped me up in those strong arms, his weight on his elbows, his fingers in my hair. He rocked his hips, the measured thrusts slow and sure.

Deep and demanding.

Edged in anguish. Rimmed in hope.

He fucked me.

Saved me.

Adored me.

Pulling pleasure.

Again and again.

Higher and higher.

His pants grew harsh, and I clawed at his back.

The threat of utter euphoria shivered through my body. It lifted and spun, a tightening inside that propelled me to another plane. Where the stars met water. Where the worlds became one.

Where shadows and light became color and darkness grew thick.

Where all sense was lost except for the feeling that you were one with something greater than you.

At one with a love that had brought me here.

One that lifted me from the depths and somehow held me under.

Where I drowned in his darkness and that storm blistered and blew and overthrew.

I gasped and hurried to meet each of his wild thrusts as his rhythm grew reckless.

I struggled for the air I couldn't find.

Because each breath belonged to him.

Darkness and light.

Life and death. Energy spun and spun and spun.

A rolling storm.

Pleasure wound.

Furious.

Unrelenting.

Austin gasped, and pulled almost completely out, my body begging for his return. He slammed back into me.

The last of that dangling thread split.

Shredded.

Lights flashed at warp speed.

Blinding, total bliss.

Austin roared.

Roared my name as he twitched and jerked, his orgasm my own.

I whimpered as beauty spread. Saturating every cell.

Two souls taken by the unending storm.

He slumped down on top of me, his hands restless as they brushed through my hair, his face buried in my neck.

"Edie, fuck. I love you. I'll never hurt you. Whatever you want, I'll give it to you. It's yours. *You are my light.*"

He dropped his forehead to mine, and an intense peace fell over me when he set a big hand on my face while we both panted for the nonexistent air. He swallowed hard, his heart manic where it pounded against my chest. He pressed his lips to mine, keeping them still, just the hint of a kiss as he breathed me in.

Life.

His eyes squeezed close, and the words flooded the room, almost pained.

"Do you feel that?"

"What?"

"Me."

I caressed his twisted brow. "I've always felt you."

He exhaled, wrapped me up, and rolled us to our sides. We lay in the middle of his bed, tangled.

"Sing to me...the way you used to," I murmured into the calm, the relentless guilt that chased us both sated to a simmer.

Wrapping us in a cloak of security.

A blanket of darkness.

Austin...

This beautifully broken boy.
He sang me my song.
Firelight.
And I knew. I would forever burn for him.

twenty-six

AUSTIN

I framed her face in my hands.

Kissing her.

She was on her tiptoes.

Trying to get closer.

The way she always did.

I fucking loved it.

Loved that it seemed like she couldn't get enough.

Like she couldn't get close enough. Couldn't get deep enough. Couldn't get *touched enough*.

I was all too eager to sign up for the task.

My chest pressed full with that emotion that gripped me every time she was near.

Joy.

I could feel her smiling under my mouth.

Damn, I loved that, too.

"I need to go."

"Why?" I said with a pout. Because hell. If this was your girl? You'd pout, too.

She giggled. "Um…there's this little thing called work. You know…pays the bills and the rent?"

"There's also this little thing called staying in bed…making love to my girl. All day."

She groaned a throaty sound. "Don't tempt me."

"Funny, 'cause that's all you do." My voice lowered. "Tempt me."

"Mmm…well, as *tempting* as staying in bed with you all day sounds, I really have to go. Cash register won't run itself, and I'm not sure Heidi is qualified to hold down the shop by herself quite yet."

A chuckle rolled from me. "I'm sure she'd be all too willing to try."

"Oh, I bet she would."

Edie and I? We'd been this way for the better part of the last month. Ever since the night I'd finally let her break down the last of my walls. When I'd let her into that place where I'd never let anyone else, and she'd turned right around and let me into hers.

Trust.

They say relationships are built on it.

And I was still kind of reeling she'd trusted me with *that*.

I pecked another kiss to her sweet mouth. "Fine. Go. But you'd better miss me while you're gone."

She tossed a grin at me from over her shoulder. "You know I will."

Leaning with my shoulder against the door jamb, I watched her perfect ass sway as she walked to her car, because I couldn't get enough of that, either, returned her small wave when she drove away, smiling like a damned fool when I turned around.

Startled, I jumped and skidded to a stop.

"You've got to be kidding me with this."

There was Deak, sitting at the table with his ankle hooked on his opposite knee, reading the paper and sipping at his coffee like he'd been there the whole damned time.

"Always so damned jumpy."

I widened my eyes. "Always so damned creepy."

He laughed at the ceiling. "I am many things, mate, but

creepy is not one of them." He waved his hand over himself, at his bare chest and bare feet, board shorts his only attire. "Ladies love it."

It was my turn to gesture at myself. "In case you hadn't noticed, not a lady."

He shot me a mocking grin. "Just keep telling yourself that."

I shook my head, fighting a smile. "Huh…if I didn't know better, I'd say it sounds like someone wants to get his ass kicked."

"I'll take ya any day, mate."

"And you just keep tellin' *yourself* that, pretty boy."

"Pretty boy?" Deak scoffed, voice oozing with offense. "I'll have ya know I've been running around the wilderness of Australia with snakes and spiders that will kill ya with just a nip since I was a boy. Swimming with sharks. This here is all man. Nothing pretty about me."

I snorted. "I bet you spend more time in front of a mirror in the morning than Edie and Blaire combined."

"Hardly. Wake up looking this good. It's a sad, sad story for the rest of you assholes."

Chuckling, I shook my head as I went into the kitchen and poured myself a cup of coffee, wandered back out and sank down in a chair opposite Deak. "What's on the agenda today? You giving lessons?"

"Nah. Off today. Jed has some shit scheduled for me tomorrow," he said, flipping through the pages of a newspaper.

"Who the hell reads an actual newspaper anymore, anyway?" I taunted, kicking up my feet.

"Real men."

"Right," I drew out. I laughed beneath my breath as I took a sip, breathing in the easy atmosphere when I rocked back.

I relaxed that way for the longest time before I felt something shift in the air.

Deak stilled. Sat up a little higher in his chair. Eyed me over the top of the paper. Something that looked like confusion moved across his normally casual expression.

He sat back, head angled as he stared across at me.

Unease flitted and fired at my nerves. "What?"

"Don't talk much about yourself."

I blinked. "What's that supposed to mean?"

He hiked a shoulder, as calm as could be. "Just wondering why this dude looks just like you and wears your last name, and I've never heard a thing about him."

Apprehension slithered down my spine. "What the fuck are you talking about?"

But I already knew. When I first left L.A., *Sunder* hadn't hit it big the way they had in the last couple years. I mean, they'd already had a huge ass following, sold a ton of records and constantly sold out their shows, but their style was too gritty and raw and hard to draw in the masses.

But something had shifted on the last album. Things had exploded. Their faces showed up on TV more and more, stories about them popping up on my Facebook feed. Didn't know if it was the song Baz had done with Shea that'd shot *Sunder* into the stratosphere or if it was just because the last album was so kickass, which it most definitely was.

Brilliant, really.

But whatever the factors, they were more popular now than they'd ever been.

Deak folded the paper in half and slid it across the table.

It was open to the entertainment section. At the top of the article was a big black and white photo of the band live on stage. Still, the static image managed to capture the intensity of the show. Beside it was a close-up picture of Baz grinning out, Shea wrapped around him, her head resting on his chest.

Emotion throbbed. Hurt and respect. Love and regret. And a fuckton of fear.

Couldn't help but feel all of them when I thought of my big brother.

Deak jabbed at the picture with his index finger, head cocked to the side. "Look familiar?"

I scrubbed a hand over my face.

No.

I hadn't ever told Deak who I was. He just figured I was some kind of stray roaming city to city playing his music, a gypsy who couldn't stay in one damned place. He had no clue about the home I'd left behind.

"Yeah, looks familiar."

"Yeah?" he pressed.

"What do you want me to say, Deak?"

"Uh, I don't know....how about why you held out on me and didn't tell me your big brother's a rock star? You could start there."

"Don't exactly advertise that fact. And if you didn't know who he was to begin with, what does it matter?"

He cleared his throat, paused while he sifted through his thoughts. "Doesn't matter who he is, Austin. Couldn't give two shits that he's famous or what the fuck ever. Think ya know me better than that by now. Just figured you didn't have any family to your name. That you moved around trying to find a place to call home and maybe you'd found it here. And for the record, I know of the band, but I'm hardly some fanboy who's gonna go searching for pictures and posting them on my Pinterest wall. My apologies for not recognizing the connection."

The last was pure sarcasm.

I scowled at him and he just kept right on. "You two not get along?"

"It's not that...it's just...my past's...complicated."

He laughed, but there was something dark about it. "Pretty sure the past is that way for the best of us, mate. Doesn't mean ya have to go hiding it."

I exhaled heavily. "I...I don't talk about it with anyone. Not you. Not Damian. So there's no need to get offended."

Only person I trusted with it was Edie.

"All right. I get it. Respect you." He nudged the paper closer. "But you might want to take a look at this."

Standing up, he walked down the hall, leaving me to my privacy and a queasy sense of dread.

I did my best not to read the caption at the top of the

article, but there was no ignoring the words. My chest tightened.

Sunder Splintering?

sun·der (sŭn'dər)
sun·dered, sun·der·ing, sun·ders
v.tr.

1. To break into two or more pieces or parts; sever
2. To force or keep apart
3. To form a barrier or border between

Warily, I pulled the article closer, swallowed around the lump growing thick in my throat when I began to read.

How long until *Sunder* lives up to their name?
Los Angeles bred *Sunder* is back at it again.
Late last week, Sunder cancelled a sold-out show in Denver just hours before curtain drop due to an *unforeseen emergency.*
Sebastian Stone, lead singer and founding member, was spotted hours later rushing into a Los Angeles emergency room.
It was announced early the next morning the last three shows of their North American tour would be rescheduled.
An undisclosed source says, "Baz is doing what is right for him and his family...and that's being there for them when they need him."
Things seemed to turn around for the troubled band when their track, *Forever,* featuring Shea Stone, hit the top of the charts two years ago. Since then, sources close to the band say Stone has shifted his attention away from the band and turned his focus on his growing family.
Sebastian and Shea Stone were wed three years

prior. Shea, who already had a young daughter before Stone came into the picture, gave birth to the couple's son, Connor, two years ago.

Guitarist Lyrik West recently said, "Family is always gonna come first for us. Whether it's our support of one another or for our growing families. That's just the way it has to be."

West was recently wed this year. He and his wife are expecting their first child this winter.

A statement from bassist Ash Evans added to the conflicting reports. "We were born to make music. Simple as that. The rest? Rumors or reality? It really doesn't matter. *Sunder* isn't going anywhere."

Can *Sunder* survive another crisis?

Or will the old adage remain true?

What goes up must come down.

Come home.
Come home.
Baz's petition spun around me.
Pushing and pulling.
Attracting and repelling.
I just didn't know if I ever could.

twenty-seven

AUSTIN

"I'm off work. Why don't I pick up take-out and I can bring it to your place? We can have a nice dinner. Just the two of us."

A grateful sigh pushed from my lungs as I listened to the quiet promise of Edie's offer, the sound of her small car accelerating the only sound in the background.

She knew how difficult today was.

Of course she did.

"I'd really like that."

I could almost hear her smile. "Okay then. Give me about twenty minutes and I'll be over."

I hesitated. A bated hush hovered around us, filled with all the things silenced that shouted to be said. "Thank you," I finally murmured.

Her voice softened in that adoring, supportive way. "This is what we do, Austin. We stand by each other. Understand each other."

"Yeah," was the only answer I could give before I clicked off the call. I pressed my hands flat to the countertop in the kitchen, dropping my head. I pulled in a deep breath, fighting to keep the panic at bay.

Fuck.

I hated *today*. Hated it just as hard as I tried to ignore its existence.

Deak walked in. Completely oblivious to my turmoil. He clapped me on the back. "How's it goin', mate? Clay just called. Gonna head out to meet him for a beer. You and Dam wanna join?"

I glanced at him. "Nah, man. Edie's on her way. Bringing dinner."

A frown pinched his brow when he saw my face. "You good? Lookin' a little peaked."

I swallowed the bitter taste in my mouth. "Yeah. All's good."

Motherfucking lie.

Because every time I thought I was getting free, loosed from the chains, they just tightened their hold.

But what did I expect?

Every year it seemed to hit me harder than the last.

"All right, then. Give me a call if you change your mind."

"Sure thing."

The door slammed behind Deak, leaving me to the silence.

That and the shrill ring of my cell phone going off in my pocket.

I tensed.

It's weird how sometimes you just know. It could have just as easily been the call of my girl. The sound of comfort.

But I knew.

I knew deep in my gut that exact same sound was the sound of death's toll.

I dug it out of my pocket, held it in my hand.

Baz.

Shakily, I exhaled the air from my lungs, tempted to reject the call and send it to voice mail. But I was so damned tired of running from shit. I answered it and put it to my ear.

"Hey," I said.

Uncertainty burned through the line. Finally, his voice came through, tight and choked. "Happy birthday, baby brother."

My eyes slammed closed. Like it could block it out. "Baz…we don't fucking do this day. You know that."

"Think it's time we did."

"God…why do you keep doing this? Pushing and pushing. I asked you for space. For time."

Without doubt, Baz was dealing with his own shit. Hurting. For once, maybe needing me. But this…this was too much. Too overwhelming. Too much to shoulder.

"I'm doing this because I fucking care about you, Austin. Because it's time for you to really live. Time for you to come home. And not with your head slumped between your shoulders but with it held high."

"Damn it, Baz. You're asking too much of me."

On top of it all, he had no clue about Edie. About the fact I had found *life*. And the last place she wanted to be was back in the middle of all that mess.

It felt like I was being ripped in a million different directions. My need to make up for all the shit I'd ever caused my brother. Knowing he was in trouble. Tied in his own way.

My penalty…my debt to Julian.

My devotion to Edie that would last forever.

All mixed up with embers of the fire I'd felt flicker around me every time I was backstage at a *Sunder* show. A slow burn that ached to be a part of what they were.

"And you're not giving yourself enough credit. You're the one who's selling yourself short."

"I've got to go," I told him, ending the call, because I couldn't handle a second more. It was all too much. The weight bearing down.

Not today.

Not today.

Without even thinking about it, I snatched a bottle from the cupboard and headed to my room. I flew back out, down the hall, and out the back, one hand fisting the neck of the bottle of Jack, the other fisting the damned monkey.

My footsteps pounded as I took the worn path down to the deserted beach. Night crawled across the heavens, a smattering of stars strewn far and wide.

I sank down onto my back on the cool, damp sand, closer to the water than I'd ever dared to come. Still, not close enough to touch. Waves rolled and crashed, climbing up just two feet away, before they fell back into the ocean.

I stared up at the endless web of stars.

Wondered if he was up there or at the bottom of the sea.

I clutched the monkey to my chest, and that emptiness throbbed. "I'm so sorry, Julian." It grated out from somewhere within my soul.

Without sitting up, I took a swig of Jack. The fluid came like a shock to my senses. It burned hot down my throat and hit my stomach like a punch. A stream of it dribbled out the side of my mouth.

I swiped the back of my hand across the wet trail.

Took another slug. Then another.

"Fuck, I'm so sorry," I mumbled, rubbing my face as the alcohol took to my veins. The wind howled and that presence thrashed. "I'm so fucking sorry."

My heart nearly went haywire when I felt the second presence wash over me. Comfort and ease. Her shadow fell across my face and her silhouette came into view.

I rocked my head back, taking her in where she stood over me.

My saving grace.

Sympathy edged her soft smile. "I thought I might find you out here."

I sat up, took another drink. There was no disguising the disgust in my tone. "Predictable, huh?"

She sat down on the sand beside me and drew her knees to her chest. She looked over the toiling darkness, then over at me. "No, Austin. I think it's completely natural. This is where you feel closest to him."

I couldn't stop the awe from pulling at my mouth. *This girl.* I reached out and touched the soft curve of her face. I didn't know if it was Edie or the alcohol that toppled my reservations, but the words flooded free. "You know what scares me most, Edie?"

She just looked at me with her head angled. Waiting. Patient and pure.

"It scares me that when I'm with you …it doesn't hurt so bad. That when you're near, the emptiness doesn't go so deep."

She chewed at her bottom lip, hesitating. "And you think feeling that way is a dishonor to him?"

I gave her the slightest nod, my hand squeezing her cheek. "It kills me I get to feel *this*, and he never will. Kills me that I took that from him. That I stole from him whoever his wife was gonna be. Whoever his kids were going to be."

She twitched in discomfort, reached for the bottle, tipped it up, and took a swig. Slowly, carefully she began to speak. "I wake up every morning and wish I could go back and change it. Erase that one mistake that started everything."

She glanced at me. Her expression twisted through me like a knife. Bleak with the pain I'd give anything to obliterate. "But I know I have to thank God for the little things. The things that are so easily taken for granted. The goofy things that make me laugh. The flowers that bloom in the morning. The flashes of *hope* when I'm having an especially hard day."

She sucked in a staggered breath. "And then I'm given something so wonderful I can't make sense of it. I'm given *you*. And I know it inside…through all the depression and hopelessness…there are great things out there, just waiting for us in the despair."

"Edie." Her name flowed from my tongue, and my fingers wove deeper into those shiny white locks, all the way back until I was cupping the whole side of her head. I pulled her toward me. My mouth fell over hers.

Her lips so damned soft.

Tongue so damned sweet.

Light.

My head spun and my gut clenched tight, my thoughts foggy but my intentions clear. "I need you."

"You have me," she whimpered as I shifted, crawling over

232

her and pushing her back onto the sand.

She ran her hands up and down my chest, and I sank down, pressing into hers, my heart catching onto the frantic boom, boom, boom of her pulse.

Or maybe it was mine.

Thunder.

I kissed her wild, this girl who got me the way no one else could.

The one who was made for me.

The light in the middle of the blackest storm.

Her phone dinged in her back pocket. Then did it again.

"Let me turn that off," she mumbled, and I barely edged back to give her enough room to dig it free. She swiped across the screen.

I knew she wanted to hide it. The sheer panic that raced across her face. She tried to contain it, but it was clear.

She fumbled and quickly tried to switch off the phone.

I yanked it out of her hand. "Don't hide this, Edie."

I sat back on my knees, eyesight blurry as I struggled to focus on the words.

Fucking whore. Keep that kind of secret from me then turn around and fuck with my life?
You owe.

Rage.

It blistered through my senses like a flashfire. I crushed the phone in my hand.

Fear clouded those brilliant features, her words shaky with turmoil. "I don't understand why he won't just leave me alone. I just want him to leave me alone."

I stumbled to my feet. My body swayed. I was hit with a rush of dizziness, my head fuzzy.

"Fuck." I roughed a hand over my face. "I won't let him do this, Edie. I won't let him. I'm gonna fix this. I promise, I'm gonna fix this."

Edie scrambled to standing. "It's not yours to fix, Austin."

I started back for the house. Blinking. Trying to clear my thoughts. Edie was right behind me.

When I got to the porch, I paced, ripped at my hair. "It's my fault, Edie, it's my fault."

She just had no clue that it was. That I was the one who had to make it right. I had to end this.

"No, it's not," she promised in all that belief. "I'll…I'll call him. Talk to him. Tell him it's over and just to leave me alone."

"No. I don't want you to ever talk to him. See him. Not ever again." I spun around, pushed her up against the exterior wall. I muttered the words between frantic kisses. "He can't have you, Edie. I won't let him have you."

I pawed at her, desperate to get her closer. "I need you…I need you…I need you."

I mumbled it, kissing her harder.

Deeper.

Needed more.

My head spun, and I yanked at the button of her shorts, desperate as I shoved them down, taking her underwear with them.

I fumbled at my fly.

Impatient.

"I need you," I demanded again.

Edie was touching me everywhere, her hands just as frantic as mine. Filling me up with all her belief.

She gasped when I suddenly lifted her from her feet and had her pinned to the wall.

I filled her in one possessive stroke.

"Austin."

The world tilted, and I gasped at the utter relief I felt in being inside this girl.

I fucked her hard and fast.

Needing to erase all the shit that threatened to come between us. Needing to get her closer. To hold her and protect her. Never let her go.

My orgasm hit me out of nowhere. So intense. Blinding. My ears rang and I shouted her name.

Through it, I could barely hear her cries. But they were there, landing against my senses like a slow reverberation.

"Wait…wait."

Wait.

I pulled out, my eyes wide with shock when my body continued to jerk and spasm, come jetting all over her belly.

But it was the fact it was dripping down her thigh that rocked me back and knocked me sober.

I might as well have driven a blade straight through the broken parts of her tender heart.

Because I saw it all unfold as if in slow motion.

Splintering.

Shattering.

The betrayal froze her face in horror. Her mouth and eyes open wide as her body reeled back.

She had an appointment next week to get a checkup and prescription for pills.

I mean, we'd had a fucking heart-to-heart about it. About her fears and reservations. It was a damned big deal. Part of her *trusting* me.

What did I do?

She began to shake. Uncontrolled. "No…no…no."

Frantic, she grabbed her underwear balled by her shorts, trying to rub me away from her body.

To clean herself of my stain.

"No."

That word? It was so quiet. Tortured. An echo of old, old wounds that had been torn open wide.

"Edie." I touched her shoulder.

She jerked, but I knew she wasn't seeing me. "Don't touch me." Her plea overflowed with tears, and she fumbled into her shorts. Her hand darted out to keep herself from falling.

She stumbled into the house.

Disoriented.

She looked around. Lost. She lurched toward the table where she'd left the bags of takeout and grabbed her keys.

She didn't look back when she ran out the front door and

toward her car.

I was right behind her, my pleas frantic and spilling out. "Edie, baby, I'm so sorry. Stop...please stop. Listen to me."

She wrenched open her car door. She shrugged me off when I tried to grab her arm. "Don't touch me," she mumbled again.

"It's not the same. It's not the same. Please, listen to me."

She started the car and threw it in drive, started moving with me still standing at the open door.

I jumped back when she accelerated. The door slammed shut and she swerved when she hit the street.

"Fuck." I screamed it.

Be careful with me.

That was the one thing she'd asked.

She'd given me everything else.

I ran inside and grabbed my keys, darted right back out, coaxing my truck to start. The engine turned over, and I gunned it.

When I got to Edie's place, she was already throwing her car in park and stumbling out.

The face I adored was blotchy and red, soaked with tears.

The front door opened and Jed came running out.

I flew out of my truck right at the moment Edie fell into his arms.

Sobbing.

I rushed for her. She whimpered at the feel of my hands on her bare arm. "Don't touch me. Leave me alone. Please. Leave me alone."

Jed turned her so I couldn't get to her, protecting her the way I was supposed to do.

Blaire was suddenly there. "Edie...oh my God...Edie."

Blaire grabbed for her, and Jed released her. Edie buried her head in Blaire's chest.

Weeping hard.

"I've got you, sweetheart," Blaire said, shushing her. Blaire glared back at me as she led Edie toward the door.

I went after them.

Jed shoved me in the chest. Hard. I floundered back. I caught myself right before I fell.

Didn't matter. I flew right back around, pushing back.

Ready for a fight.

To fight for her.

Couldn't let her go.

Wouldn't.

"It's not the same, Edie," I heard myself yelling. Begging. "It's not the same. Don't do this. I love you. Please. Edie…fuck…please. Listen to me."

I love you.

Jed got in my face. "Warned you if you hurt her, I'd be coming for you."

All my attention was on the door, the sounds coming from inside. I angled that way. "I need to—"

He shoved me again. "Only thing you need to do is get the fuck out of here. *Listen* to her. She told you not to touch her. To leave her alone. And that's exactly what you're going to do."

Be careful with me.

I stumbled back.

Panting.

I could feel my world crashing down around me.

I couldn't even do that.

Hate thudded through my veins.

Because that was me.

Always taking the good I was given and crushing it in my hands.

I always fucked everything up.

Hurt those who meant the most to me.

But if it was the last thing I did? I'd set Edie free. Loose her from the chains that still kept her bound. Protect her from that bastard so she could live.

Just once.

Just once.

I would do something right.

twenty-eight

EDIE

"*E*die…calm down…calm down."

Blaire brushed her fingers through my hair, pushing my head back as she did. Forcing me to look up at her and into the blank worry flooding her expression.

"Shh. It's okay. Calm down. Just calm down, okay? Take a deep breath."

I attempted it, but my throat was too raw and my lungs were too tight. I wheezed around another tremor that rocked through me and my chest heaved.

"How could he?" I gasped.

How could he?

He promised. He promised.

Blaire gripped my face. "Did he hurt you, Edie? You need to tell me if he hurt you."

"Yes…" Another wheeze, and then I shook my head. Trying to make sense of what had just happened in the last fifteen minutes. "No…not like that."

How had we gone from the highest high to the lowest low?

Austin.

I ached, and I wanted to push back out the door to where

he was yelling for me and promising it wasn't the same. I wanted to run to him.

I wanted to *believe*.

I didn't know how to process it. How to separate the two.

Instead I cried toward the floor, my ears filled with the harsh tone of Jed's voice and Austin's panic. I dropped to my knees when I heard the roar of his truck take to the street.

"Austin." His name left me on a landslide of grief.

Blaire got to her knees in front of me, smoothing back my matted hair. "What happened?"

Jed blazed inside. Aggression and rage. "What did that motherfucker do to you? I'm going to kill him, Edie. Swear to God. I knew it…I fucking knew it."

I gasped out a cry.

"Jed…stop it." Blaire shot him a warning glance. "You're not helping anything."

Heavy footsteps thudded as he approached. Jed's boots came into my vision where I cried toward the floor. "What did he do to you, Edie? Tell me."

Blaire kept smoothing back my hair while old turmoil crested and broke over me.

Wave after wave.

All my fears.

All my insecurities.

The stolen hopes.

The things Austin made me want.

Only for the wants and desires Austin inspired in me to trigger all the fears again. I felt consumed by the loss. It was the type of loss I didn't think I could ever survive again.

So I'd run from the possibility.

Threw up walls all around me in hope it would protect my fractured heart from being completely obliterated.

This was the very thing that had held up the barriers between Austin and me all those years ago. What had filled me with fear when I first found him here. What had filled his touch with caution while I'd slowly succumbed to what had always roiled between us.

All of it because I'd been terrified of ever experiencing anything so horrific again.

Only I'd just lost it all over again because losing Austin hurt almost as bad.

Different.

Still, it was enough to gut me. Rip my insides to shreds.

Austin.

Would I forever allow it to dictate who I was? Who I was going to be?

I sank all the way to the ground. I hugged my knees to my chest. Through bleary eyes, I looked at my friends. Those who'd taken me in when I was at my lowest.

"I…" It broke in my throat, and I squeezed my knees tighter, as if it might fill up the emptiness throbbing in my chest. "I…when I was fourteen I…"

twenty-nine

EDIE
AGE FOURTEEN

*E*die pulled the fat roll of packing tape across the top of a box.

Sweat dotted her temples and rolled down the column of her neck.

Nausea swelled.

A rush of dizziness swirled, and her hand shot out to hold herself up on the box to keep herself from swaying. She dropped her head and fought the bile that worked its way up her throat. She fought hardest against the awareness that hovered just out of reach.

Floating around her conscious and teasing at the periphery.

Six weeks ago, she'd come home from that party and forced herself into a scalding hot shower. She'd scrubbed herself until her skin was raw and red. Until she could no longer smell the sickening smell, the foul stench made up of sex and man and her own stupidity.

She'd stepped from the shower, a towel wrapped around her shivering body, and looked at her haunted reflection in the mirror.

She'd felt so stupid and naïve. Used and dirty.

Never again.

Standing there, she'd promised herself it would never happen again. She'd never allow another man to use her that way. No man's touch would ever again be unwanted or fill her with fear and dread.

She'd promised herself a lesson learned, but an act forgotten.

One mistake.

One she was leaving in the past.

Now beads of sweat gathered like sickness and slicked her flesh.

Nausea swam.

She flew to her feet and slid onto her knees on the bathroom floor a second before she purged her despair into the toilet.

"No. No. No." She clung to the seat and begged the prayer. "Please, no."

On trembling feet, Edie exited the city bus. She stepped down into the neighborhood she'd never wanted to return to. The bus accelerated. She held her breath as a thick plume of black diesel fumes spun through the hot, stagnant air.

Butterflies tumbled in her belly.

But not the good kind.

These flapped and whipped and scattered in fear, and she swallowed hard, her hands in fists, balled up as she hugged her arms across her chest and forced herself to move in the direction of the house she'd snuck out of eight weeks before in the middle of the night.

She had no other options or choices but to come here.

You don't have to be afraid. You can do this. You can do this.

It left her mouth on a whispered chant as she followed the street signs, heading north, deeper into a worn down neighborhood where the houses were dilapidated, as seedy as they were shoddy.

Someone honked as they flew by, obscenities cast into the

air, and she cringed, shoulders drawn to her ears as if it could protect her from the unfound fate lurking in the distance.

She sucked a bolstering breath into her lungs when she stood at the gate of the house.

It looked so different in the day than it had that night when it'd been little more than a blur.

A short chain-link fence blocked off the property.

Within, a tiny weathered house was hidden in a mess of overgrown trees and shrubs. Garbage littered the unkempt yard, and a broken-down car sat in front with the hood removed, deteriorating off to the side.

You can do this.

She repeated the pep talk, really having no clue what she was truly doing or what result she was hoping for.

A ball of dread spun up her already unsettled stomach as she thought of who was waiting inside.

But she'd done this, and she needed help. She had nowhere else to turn.

So she marched up the walk, didn't slow or pause before she pounded on the door.

That sudden burst of courage withered when the door jerked open.

He stood there with a salacious smirk lifting at one side of his mouth, shoulder leaned up on the jamb. "Well, well, well. Looks like someone's back for more. Wasn't so bad after all?"

She shook, twisted her fingers into knots. "No...that's not..."

That smirk curled into a sneer. "Then what the fuck are you doing here? We had an agreement. I told your brother you were sick and you skated off without him ever having to know what a hot little slut you are. No harm. No foul. Now it's on you to keep your end of the deal."

No harm, no foul?

Her world tilted with all the *foul*.

"I need your help."

Mocking laughter rumbled from his mouth. "How's that?"

"I'm pregnant."

He froze, before he shook his head. "And what's that got to do with me?"

Her frown was unconscious, tight on her brow as she tried to process what he was implying. "I…we…"

His laughter went hard. "Little whores like you…always playing the same damned game. Pretending we got you in trouble to drain us of a dollar or two. Don't think you're the first one who's come knocking at my door. How many other guys did you hit up?"

"Other guys?" Her head shook. "There was only you."

He huffed toward the sky. "Right."

"I swear to you." It came out a pleading cry. "Please, I need you to help me."

Disgust shook his head, and he swore beneath his breath, left the door open wide while he disappeared inside.

Her guts coiled too tight as she waited, apprehension lifting when he reappeared.

He grabbed her by the wrist, squeezed open her hand, forced a wadded-up ball of money into her palm.

"Three hundred dollars. Three hundred dollars more than you're worth. But hey, sometimes you have to pay the bitch."

Confusion clouded everything as the door was slammed in her face.

Edie lifted her hand, staring down at the payoff.

Three hundred dollars.

God.

She shook her head, fighting more of the tears she'd been fighting for days.

She was so stupid. It was only then she finally caught onto what he thought she wanted.

She squeezed her eyes, like it might block it out.

Then, just like the naïve little girl she knew she was, she turned and ran.

Rain pelted at the window, big fat drops that gathered and streaked in thick rivers down the pane. Edie stared out of it, at the green landscape of her new Ohio home, her hand on her belly that had barely begun to show.

Her secret.

Her life.

A tender smile threatened at her mouth, all wound up with the fear.

Fear of being completely out of control.

Fear of the future.

Fear of *fate*.

She knew it would come. She was a fool to think it wouldn't come sooner.

Her mother's gasp had her jerking her attention to the side. Her mother reached out and clung to both sides of the jamb to keep from falling. "Edie...baby...what did you do?"

Her mom held her on the floor while Edie sobbed, rocking her like the child she was. "It's okay, baby, it's for the best. It's for the best. You have your whole life ahead of you. You'll thank me later. I promise, you'll thank me later."

"No, momma, no."

Her mother pressed a kiss to her forehead. "It's so hard to see the future, Edie. We don't realize how big it is, stretched out in front of us, when all we can see is the here and now. But I can see yours. I always have. The dreams I've had for you. All the opportunities you can attain. The amazing things you can achieve. Who you can become."

But Edie.

She saw images of the future unfolded out in front of her. Like snapshots of what could be.

Only these frames. These frames looked so different than what her mother could ever imagine.

Edie curled into the tightest ball. Night pressed down from all sides. Her knees were tucked around her round belly, as tight as she could get them, but not nearly as tight as her arms.

She kicked, and tears slid free. Overwhelming emotion swamped Edie.

Joy and sorrow. Joy and sorrow.

It slammed her from all sides. Tripping her from below and burying her from above.

She wasn't supposed to love. Not like this. But she did. God, she did.

Edie wailed, her head pressed into the pillow. Her face lifted toward the ceiling as she released a tortured cry, her mother's hand squeezing hers almost as fiercely as she squeezed back.

"You've got it, Edie. One more push. One more push and you're all done."

Done.

Edie didn't want to be.

She wanted to hold on. Keep *her* where she could hold her. Where she could protect her and love her.

"No." It was a scream, a raspy, broken weep, her head frantic as she shook it back and forth.

But there was nothing she could do, her instincts alive, and she bore down, her teeth gritted.

She pushed.

And everything went silent.

Her heart stopped as the entire world froze.

A tiny shattered cry.

A tiny perfect body.

Edie's heart took off at a sprint.

Love. Love. Love.

It engulfed and immersed and overthrew.

Quickly, Edie pushed up to sitting, hands reaching. Desperate as she fumbled for the child. "Please," she whimpered.

And *she* was there, placed in Edie's arms, swaddled in a small white blanket, a blue and pink cap on her head.

Lips red.

Eyes swollen.

She blinked the bluest gray.

Edie's mother looked down, and tears were soaking her face. "It's time."

Edie locked her against her chest. "No...I changed my mind. I changed my mind."

Her mom shook her head. "Don't do this, Edie. Please don't make it harder than it already is."

A nurse reached for her child, and Edie held her closer.

"No...no...I changed my mind."

No one listened. Hands ripped her away.

Her mother's voice was at her temple, a hand in her hair as if it might soothe and ease. "You'll thank me later. I promise, baby, I promise. Soon you'll forget."

Edie watched as the door fell shut behind them, her breaths gasped and strangled, her hair matted and stuck to her face.

Every inch of her ached.

Torn open wide.

Edie screamed.

Screamed toward the heavens.

"Wait. Please, wait."

And this hollow space.

It just echoed back.

Loss. Loss. Loss.

"No," she wailed. "No."

And Edie promised.

Promised she would never again be left without a choice. Promised no man would ever touch her again.

Edie forced herself to stand. To move. To leave the house.

Each footstep felt as if it required the greatest effort, and her next breath felt as if it might never come.

Days and weeks and months were spent trying to convince herself that it'd been the right *choice*. That *she* was safe and loved and cared for the way she should be.

Edie's head knew it.

She just didn't know how to convince her heart.

It just hurt *so* bad. A crippling anguish that never seemed to abate.

So she searched for her, in the face of every baby that passed, with every cry that echoed through the air, through the years that didn't erase the emptiness or grief.

Edie shut herself off. Locked down her heart and spirit. Let herself grow stagnant and stale.

Because she couldn't do it again. Couldn't risk the loss of that kind of love.

Not ever again.

She trudged through the days and years and allowed herself to grieve at night.

The door creaked open, letting in a wedge of muted light. She tensed as footsteps echoed. She gasped in a startled breath when soothing fingertips gentled through her hair. "Shh…I've got you."

And for the first time, fear didn't come, and when he crawled into bed next to her, she didn't feel so hollow.

The boy with eyes like hers.

Haunted.

Lost.

He wrapped her in his arms. Tender arms that shook and a body that trembled. She breathed out and pressed her head against his chest where his heart thundered against his ribs.

He lifted a dream catcher above them. "See. You don't have to be afraid. This…it will hold all your dreams. They have no power over you. They can't hurt you. Keep it with you always, and it'll give you peace and safety."

It was the first time Edie had felt it since she let *her* go.

Peace.

thirty

AUSTIN

The plane touched down in L.A.

I climbed in the back of the waiting town car, shot my brother a text.

In LA.

His return was quick.

You're here? Why didn't you tell me you were coming?

I tapped out a response.

Last minute decision. Where are you?

Guilt pressed down on my shoulders. I knew I was misleading him. That I wasn't here for the reasons he wanted me to be. But I couldn't tackle that right now and take care of Edie. And fuck…Edie came first. If Baz had the first clue about what was going down, I knew he'd agree, too.

Old Sunder house. Band meeting. All the guys are here.

Be there soon.

My knee bounced a million miles a minute. My fingers tapped just as fast against my thigh.

Forty-five minutes later, the car began the ascent into the Hills. Houses were butted up close to the narrow, winding road, and evergreens and palms swayed in the summer breeze. That endless expanse of city sky was dyed a dingy gray by the heavy smog.

A swell of homesickness hit me hard.

I both welcomed it and hated it all the same.

Because with each second that passed, anxiety fired through my nerves. It was an antsy, sick feeling that ratcheted higher and higher.

Tick.

Tock.

Like the slow turn of the wheels that cranked a vintage clock.

Going to fix this, Edie. Promise you. Even if you never talk to me again, I'm going to fix this.

The words were a grated promise held silent on my tongue.

I fisted the tattered green monkey I'd stuffed in my backpack when I'd rushed through my place this morning, grabbing things I thought I might need.

Damian had been on my heels, demanding to know what the hell was going on and how long I would be gone. Told him I didn't know for sure, but I had to go home for a while, and if by some miracle of God Edie showed up, to tell her I'd be back as soon as I could.

I crushed the worn plush monkey in a fist, like if I squeezed it hard enough it would cry out the answer to the abounding questions.

Instead it echoed back the loss, whispered the moans of

that snuffed out presence that haunted me like a ghost.

The car pulled into the hidden brick drive. A row of flashy cars, some I recognized, some new, lined the front of the massive stucco mansion. Most of the impressive structure was concealed by towering trees, hidden by the sweeping span of their lush, secreting leaves.

The anxiety lighting up my nerves ratcheted another rung higher.

We came to a standstill.

I opened the door, climbed out, and slung my backpack over my shoulder.

I muttered a quiet, "Thank you."

Feet echoing, I trudged up the walkway to the ornate double doors.

I had no clue if I should knock or ring the bell or walk right the fuck in.

Because I no longer knew my place.

Didn't know where I belonged or where I fit in.

Didn't know if the second I stepped through the doors if I would regress back to the sniveling kid who shredded his life and the lives around him without a second thought.

Careless.

Reckless.

Mindless.

Just like last night.

But fuck. I was determined to hold together the few pieces I'd found.

I wasn't leaving here until I made this *right*. Until that fucker Paul was no longer a threat. I set my hand on the handle, thumb tentative before I finally pushed down the latch. Metal grated against metal as it disengaged.

The door dropped open to the interior that was nothing less than a rambling expanse of extravagance.

The foyer was wide and open and high. A set of double doors sat off to the left. Behind them was the kitchen that was every bit as lavish as the rest of the place.

On the right was a hallway that led to the downstairs offices and den, and next to it was the broad staircase that climbed to the two wings sheltering the six bedrooms above.

Emotion throbbed as memories rushed. I couldn't stop my thoughts from going to the room right above.

It was where I'd first found Edie and she'd found me.

In the middle of the ground floor was a huge living area that opened up to the bank of sliding glass doors overlooking the pool and sprawling city below.

Trembles shook my body.

Something about it felt like home.

Confusion mixed with it, careening left and right, making my head spin.

Because I was more unsure about where I belonged than I'd ever been before.

My backpack slid from my shoulder and landed with a thud on the marble floor. My boots echoed against the shiny tiles as I edged deeper into the house. The sound answered back with something that rang like loneliness.

I jerked when I heard the heavy footsteps banging down the staircase.

My attention flew to the right. Ash bounded down, completely unaware.

Seeing him was like a punch straight to the gut.

Blond hair a mess, big, hulking tattooed arms, smiling face.

The weight I shouldered for his sister hit me like a full-body blow.

He reared back when he saw me. He grabbed for the railing and stopped midstride.

Surprise pulled all over his face. Blue eyes, so much like Edie's, flashed. But his surprise? It was all in welcome because he didn't have a clue. "Well, holy shit, if it isn't *the* Austin Stone. In the flesh."

His head began to shake, and the smirk he loved to wear ticked up at the corner of his mouth. "Our very own vagabond returning after years of adventure."

He took another step down. "How the hell are you?" He didn't pause for my answer, just kept shaking his head and grinning as he headed my way. "Look at you. Strutting in here, all grown up. For a second there, thought you were Baz. Blows my mind. And at the risk of sounding like a pussy, which obviously I am not, I'm gonna go ahead and lay it out there and say the ladies will be pleased with what they see."

Leave it to Ash, his thoughts always salacious, heading straight to his endless hunt of women.

I chuckled. Because, hell, I couldn't help it. It was damned good to see him. Didn't know how much I missed him until right then. "And I see absolutely nothing has changed around here."

He laughed, the sound incredulous. "Dude…that is where you'd be wrong. All these assholes? They've gone and lost their ever-lovin' minds. Shacked up with their ladies. Put rings on their fingers. They're pumping out kids faster than my new Maserati. It's just me and Zee filling up these walls and whatever fun we can find for the night."

Of course because it was Ash? He said it with pure affection and a smile riding his face.

"For real…thank God you're back. Time to tip the scales back our direction. You know…to those of us who aren't dragging around a ball and chain."

Back.

Unease itched my skin.

I wasn't really.

Couldn't be. Because this was the last place Edie was ever going to want to be. And I doubted the dude would be all smiles and welcome if he knew I'd been living in his little sister for the last month. If he had the first clue why I'd returned. Here to fix what I'd fucked up a long damned time ago.

He strolled the rest of the way down. Like he owned the place.

Guess he probably did.

He shoved his hand out in front of him. I shook his hand, completely caught off guard when he yanked me forward, hugged me hard and clapped me on the back.

His voice came low at my ear. All jest evaporated like a

mist. "Hey, man, want you to know it's really fucking good to see you. You've been gone far too long. All of us…we've missed you. But your brother has needed you. He's struggling, man. Feels stuck."

It felt like a warning.

Stepping back, he inclined his head toward the stretch of windows.

My heart seized in my chest.

In the distance, I caught sight of my big brother.

The guy who'd sacrificed so much for me.

Guess I wasn't prepared that seeing him would affect me this way.

Emotion ripped me all over.

Regret and joy and suffocating sorrow.

I watched him lift a little boy from under the arms and toss him in the air. Catching him, he smothered him in a barrage of kisses to his chubby cheeks and chin. All over his entire face. The little boy giggled and burrowed deeper into my brother's embrace.

This little boy I didn't know.

Connor Stone.

One I'd been too much of a coward to meet.

Ash's voice broke through the daze clouding my head. "Go on, man. Nothing is gonna make him happier than seeing you here."

I didn't answer him. I just started in that direction. I moved slowly—cautiously—toward the guy I wanted nothing more than to make proud. Then time and time again, I turned around and constantly let him down.

Edie flashed through my mind. The way she always looked when she was lying beneath me, conflicting with the expression she'd worn when I'd crushed her anew.

Fuck.

When was I going to stop?

It felt like my guts were tied all the way up in my throat.

I pushed open the sliding door and stepped out.

A blast of heat and sun and city pelted me. The sounds of

Hollywood shouted back, a vibe of energy, horns, and the roar of the freeway in the distance.

Sebastian stilled, and his back went rigid, before he hooked his little boy on his hip and slowly turned around to face me.

Relief.

His or mine, I didn't fucking know. But it was there. Zipping between us on that invisible tether that bound us.

Family.

Blood.

Devotion.

"Austin." His eyes wandered, taking me in.

I stood there like a guilt offering. Because shit. I had no clue what I'd really put him through while I'd been missing for all these years.

Guarded, he took a couple steps forward.

My gaze was drawn to the little boy tacked to his side. The kid was all joy and light and smiles, sandy-blond hair, and the same eyes made of *Stone*.

Affection clutched me. Pulsed and pulled me every direction. Fuck, if I didn't feel like weeping.

Right there.

Sure, I'd seen pictures.

But it wasn't close to being the same.

A distinct rawness made its way into my tone. "He's amazing, Baz. Looks just like you."

My brother grinned in a way I didn't think I'd ever seen him do. He ran a tender palm from the top of the boy's head all the way to his chin. "Think so?"

"Yeah, man."

Connor giggled, the kid's attention short-lived just like you'd expect from any two-year-old. Wiggling, he pointed with a little finger across the expansive lawn that sat off to the right side of the pool.

If Ash's mind was blown, mine had exploded.

It was a pool that had played partner to all kinds of depravity. Now it sported one of those ground-level covers to keep little ones safe.

Ash was not joking. Things had changed.

"Ball...down," the little guy demanded.

"In a minute, buddy. Want you to meet someone really important first. How's that sound?"

Baz carried him my direction. Grey eyes glinted their curiosity. Connor smiled an adorable, shy smile. All I could do was give him a wobbly one. He turned his head on its side, tucked against his daddy's chest, staring at me, like he wanted to interact but wasn't all too sure what to make of me.

Something wistfully sad hit me like a hammer.

The soul-deep realization of what I'd been missing.

The awareness of the time I'd lost.

"This is my brother...your Uncle Austin. Can you say that? Austin?" he coaxed. Baz slanted his voice in a doting way I wasn't entirely sure I'd ever heard my brother do before. Except maybe for that sweet little girl who'd come in and swept him off his feet, the tiny thing as irresistible as her mother.

No wonder Baz had been done for the second Shea had come barreling into his life.

I shook Connor's fisted hand. "Hey there, little man. It's nice to finally meet you."

He grinned wide, repeating what his dad had been cajoling him to say. "*Auffin.*"

Yeah.

That damned near slayed me.

Warmth spread. Infiltrating. Penetrating all those dark corners.

It was so intense I didn't quite know what to do with it. A feeling so right clashing with the horror I'd done Edie last night.

Broken her trust in the worst way.

I had so much to atone for.

No question, I was here for a reason. A goal.

To silence Paul.

No longer would that name need to be a part of Edie's vocabulary.

But there was no chance I could ignore my brother altogether. Not him or the questions that remained between us.

The intentions he'd implied.

They'd been blatant in his texts and letters. Clearer and clearer with each one that passed.

No. I couldn't accept it. Couldn't stand in his shoes.

They were too damned big to fill.

And Edie...this was the last place she wanted to be.

But maybe I could do a little of that setting straight with Baz while I fixed the mess with Edie.

It fucking sucked that plan included leading Baz on more. But I had to believe he'd get it in the end.

Then I'd return to Edie and beg her for one more chance.

One I didn't deserve.

But I wasn't going down without a fight.

"Yeah, little man, I'm your Uncle Austin."

Just as fast as his interest lasted, he was pointing at his ball again.

Ball...down...Daddy, down."

Baz set him on his feet. He scampered off, toddling after it.

Baz slanted away for a second to watch him go. The second his back was turned, a blast of tension gusted through.

It stagnated the air between us.

Baz turned back. Wary. "Austin." My name slid from him like it was wrapped in caution flags.

My throat was doing that burning thing. I beat it back, forced out the chopped-up words. "It's good to see you, brother."

An incredulous sound puffed from him. He smiled a smile full of disbelief. "God...I was right. Almost don't recognize you. Except for the fact I kinda feel like I'm looking in a mirror."

Discomfort had me scratching at the back of my neck. "Time has a way of doing that, yeah?"

"Yeah. And it sure looks like time's been good to you."

I quirked a brow, hoping to throw a shot of lightness into the mood. "Oh, getting cocky now, are we, considering we're now damned near close to twins?"

Second I said it? We both fucking winced. Pulled right back down where we were slammed into this brutal reality. Wished I could take it back. But, no. I'd tossed it out there into the light where it strutted around, begging for attention.

Desperate to be recognized.

Refusing to let us forget.

Like there'd ever be a chance of that.

Pain coated his tone. "Austin."

My hands fisted at my sides. "I'm so sorry, man."

His brow dented, lines cutting all over. "What the hell are you sorry for?"

"For everything."

He gave a harsh shake of his head. "You think I've been sitting over here disappointed in you?"

Of course he had.

Why wouldn't he be?

"I left."

So maybe that was the culmination of it all. Because God knew it'd begun on that day when I was eight years old.

When I'd committed the worst crime.

The greatest sin.

Seemed I couldn't stop making them since.

Another shake of his head. But this one was almost a rebuke. "You think I didn't get that you needed to go? You think I didn't respect what you were doin', Austin? Fuck...I missed you like crazy. Worried about you night and day. But that didn't mean I wasn't behind you. One-hundred percent."

Always having my back. That was my brother. Even when doing so cost him so much.

He averted his gaze toward his son, before he looked back at me, a hand raking through his hair.

"Fuck, man, I messed your life up so bad. Dragging you into all the bullshit that ruled my world. You were just a little kid, and there you were, right in the middle of the mess, every kind of sin going down right under your nose. Think I don't know it was my fault you got mixed up in it?"

"You know that's not close to being true. It was all on me, Baz. I was the one who was looking for a way to dull it. To fill up some of that void. I would have found it...one way or another."

His lips pressed tight. I could feel the disagreement rolling through him. "Maybe we both were to blame. I don't fucking know. All I know is when I found you on the tour bus, sprawled out face down on the ground, lost to that shit..."

Grief clutched his tone. "I thought you were dead, man. Thought I'd lost another brother. And it was my fault."

I blanched, assaulted by his words. He didn't give me time to take a breath. "Then you lived, Austin. *You lived.* I felt like we were given a second chance, and I kind of lost it, doin' my best to keep you sheltered and isolated so nothing bad would ever happen to you again."

He gave me a slow shake of his head. "But I know now that wasn't right, either. I wasn't doing anything but stunting you. Holding you back from who you were gonna be."

Tendrils of joy and sorrow weaved through my senses. Taking hold. "Only thing you ever did was look out for me, Baz. Knew I had to go... If I was ever going to be something, *be someone*, I had to go and find my way."

Crazy thing was, I'd found Edie.

The urge nearly knocked me from my feet. *Tell him.* Lay it out. I bit it back. I refused to betray Edie. Never again would I tell secrets I didn't have the right to tell.

Emotion plucked at one side of his mouth. "I see the guy now. Standing right there in front of me."

Voice raw, I managed to ask, "And who's that?"

Because fuck.

I needed to know.

"Someone strong. Someone who's still hurting and suffering from the past. But he's there. Someone brave enough to step back into the middle of it. Someone who's a million miles apart from the scared kid who walked out that door three years ago. And still...he has the same soft spirit. I see him, Austin. And he's a good man. I've always known he was there.

Waiting for the opportunity to be great."

My jaw clenched.

God.

His assumptions were both merciful and cruel.

"That's who I want to be, Baz. I'm just not sure I've made it there yet."

Unease wound between us. I swallowed hard. "I saw that article, Baz. One about the shows getting cancelled. You showing up at an emergency room here in the city. Your texts. Rumors flying. You wanted me here, and here I am. Now tell me what's really going on."

Baz blew out a breath toward the sky. He shook his head as he shoved his hands in his pockets.

"You always thought you were the lost one, Austin. But I'm the one who's been searching my whole life. Never quite sure where I wanted to be. Think I knew it the moment I met Shea. Knew I was meant for something different. And I'm not sayin' it's bad or wrong to want both. But I've felt like I've been in limbo since the second I found my family."

He glanced at his son. "We've been going back and forth for the last three years. Sharing our time between the house we bought here in L.A. and Shea's old place in Savannah. Damned near kills me every time they don't come with me."

He looked back at my frozen gaze. "Shea decided to bring the kids out here for the summer so it'd be easier for me to come home between cities during the tour. Every time I get on a plane to leave? I don't want to go."

His head shook. "We were in Denver and I get this call from Shea. She's super calm. Not agitated or anything. She's just letting me know she's taking Kallie to the emergency room because she had a fever that wouldn't break and Shea wanted to be sure she was fine since it was the weekend."

Without taking his hands from his pockets, he shrugged toward his ears. "I panicked, man. Took off for the airport without letting anyone know. Because I *couldn't* handle the thought of not being there if they needed me. Got off the plane to find all these missed calls, wondering where the fuck I was."

He looked out over the city. "Let the band down, Austin. I've been doing it for a while now. Because my heart's not in it. It's with Shea. With Kallie. With Connor. I'm stepping down. One way or another."

Apprehension twisted up with the spark of those old dreams.

Baz stared across at me. "I heard you all those nights in your room, Austin. Playing. So fucking good you made me sound like a hack. Know you've been playing all these years, too. Different stuff, but the same. The same heart. The same soul."

"You're wrong, Baz. I...I fuck everything up."

He shook his head. "No. Might feel like it. But you don't. You've just been searching, too. Just like me. And fuck...I won't pretend like I know where you should land. But what I do know? I know there's no one else I'd rather take my spot than you. And that's the truth of it. It's not because I'm trying to save you or give you something you didn't earn. If this is where your heart belongs? Then step up and take it. If not? Then that's okay, too."

That heart?

It flew into a riot.

Because I knew when I came here that would

be Baz's offer.

And there was a huge part of me that wanted it. A part that had wanted it forever.

But my truth? My heart? I knew where it belonged. It belonged with Edie. But for right now, I would pretend.

thirty-one

AUSTIN

A ring of shot glasses met in the middle of the table.

Excited, Ash's gaze bounced around at everyone sitting in our circle.

Baz, Lyrik, Zee.

Me.

"To an endless well of inspiration and songs," he said with that easy-going smirk he couldn't help but wear. "To our fans. To our friends. To this mismatched family that's always gonna belong. Most of all…to Austin for stepping up into his rightful place. Deserve it, man. Welcome home."

A ripple of disquiet weaved through my insides. It bound with an overwhelming sense of right.

God. I couldn't make sense of this. The push and pull. Seemed the longer I was here, the stronger it grew.

The truth of it was, it felt good being home. Like I'd reclaimed something I'd lost.

But it didn't come close to touching how fucking bad I missed Edie. It'd only been three nights since I'd destroyed another piece of her. Two days since I'd come here. But each of those nights? They were spent wide awake. Arms aching.

My body a void.

Lost to that black, black sea.

Desperate to climb back onto land.

From his spot across from me, Baz eyed me.

Toasting before a show?

This was one of the traditions I'd been excluded from long ago. Back when things had gone south and I started pumping my body full of shit that had only served to fuck things up more.

Seemed all of us had that proclivity. Save Zee. Dude was without a doubt hands over fists wiser than the rest of us.

Thick, dark liquid sloshed down the side of my glass as I knocked it against the guys'. I poured it back into my mouth. It slid down my throat, hot in my gut.

"So tell me how this is going to go down."

Lyrik leaned forward, all sly and dark, way he always was. He raked a tattooed hand through his unruly black hair that was just as black as his eyes. "You keep up with the songs?"

I nodded. "Yeah."

Of course I did. Think everyone here knew there was no chance I'd just up and stopped listening to the words they wrote. To the songs they played. Didn't matter how much distance separated us. I never could have gotten that far.

Like Baz had told me when he'd given me my first guitar.

Music beat in my blood.

It was part of what tied all of us together. The threads of their songs were just another part of the bond.

Lyrik nodded. "Then you go out there. You play. You see how it feels. Then you make the decision if you want to stay. Simple as that."

Incredulous laughter threatened. Because there was not one simple thing about it.

Lyrik sat back with that dark gaze. "You willing to take a chance?"

A chance for my brother?

A chance to make this right with Edie?

"Yeah, man, I'm willing to take the chance."

Ash slapped both hands on the table. "Hell yeah. This is gonna be epic. Baz's baby brother taking his brother's spot. Girls are gonna lose their heads." He lifted his arms out at his sides. "This boy right here needs some lovin', but I'm pretty sure this asshole is gonna give me a run for my money."

A chuckle rolled from me, all mixed up with more of that guilt. It felt wrong keeping something so significant from Edie's brother. But what the hell else was I supposed to do? "No worries about that, man. They're all yours."

Zee widened his eyes. "Like he needs more encouragement."

Tamar and Shea, Lyrik and Baz's wives, appeared at the door.

"Knock, knock," Shea said with a smile as she peeked her head inside.

God. It was weird seeing Shea after everything we'd been through. Part of me felt so removed. The other? I felt as close to her as I could be. The things about her past I'd unwittingly known, not having the first clue how tied we were. Not until it'd almost been too late.

Thank God it was behind them.

Behind us.

Now Baz and Shea could live in peace.

Peace.

Fuck.

That's all I wanted for my girl. Sitting there? I felt antsy. Desperate to make it happen. Unsure if I could.

Tamar walked into the room ahead of Shea. Her stomach was just beginning to hint with the swell of the child she carried inside.

Lyrik had to be one of the hardest, most intimidating guys you'd ever meet. But the second he saw her? Swore the guy turned to goo. "There you are," he murmured as Tamar weaved his way to him.

Ash swiveled in his seat, grinning wide like the cocky bastard he was. "Ahh, Tam Tam. We were just talking about the fact I need some lovin'. And here you are. Come give me some kisses."

"Watch yourself, man." Lyrik's words were almost a growl, but he was too busy pulling his wife onto his lap, kissing her obscene right in the middle of the room.

"Hey, now. Why do you always have to go and get hasty with the assumptions? I was just gonna tell her hi."

Zee flicked a pen at Ash. "Maybe it's because we've all been subjected to the way you like to tell girls *hi* for far too long."

Ash dodged it, gave one of his dimpled grins. "What? I can't help it if I'm irresistible."

Shea smacked him on the back of his head as she passed by. "You wait, Ash. I still have one hundred bucks on you filling up your ridiculous house back in Savannah. All those rooms painted pink and blue. I saw some super cute boots that are just calling my name."

She gave me a soft smile as she rounded the table, heading toward my brother.

Ash shook his head like he was getting ready to tell the saddest story. "Guess those boots are going to sit there…going out of style."

"We'll see," she said, winding her arms around my brother's neck from behind.

I laughed, propped my elbows on the table.

So confused.

Because God. Being here, with the guys? With Shea and Tamar? It felt like home.

All the while my spirit thrashed for the one thing that set it at ease.

Do you feel me?

Thoughts of Edie out there, alone again, swamped me. Sucking me deeper toward that storm.

I could feel it.

Building in the distance.

"How was your day?" Shea asked, her mouth soft at my brother's ear.

Baz looked directly across at me. Holding me in his gaze. "It was a good day. A damned good day."

For the next two hours, we all hung out in the solitude of Lyrik's basement at the house he shared with his family.

Baz handed me an electric guitar and the four of us worked through their set list. Making sure I was on. That I could handle it.

Baz paced behind us, tapping out a beat on his thigh as he bobbed his head, already taking the position of support. In the background for input and advice, a shift of key and a lift of voice.

It felt so fucking good.

So right.

With each screaming lyric I sang, with the hard, chaotic, thrashing beat I tapped into—that one glaring, bitter piece screamed out from within me.

Fix this. Set her free. For once, do something right.

"Anyone mind if I step out to get some air?" I asked.

Baz inclined his head toward the stairs. "Take all the time you need."

I set the electric guitar that belonged to my brother aside. An overwhelming sense hit me with the force of a freighter.

I gasped around it, climbed the stairs to the main floor of Lyrik's enormous house. The two upper levels were all luxury and opulence and clean lines.

Still, there was something homey about it. Maybe it was the way a bunch of toys were strewn about, evidence of the presence of Lyrik's son, Brendon. Or maybe it was the way Tamar scurried around on her bare feet. Or the way Shea's and her laughter rang out and echoed on the stone tiles.

Maybe it was the joy climbing the walls.

And that's what I wanted for Edie.

Her joy.

Her freedom.

For my girl to finally be free of all the bullshit.

Then maybe she'd finally see the decision she'd never wanted to make was the right one. Maybe then she'd be free of the guilt and shame.

Free of Paul's vile and vengeance.

All of that belonged on me.

Whatever it took, I was going to protect her.

Set her *free*.

I opened one side of the massive French doors framed in carved, ornate wood and centered in ten-foot plates of glass. I stumbled out into the hazy heat of the late afternoon light, the City of Angels rambling forever below.

I pulled out my phone, entered the number I'd memorized. The one that had been haunting Edie for the last two months.

I played the fool as I tapped out the message for the bastard I had every intention of destroying.

Every intention of finally silencing the voice at the helm of her regrets.

The root of it all.

One mistake.

That's all it took for a cataclysm to ensue.

But this was a choice I wouldn't ever regret.

Hey man, it's Austin Stone. Heard you're out. *Sunder's* playing tomorrow. Lucky's @9. You should hit us up. Been a long time. Want to talk to you about an opportunity with the band.

I pressed send.

Knowing full well he'd be shocked I'd texted.

But I also knew with all of me the piece of shit would be chomping at the bit for the chance of having any part of *Sunder.*

He'd come.

And I'd finally stand up and take the responsibility that was mine.

For Edie, I was gonna be sure I made this go away.

Once and for all.

thirty-two

EDIE

Gripping the door handle, I stared out the car window. Fighting the fingers of panic and fear that wanted to sink their nails into my skin and hold me back.

Keep me under.

The way they'd always done.

"Are you okay?" Blaire asked quietly. She was sitting in the backseat, and she leaned in between the two front seats.

I shook my head, still looking out at the awaiting terminal. A single tear slipped free. "I don't know. I'm just…I'm so tired of being driven by the past. I'm so tired of running. I want…"

I wanted life.

I wanted the breath I couldn't find since my fear and insecurities had forced him out of my life three days ago.

I wanted Austin.

God. I wanted Austin.

That intensity shimmered in the distance.

Calling out to me.

Asking me for once…for once to stand up and be brave.

I turned, caught the flash of sadness in Blaire's expression, the pride that flared behind it.

Telling Blaire and Jed about *her* had been liberating, speaking the words that seemed so dirty and wrong.

All along I'd been afraid of the judgement that would come. The words that would only affirm what I already knew.

But Blaire...she'd just hugged me, rocked me for hours, while Jed had sat on the couch with his hands clasped between his knees, offering me his silent support.

I'd spent the last three days dealing with the mess of emotions toiling within me. Hurt by what Austin had done, but knowing my demons weren't the only ones we were dealing with.

My broken boy.

My spirit danced and thrashed.

A riot of intense, overwhelming longing.

I knew he needed me just as desperately as I needed him.

Last night I'd broken down and gone to his house. I'd gone knowing we had major issues, but sure I wanted to work through them all the same.

Willing to finally fight.

Fight for us.

Damian had met me at the door and told me Austin had gone home. He'd told me Austin said if I came, to tell me he'd be back soon.

To *wait*.

But soon wasn't soon enough.

Fear slithered strong.

Paul was in L.A.

But until I faced him? He was always going to be there in the background. Lurking like the darkest threat.

He'd stolen my safety.

My hopes.

He'd stolen years.

I wouldn't allow him to make me afraid for a second longer.

Blaire gestured with her head toward the terminal buzzing with people. "You're going to miss your flight if you don't get going."

I nodded. "Okay."

I grabbed my duffle bag from the floor between my feet and cracked open the door, while Blaire scrambled out the back.

"See you later, Edie." Jed's voice was rough. Choppy with emotion.

"Goodbye, Jed," I said, not sure how to leave things between us. If saying something would make it better or worse.

I started to duck out.

I froze when he suddenly snatched me by the wrist. I shifted, looked back at him as he stared across at me, the big, burly man's expression so entirely soft. "Go, Edie. Find your peace. You deserve it and he's out there waiting for you. That's where you belong. I get it now."

Air rasped from my lungs. I offered him the saddest smile that brimmed with all my appreciation I had for him. My affection.

Because he was so good.

So right.

He just wasn't right for me.

"Thank you." I squeezed his hand. "Your peace is out there, too, Jed. You'll find it. I promise. Just wait."

His eyes crinkled at the corners like maybe he disagreed, but he let me go.

Out on the sidewalk, Blaire wrapped me in her arms. "I'm going to miss you."

I fought the moisture that grew thick in my eyes. "I don't even know how long I'll be gone. I might be back on the next plane."

She stepped back, holding one of my hands. She shook her head as if she might never see me again, wiped at a tear that ran down her cheek.

Then she smiled.

"No, Edie. We all know what this is. And it's time for you to go home."

thirty-three

AUSTIN

We all clamored down the dank hall of the music theater to the welcome of claps on the back, voices lifted and filled with the type of thrill that was impossible to escape in a place like this.

Something both dark and alive.

The Hollywood venue was one I'd frequented many times. A place that had been happy to play host to *Sunder* before the guys had made it big, me little more than a kid tagging along, hanging out in the back rooms that acted like a bedfellow to sin.

A partner to all the crimes and transgressions.

A bedlam of immorality.

Sex, drugs, and rock 'n' roll.

Within these walls, that old cliché had earned its keep.

But that didn't mean it wasn't bigger than that.

That this place didn't hum with possibility.

It'd housed the dreams of those who meant the most to me—Baz and the rest of the boys who'd worked their asses off to get a break. Opening for whoever would have them. Playing places just like this across the country as they begged and

271

scraped by, until someone had noticed their talent and took a chance on them.

Now, they were passing it on to me.

No dues paid.

And I didn't know if it made me feel cheap or proud.

Like a beggar who'd somehow stumbled upon the greatest windfall.

For years, I'd been playing my music in the quiet of small clubs.

A prisoner to that unending loss. Chained to the sea and the songs. All the while knowing I couldn't ask for anything more than the opportunity to honor Julian in rhythm and words.

Now...now I'd step out in front of *Sunder's* oldest fans. Those who'd been there from the beginning. I'd stand in my brother's shoes and pray I could do him an ounce of justice.

All the while feeling like a bastard because I knew after I faced Paul tonight, I'd have to turn around and walk.

We emerged at the end of the hall and stepped out into the darkened backstage space. Heavy maroon curtains did nothing to conceal the chant of the crowd demanding their beloved band.

Sunder. Sunder. Sunder.

It pulsed through the dense air as if it breathed. A living force that compelled and stirred and sent this compulsive feeling jetting through my veins.

The itch.

The urge to step out onstage.

How many times had I felt it before? Just a kid on the outskirts, not brave enough to even *wish* I belonged in my brother's world?

My fists clenched, and a big hand clapped me on the back.

I turned.

Anthony Di Pietro. *Sunder's* manager. A guy who'd been there through thick and thin. Through arrests and overdoses and deaths. His presence was fused to the struggles and the victories of this band. Never once had he wavered in his support.

He watched me with keen eyes, deep with encouragement. "You've got this, Austin. Seen it in you all along. Now I want you to get out there and own this stage."

Anxiety fired through my nerves. My guts were tied up in devotion, all the old insecurities and fear I felt at an all-out war against the soul-crushing need to honor my brother, that call vibrating within the cavernous space hollowed out inside of me.

To honor both my brothers, really.

It damned near made my head explode to realize they'd become one and the same.

Scariest part? It was the bone-deep urge to do this for myself.

But it was the all-consuming need to do this for her that had me giving Anthony a tight nod.

I looked to the side when I heard Ash call my name. He lifted his chin, gesturing to where the rest of the guys stood up close to the side entrance of the stage. "Hey, man, it's almost go time. You know the drill. Let's go."

Over my shoulder, I cast a fleeting glance at Anthony who made himself comfortable by leaning a shoulder against a big speaker.

My footsteps became restless as I made my way to the huddle.

Fuck.

What was I doing?

But there was no stopping it now. Every inciting factor propelled me forward.

Seemed crazy that now my brother was the one on the outskirts, lingering off to the side. He gripped me by both sides of the neck, pressed his forehead to mine. His words were raw when he whispered, "You were made for this. Don't ever question that."

Throat heavy, I nodded, not having the strength to speak, and I turned into the huddle made up of *Sunder*.

Lyrik. Ash. Zee.

And me.

Lyrik and Ash slung their arms around my shoulders, Zee in between the two of them. All of us came together like we were some kind of sports team, which was just about laughable considering none of us had ever hit a field.

But here we were, hitting the stage, and Ash was feeding us all the cocky shit he loved to spew. Amping us up. Feeding the frenzy that sizzled beneath our skin and flamed in our stomachs.

Sunder. Sunder. Sunder.

They chanted it louder.

Demanding.

A rush of energy bristled across my flesh, and I gulped down the air that was alive with the frenzy.

My lungs were so damned heavy. My heart a manic pound, pound, pound.

"Tonight belongs to us." Ash shouted it, pushed off to break the circle, bouncing on his toes.

Zee went striding out onto the stage. He shoved two drum sticks above his head.

A tribute to his fallen brother.

My chest tightened at the sight, and for the first time I wondered how much Zee and I might be alike.

I paced.

Back and forth.

Three steps one direction, three steps the other.

What was I doing? What was I doing? I didn't belong.

Sunder.

The crowd screamed it, and I was hit by another rush of energy.

Ash sauntered out.

Cheers and screams.

Something close to hysteria blistered through the space.

Growing stronger.

More complex.

As if it understood the intricacies of this night.

Lyrik rode out on his intimidating way. Slow, sure, and

confident.

From where I stood, I could feel the way the crowd surged. Standing-room only. A crush of bodies vied to get closer to the stage.

I stood there at the side.

Fisting my hands. Wanting to fist my hair. For the first time in months wishing for the security of that damned hoodie.

Fuck. Fuck. Fuck.

Wasn't worthy to stand in my brother's shoes.

In his light.

In his legacy.

His hand was on my arm, his eyes telling me he'd heard every single fear playing out in my head.

He didn't need to say a word.

Everything in his expression promised me I was wrong.

That he believed in me.

That after all this time, what he saw? He saw something good.

I sucked in a breath. Steeling myself.

The frantic air drawn into my too-tight lungs only amplified the thunder of my heart.

I stepped out onto the stage to shouts and screams.

The swelling mass undulated with the confusion of my presence and not my brother's. All of it was messed up with the profuse excitement. A living, breathing ring of intensity.

Lights flashed.

Strobed across the toil of bodies and indistinct faces.

With my heart in my throat, I slung my brother's electric guitar over my shoulder and got up close to the mic.

There was no missing the weight of the eyes brimming with questions. Like everyone present was trapped in the bated, bottled anticipation.

An expectancy waiting to snap.

Energy stretched taut and tight.

No chance it wouldn't break.

"Evening," I called out. I dug deep for the confidence my brother had done his best to instill in me. Even after everything I'd done, he'd believed, and I wasn't about to let him down.

I strummed an echoing chord.

Cheers went up, the shriek call of whistles.

"Things look a bit different up here to y'all?"

Shouts, mostly of approval, but a few boos made their way to my ears.

And somehow…somehow that was okay.

A grin pulled at my mouth. "Look a little bit like my brother, yeah?"

Screams. Mostly of the female kind.

And that buzz lifted, a constant throb, throb, throb.

Propelling me forward.

"Let's see if I can play and sing like him, too."

That was all it took for the thrill to go lurching out of control.

For the energy to snap.

I jumped into the hard, hard chords of the song. A riot of chaos slammed at the bottom of the stage. And the rest of the boys…they were right there. Playing strong and sharp.

The music.

I'd always known it was there. Seated deep in my soul.

Tonight it flowed free and fast.

Fierce.

And I sang…sang the song my brother had written years ago.

Back before he found a way to be free.

Before he found love.

I tapped into the lyrics. Into the feel. And I thought maybe for the first time I really got their meaning.

> I can't touch time
> There's no remedy for this space
> How long will you hold me under?
> Just end it now
> End me now

And I knew.

I knew with the crowd a tumble of energy.

With the song weaving its way into my spirit.

With this overwhelming feeling of being one with the guys.

With the way it crashed over me with the force of a tidal wave.

All-consuming.

Overpowering.

Uncontrollable.

Wanting to be up here wasn't some distorted sense of loyalty.

It wasn't obligation or duty.

It was just like Baz said.

Right here was where I belonged.

But I was willing to give it up.

To forever let this feeling go.

Because nothing was worth it if Edie wasn't by my side.

thirty-four

EDIE

Do you know what it feels like to stand at the precipice of life?

Teetering on the edge of the here and now?

You know in your gut you're only one fumbled step away until you're in a free fall.

Tumbling down, down, down.

On a direct collision course with your past.

Even when you've done everything in your power to leave it behind.

So careful not to travel the same roads littered with mistakes and regrets and unbearable pain.

And there those roads were.

Circling right back around again.

Bringing you face to face with the past you'd give anything to forget.

Funny how I'd done everything to avoid this.

Facing my past.

But I didn't want to be afraid.

Not anymore.

I wanted to be brave. Filled with the kind of courage Austin swore he saw when he looked at me.

That didn't mean I wasn't trembling when I unlatched the door of the taxi, mumbled a quiet *thank you*, and slipped out into the Hollywood night. The thick air was warm against my already heated skin.

I felt hot.

Shaky.

I stepped up onto the busy sidewalk.

I stood in the middle of it while a hoard of people bustled around me, voices lifted and carefree as they headed to whatever spot would keep them entertained for the night.

And I just remained there. Frozen. My heart pounding in my ears as I stared up at the vintage-style marquee. The sign was all lit up, big, bold, black letters proclaiming tonight's act.

Sunder.

When I first got to L.A., I'd gone to the one place I knew to find him.

Where we'd started.

Praying we weren't at our end.

The old *Sunder* house in the Hills.

It'd been dark.

Quiet.

Almost eerie.

Or maybe it'd just been the stunning amount of discouragement and dread I'd felt in the possibility that I'd missed them. The irony that after all this time I'd finally gained the courage to step out and they were gone. On the road.

With a dash of hope, I'd looked up their tour schedule.

And here I was.

Standing in front of the glitzy, flashing lights.

A beacon.

The faint beat of the loud, hard music seeped through the thick block walls, stretching out to touch the night.

Sunder.

My head spun with the old fears and insecurities, with the old shame I no longer wanted to wear, and I forced myself up to the window.

My tongue darted out to wet my dried lips, and my voice

cracked. "I need a ticket, please."

A girl with teal streaks in her platinum blonde hair and a ring in her lip leaned toward me. "Sorry, you're about a month late. Shows been sold out for weeks."

Desperation rippled through my senses. I gripped the edge of the counter. "Please...I have to get in there...my brother..."

What was I supposed to say? My brother was on stage? That I clung to the hope that the boy I needed was somewhere in there, sharing in the show with his own brother?

That I belonged?

I guess I looked just desperate enough, because she shook her head, gave me a wry smile. "Go on. It's open floor. Don't tell anyone I let you in."

Relief flashed. "Thank you."

"Sure thing." She said it like it meant nothing. She had no idea how wrong she was.

I moved through the double doors and into the lobby area. People were everywhere, mostly youth, here to lose themselves to the hard, chaotic songs that spoke to them. The lyrics intense and pronounced.

As if they, too, had come here to be set free.

Free.

Nerves fired fast, and my pulse thundered, my breaths getting spun tighter and tighter as I shouldered through. Each step spun me higher.

Finally, I made it into the main room.

The lights were completely darkened.

All except for the bright bursts of light flashing on the stage.

Glowing silhouettes.

Strumming guitars.

I pushed deeper through the raving crowd.

Drawn.

Deeper and deeper.

Everything locked in my throat.

Bewilderment. Love. My spirit danced in recognition.

I blinked.

Austin.

I blinked again, trying to make sense of what I saw.

Austin.

He was here.

On stage.

With *Sunder.*

Singing.

Playing.

In place of Baz.

What was happening?

A tumble of confusion rippled in waves, and my attention was drawn to his right.

To my brother.

My blood.

I'm going to miss you when I'm gone.

Never before now had I felt the full magnitude of that claim. The fourteen-year-old girl who'd just wanted to be around her older brother, desperate for a moment to feel important. The one who'd been ripped up and tossed aside.

I missed. Oh my god, I missed.

My heart clenched, and I was trying to swallow around the clot of emotion at the base of my throat. I fought to get closer.

A tumble of dark faces and thrashing bodies went wild at the foot of the stage.

I pulled in a breath to steady myself. It felt as if I did nothing more than suck down more of that throbbing turmoil. Pulled it deep inside. Where it penetrated muscle and bone.

Calling me back.

Closer.

Nearer.

Something severe simmered across my flesh.

A sizzling, powerful force.

A raging storm building in the distance.

A bristle of energy and a lash of wind.

I'd run so far from this. And here I was. After all these

years. Crawling back like a broken, beaten-down vagrant begging for a return ticket home.

Austin screamed into the mic, that gorgeous mouth twisted and harsh. His fingers flew in precision across the frets. Up and down the neck of the electric guitar, his other hand strumming the reckless beat.

Oh god.

No boy should have the right to look that good.

My beautiful, broken boy. And I spun and spun and spun.

Darkness.

Light.

Chaos.

And this unyielding ration of hope.

It was stunning.

The fever that raced inside me.

I battled to get closer, weaved and squeezed through the tight-knit bodies who fought for the same position as me.

Closer. Closer. Closer.

My body canted with the dizzying tilt of the room, my steps bringing me nearer.

Wanting more.

That's why I was here.

I finally was ready for more.

I was ready for it all.

Strobes flashed. Bright strikes of colorful lights streaked across the defined lines of his face.

This boy who I should have known would always be a part of me.

I wanted it.

I wanted him.

Wanted everything he had to offer.

I stood there in complete awe in the middle of the bed of disorder. Bodies slammed, thrashed, and screamed all around me. Fists in the air. Voices lifted to sing along with this beautiful, mysterious boy.

A boy who without a doubt had belonged there all along.

I'd seen his fear of standing there. Heard it in his words and felt it in his reservations.

But I knew...I knew he belonged.

Joy lit.

Hope and peace in the middle of the darkest night.

Unable to take it any longer, I pushed back out through the crowd. I guess I shouldn't have been surprised the task was so much easier than my endeavor to get closer to the foot of the stage.

But that's exactly where I was heading.

Closer.

Moving toward forever.

The need pounded through me like the beat of Zee's drums.

With the manic chaos of their songs.

I moved to the backstage side entrance and started up two steps. My approach was cut off by a big, burly, bouncer.

He probably could have doubled for Jed.

He crossed his thick, tattooed arms over his chest.

"I need to get back there." My voice was both weak and strong.

Needy.

He laughed. "Yeah...you and every other girl here, sweetheart. Invitation only."

"Please...Ash Evans...he's my brother."

And I wanted to say it.

And Austin Stone is my life.

It froze on my tongue.

The big guy shook his head. "Nice try."

His smile turned almost sympathetic. "Maybe hang tight right out here...your *brother* is likely to go scouting through the crowd sometime tonight. Never know what flavor he's looking for."

My stomach turned, and I fought the burn of moisture pricking at the back of my eyes.

Tears of protest and hope and this elusive freedom that taunted me.

Hovering in the distance.

The future I hadn't been brave enough to hope for just out of reach.

I noticed movement behind the bouncer, and my eyes adjusted to make out the lines and curves. The familiar face came into focus.

Relief slammed me from all sides. "Anthony!" I yelled.

Desperate, I struggled to peek my head around the hulking mass who stood like a concrete barricade in front of me. "Anthony!"

Anthony di Pietro, *Sunder's* manager, stumbled in his confident stride. He took a curious step back, brows dented as he peered at me through the haze of darkness and smoke.

"Do you remember me?" I all but begged.

"Edie?"

Deliverance.

"Oh my God, yes, please, I need to…"

I needed to *live*.

Bouncer guy was already swiveling to the side. He muttered an apology, letting me by just as Anthony was scooping me into the warmth of his chest.

As if I were his long-lost child.

I clutched him and let free the sob that rattled against my ribs.

Relief.

His voice washed with concern. "Edie Evans. Where the hell have you been? Ash…your brother…he's going to be so relieved to see you. He told me he hasn't talked to you in forever."

Regret fisted my heart. I knew the one letter I'd sent my brother was no less than a feeble attempt at covering my grief. Ash would have worried about me all these years.

I knew he would.

I just hadn't known how to stand.

Now I was ready.

"I can't believe you're here," Anthony mumbled at the top of my head.

Tears streamed down my face. He just hugged me, rocked

me, soothed me in a way that let me know I was welcome. "Hey, it's okay. He's going to be happy to see you. I promise."

Shame.

It hovered in the periphery. Taunting me from the shadowy fringes. A dim, wavy hue of red that simmered and glowed.

At the ready to strike.

To pull me back into the depths of loneliness and nothingness.

I refused to let it.

Anthony peeled me away, held me at arm's length. "I've got to run up front to take care of something really quick. Why don't you head over to VIP at the side of the stage. Boys'll be off in less than five...only have one more song after this one."

Sniffing, I nodded, raked the sleeve of my shirt across my face to mop up the moisture.

I offered him a small, thankful smile while freedom bounded through me.

"Okay, thank you."

He slanted a nod, lips pulling at one side. "Welcome home, Edie."

He strutted away, and I moved through the shadows, hugging my arms across my chest.

Every cell in my body felt drawn to the sound of the voice that lifted from the stage.

Mesmerizing.

Spellbinding.

Hypnotizing.

This haunted boy, so dark, so grim, so full of life.

I edged up to the side where I could see him. I was hidden behind the sweeping curtains that blanketed the stage, the rise of them high and heavy.

They kept me veiled as I looked out on the future waiting in the distance.

Trembles rolled, desire and devotion as I looked upon a face too brilliant.

His talent too beautiful.

His body a straight shot of devastation.

All my defenses were obliterated.

He was lost to the vibe and the sound and the call of the fans.

Emotion swam through me.

It dragged me into waves of murky, impenetrable waters.

So deep and dark.

I floated through them.

Drowned in his comfort.

This boy my perfect air.

My breath.

My lungs burned with the weight of him.

So full.

Brimming with hope.

With belief.

Love.

I wanted to lose myself in it forever.

That darkness fluttered and flashed. But this time it was different.

Vicious.

Vile.

The air locked in my lungs.

I froze.

Awareness pricked at my consciousness, and the tiny hairs lifted at the nape of my neck.

Chills skated my skin as dread crawled across the surface.

Darts of fear pierced me everywhere.

Stabbing.

Torturing.

Tears threatened, and I tried so hard to keep them back. To keep from showing him I was weak and vulnerable. Refusing to allow him to ever hurt me again.

But the reaction was already there, and Paul laughed low and menacing at my ear.

I'd known I'd have to face him. Someday. And soon.

But not here.

Not like this.

Hot breaths panted against my cheek.

Memories spun.

His corrupt body against mine. His vulgar breaths in my face.

Bile climbed up my throat. Sickness clawed like the sharp bite of nails.

A sob.

I tried to hold it in. But it erupted.

Tight and shrill.

As if my coat of protection had been ripped away to reveal the sickening shame.

The morbid loss of being used up.

Panic took center stage.

Clotting off all other feeling.

Fight or flight.

And God. I wanted to fight.

But I didn't have the strength.

I pressed my hand to my face and turned to run.

I rushed to get around him. To find a safe place to hide. I shrieked at the repulsive grip that clamped down on my forearm. He forced me back. "Where do you think you're going?"

I attempted to yank my arm away. "Stay away from me."

He jerked me up against him. "Want to talk to you…maybe get a little bit of what you owe. Seems like a good enough night to start. What do you think?"

I pulled back and he yanked me toward him. Hard. I stumbled forward. He turned me so my back was against his chest, his arms banded around me like chains.

No.

I thrashed and kicked my feet.

My screams were buried in the music.

He tightened his hold.

We were in the shadows.

Hidden.

Every inch of me rejected the idea of ever being touched by him again.

The heavy curtains surrounding the stage disguised us, the darkened wings keeping us obscured.

He dragged me back until we hit a door. He opened it and hauled me inside.

The small space was dark as pitch.

The second we were inside, he spun me and tossed me out of his hold.

I gasped and reeled back. I barely caught myself when I tripped over something on the ground.

He fumbled with a switch.

An overhead lamp blinked to life, and I registered we were in an old dressing room that was being used as storage, the messy space stuffed full of boxes and equipment.

An unorganized path cut down the middle.

Paul stared across at me, a sneer written on his face as he reached back and locked the door.

Revulsion curled my stomach.

"What do you want?" I demanded. I hoped it sounded strong, but it came off weak.

Enclosing, he inched closer. I took a fumbled step back. "Stay away from me."

Outside the walls, I heard Austin shout into the mic, "Goodnight!"

"Austin." His name came out without my permission.

Disdain filled Paul's dark eyes. "You always did like him better than me, didn't you?"

Fear came alive. Churning in my gut and stampeding through my spirit. Not the fear of the crushing emotional impact he had cast on me.

But true, gutting fear.

The kind that screamed of self-preservation.

Of the fight for life.

"Been telling you, you owe. Of course I had a whole different idea about how tonight was gonna go down...but hey...when opportunity strikes."

My head shook, the words sticking to my dry tongue as I took another step back. "I don't know what you want. I don't have anything to say."

He laughed, this maniacal, malicious sound that cut through

me with sharp barbs of hatred. "You don't have anything to say? I've been rottin' in a cell for the last four years, and you don't have anything to say?"

"I don't know what you're talking about." I shook my head in confusion, my voice clogged with fear. "You…you…got caught with drugs."

Austin had told me he'd been arrested the night after I left. After he *found* out. He'd been pulled over for driving without a license plate, drugs in his car, possession, repeat offenses.

He cracked a smile that cut through me like a rusted knife.

He ambled forward. Almost casually.

But there was no missing the threat behind it.

He encroached.

I moved backward, just as slowly as he stalked forward.

Nowhere left to go, I knocked into a big box behind me.

"Austin." His name was a trembled yell. The sum of it a plea. Knowing it wasn't loud enough.

He didn't even know I was here.

"Keep yelling, *baby*. No one's gonna hear."

Paul raked a nail down my cheek.

Vomit churned in my gut.

"But before we get to the fun part, let's say you and I have a little chat about this." He dug into his pocket and pulled out a crumpled piece of paper, unwrapped it, and shoved it in my face.

I flinched, but I forced myself to focus, to make out what it said.

To comprehend what it meant.

My wild eyes took in the words written on the tattered note.

Three hundred dollars. Three hundred dollars more than you're worth. But hey, sometimes you have to pay the bitch.
And sometimes payback is the bitch.

My head spun and I struggled to process it. Those vicious words roared back as if I were hearing them for the first time.

The memories I'd wanted to suppress.

Standing there begging for help and receiving nothing less than a slap to the face.

The fear.

The sorrow.

The *grief*.

The empty place inside me throbbed, and I squeezed my eyes closed while the words that had been added at the bottom prodded at my awareness.

Doubt and disorder.

My mouth dropped open, my tongue tied in knots. Just as tight as the knots tied in my stomach.

Paul crumbled the note back in his fist. "Funny, you know, gettin' pulled over in your own damned car." His tone was hard, laced with sarcasm as he spit the words. "License plate that had been there that morning gone. Five baggies of coke under your seat that you sure as fuck didn't put there."

Oh God.

Oh God.

My eyes squeezed tighter. Fighting the awareness.

No.

He wouldn't.

Paul edged me farther against the box. Rancid breath choked me as he spewed his rage all over my face. He leaned in close to my ear, the oppressive weight of his forearm pressing against my chest.

Bitter laughter bled. "Sat there for four fucking years wondering who was out to get me...thinking there was no chance a stupid little slut like you would have the balls to pull off something like that."

Slut.

The word cut and sliced and slayed.

Harshly, he shook his head. Struggling for his own control. And then he was giving in to it, and his forearm slipped up and under my chin.

I wanted to scream.

To beg him to stop.

To tell him I wasn't responsible.

Instead it was a mumbled cry. "Please…don't. I didn't…"

The pressure increased on my throat. Paul's arm pushed in deeper, cutting off my flow of oxygen, forcing up my chin. The heavy box creaked beneath me.

A whimper escaped, and I clawed uselessly at his arm.

Weak.

Please, God, don't let me be.

I wanted to be strong.

To find the courage that Austin saw in me.

All the while trying to make sense of what he'd done. Why he'd done it.

My mind didn't want to wrap around the fact he was responsible. The fact Paul had been texting me all this time and he'd never confessed.

I don't understand.

Austin promised I was the only one who did.

Paul laughed again. Eyes wild. Raging with the thirst of revenge. "Such a stupid, stupid girl. They let me out early on account that I was such a good little boy on the inside. Of course they gave me back my things they'd confiscated. My clothes and my cell phone. And there it was, right in my wallet, evidence it was you all along. But that's what you wanted, right? For me to know. What did you think it would accomplish?"

Fear shivered and raced, and I blinked through the tears that wouldn't stop falling.

Once again, I was the fool, subject to the cruelty of Paul's depraved, wicked hands.

"What'd you think, Edie? When I got out…what exactly did you think was going to happen? Did you think I was just gonna let this go? Because you're going to pay like the dirty slut you are."

A ragged cry ripped up my throat.

"No. Please. No."

He leaned in, his breath lifting the vomit to my mouth, his murmur a blade in my ear. "Yes."

thirty-five

AUSTIN
AGE EIGHTEEN

*M*usic blared from the speakers. The house in the Hills was packed.

Overflowing with bodies just wanting to be seen.

Sunder had played tonight.

For the first time ever, it was to a sold out stadium.

Seemed overnight, droves of people were salivating at the mouth, dying to get a taste of what the boys in the band had to offer.

Wanting to bite off a chunk for themselves.

Fucking vultures.

It made me itchy.

Ill at ease.

I drifted around the outskirts of the mayhem, the way I always did, keeping to myself.

The two things that used to draw me down to the unending parties? They no longer seemed a temptation. Not the lines cut on the table in the den or the half-dressed women hanging on whichever guy they could sink their claws into.

Didn't want any of that anymore.

I'd made Edie a promise.

I'd promised her I'd keep my nose and my body clean, because the thought of me slipping back into that mess was more than she could bear.

You're too good for that, she'd begged me in the night. Washing me in a well of that sweet, sweet confidence and steadfast belief when I'd confided in her some of the shit I'd gotten myself into. The chaos and turmoil. My quick stumble right down the rabbit hole. So fucking young, I'd followed that dark, dark path with the rest of the guys.

For a lot of years, it seemed the only direction any of us could go.

You'd think that once everyone had kicked, this shit wouldn't be going down right out in the open in the *Sunder* house. But there it was, that temptation right under our noses, the seedy glitz that seemed to go hand and hand with this lifestyle spread out like a buffet.

Any of us could just reach out and gorge ourselves on it.

Feeling suddenly swept along the floor.

Fueling and feeding.

Coming faster and faster.

Drawn, I looked up. My gaze snagged on the only one I wanted to see.

My favorite secret.

From across the room, Edie cast me a shy, sly smile. She dropped her head just as fast as she'd glanced, turned back to whatever her crazy-ass brother was spouting to her.

The guy was larger than life.

Loved living big.

Out loud.

One tattooed arm was slung around some chick, the other gesturing wild as he told a story that was probably nothing more than a tall tale.

Damn, did I ever want to be close enough to hear.

Okay. So that was an outright lie.

I wanted to be by *her.*

I wanted to be by the girl I was having a damned hard time

not reaching out and touching. But that would be exposing us. And since the whole *us* thing was already such a muddled, complicated mess, I knew that wouldn't be the best thing.

Best thing?

It was that this girl was out of her room.

Smiling.

Showing her face when before she'd always tried to hide.

What the hell could it hurt to say hi?

Stuffing my hands in my pockets, I strolled her direction, as casual as could be while some kind of frenzy sparked inside of me.

She cut her gaze to the floor, so sweet and shy, chewed at her lip as I approached.

Even then, there was no missing the way her body twitched the closer I came.

Needing me the way I needed her.

And that need?

It just kept growing and growing.

Strong and overpowering.

Life and light.

Gripping me everywhere.

Ash grinned like a fool. "Well, well, well. Looks like we have another Stone who wants to come out and play."

He smirked at me, tightened the arm he had looped around the back of the chick's neck. "Darlin', why don't you go grab a friend or two? Introduce them to my boy Austin here."

He jutted his chin my direction, all smiles and tease. "Dude looks like he could use a little company."

Edie flinched.

I was sure no one else noticed.

But I sure as fuck did.

Without removing my hands from my front pockets, I lifted my elbows out. "Just fine, man. Don't need you trying to hook me up. Pretty sure I do fine by myself."

Blue eyes danced. "Ah. That you do. And tonight there are lovely ladies for miles, and all of them are beggin' for a little fun. I'm all too glad to provide it, but I'm not sure I can handle them all."

I raised a brow. "Pretty sure you'd make a good go of it."

He laughed. Loud. "Guess I just might."

His gaze slanted toward his sister. "Since you're down here, why don't you keep an eye on Edie-girl for me?" His smirk twisted into an affectionate smile when he looked at her. "Prettiest girl in the whole house."

Edie blushed the way she did.

Angel.

He turned his attention back to me, emphasizing the fact with a cock of his head. "Don't need any of these fuckers trying to make a move on my baby sister. You know that shit's not gonna fly."

Damn right, it wouldn't.

"Sure thing." I said it like it didn't matter. If he only knew his baby sister was the only reason I was down here.

I looked at her, into that ocean blue, feeling it swallow me whole. Taking me under.

"You want to go somewhere where it's quiet?"

"Please."

I started to walk backward, inclining my head back. "Let's go out to the courtyard. It's nice out there tonight."

"I'd love that."

We walked side by side into the kitchen, which was packed wall to wall. "I'll grab us a couple waters. I'll meet you out there."

"Okay," she said thankfully, because I knew she didn't want to be stuffed in there with a shitton of people she didn't know. She squeezed through the crush, white hair swishing around her as she made her way to the other side, quick to slink out the back door.

I said a couple of hellos, dug around in the fridge for waters, which was about the last thing most anyone wanted around here, before I was moving the direction Edie had gone.

I stepped out into the night. Huge trees grew tall and proud at the side of the massive house, stretching out to offer protection and shade, the party a raucous echo I was all too happy to leave behind.

I walked down the path to the small courtyard made up of hedged bushes and trimmed flowers secluded at the side of the house. Rays of moonlight slanted down to illuminate the space.

The air punched from my lungs when I saw Edie in the middle of it.

Chills skated my spine.

Licks of ice-cold flames.

My hand clenched down and the plastic bottles creaked, razors raking my throat when I attempted to swallow.

Paul towered over her, his head dipped down as he tried to get in her face, no doubt saying something vulgar.

Depraved.

Edie's head was tipped down, turned away. Like she was trying to shrink into nothing.

The girl a prisoner to the undeserved shame.

Possessiveness surged and fire flamed through my veins.

Red blotted out my sight, and I dropped the bottles, hands fisted when I rushed toward her.

I felt myself coming unhinged when I finally got close enough to hear what he said.

"…only fair we go another round. You owe me, *baby*, don't you think?"

His voice was saccharin sweet. Wicked and base.

Rage blistered and boiled. And I was there. Chin lifted as I tried to contain it all.

My favorite secret.

He glanced at me, dismissed me just as fast. "Kinda clear I'm busy here, don't you think?"

I just stood there.

While it built and built.

The hatred for what he'd done.

For her anguish and sorrow.

For her loss I tried to hold every night.

The fact this bastard was the one who stood in our way.

He was the barrier to the happiness teasing us. So close, but so fucking far out of reach.

"Said fuck off, asshole." With that, his voice came a little harder, and I stepped closer.

Just as he cinched a brutal hand around Edie's wrist.

"Let her go." It grated and rocked.

He laughed a mocking sound. "That's not gonna happen. She and I have some unfinished business to take care of. Bitch owes me and she's gonna pay."

The violence simmering inside me exploded.

I surged forward. Pushed him in the chest with both hands. "She's not going anywhere with you."

Paul reeled back. Anger struck harsh lines into his disgusting face. "And it's gonna be you who stops me?"

"Yeah, it is."

I said it so cool.

Like I wasn't a scrawny kid staring down a pissed-off full-grown man. But the man I wanted to be was bursting at the seams. Flailing for a way out. To break free.

I'd fight for her.

Willingly.

To the death if that's what it took.

"Austin." My name was a plea from her mouth. It was a request I couldn't quite grasp as I was pushing her behind me and wedging myself between them.

Paul chuckled low. Clearly it was then my intentions sunk in.

"Ah…isn't that cute. Looks like someone has a crush." He cocked his head, his tone pure insult. "Dumb kid willing to get his ass kicked for a worthless slut. She's a nice lay, though, isn't she?"

Slut.

It struck the air like a bolt of lightning.

An inciting fire.

Edie gasped with the blow of it.

My angel.

I flew at him.

A flashfire of fists and hate and curses from my tongue.

Paul struck me.

It was a direct blow to my chin that nearly knocked me from my feet.

My head rocked back.

It didn't matter the pain nearly split me in two.

I fought back.

Attacking with everything I had. "I will kill you, motherfucker. You used her...knocked her up, you piece of shit. You didn't even fucking care. I'll kill you. I'll kill you."

I caught him up high on the cheekbone.

The skin split, and he stumbled back, wiped the blood gushing from the cut I'd inflicted. "I took advantage of her? Little sluts like her are all the same. Crying wolf for a few extra bucks like the whore she is. Probably wasn't even pregnant."

Blinding.

The rage.

The hate.

Didn't give two fucks he was bigger than me.

He was going to pay.

If it was the last thing I did, he was going to pay.

I kicked and punched as a mumbled disorder of words tumbled from my bitter tongue.

"Wasn't pregnant? You ignorant piece of shit. She had her. She had her. She had to give her away. Do you have any idea what that did to her. Do you have any idea?"

The words were as jagged as my breaths.

The stars and sky spun in a kaleidoscope of madness.

The agonizing violence that couldn't be sated.

The love I had for this girl excruciating.

Edie suddenly wailed.

A cry so deep it penetrated the fury.

She was buckled in two when I turned to look at her.

Her gaze was on me.

Broken.

Betrayed.

"You....you told him? He was never supposed to know. How could you...how could you?" She backed away, clutching her middle. The spot where her daughter had been.

Paul froze, then inched forward. "What the fuck did he say? You tellin' me there's a fucking kid out there who might be mine?"

He flew in, dipped down where he spit the words toward her horror-stricken face. "That what he's saying? That someday I'm gonna have some snivelin' kid show up, knockin' at my door, claiming I'm their long lost daddy?"

Edie choked over her tears. Head between her shoulders. Trying to hide.

Shame.

Fear slicked my flesh.

Clammy and cold.

What did I do? What did I do?

Always taking the good things I was given and destroying them before they got the chance to grow.

"Edie," I whispered.

"Fucking stupid whore. You get paid for that, too? How much did you get for her? Tell me."

"Edie," I begged.

She wasn't even looking at Paul when he lashed and spewed appalling words from his mouth.

She was staring at me in disbelief.

I could feel it, that hope sucked out into the open air. Dissipating like the trust I'd just crushed. A whirlwind beaten and stirred with the fury. Colliding and crashing until there was nothing left.

I stood there as she fled back into the house. I fisted my hands in my hair. Trying to breathe.

Paul spit toward the ground. Pointed at me. "This isn't over."

My voice was deathly quiet. "You can go to hell."

He scoffed out a laugh, before he took off, tossing the casual words over his shoulder. "We'll see about that."

I paced.

Wondering just how I was going to make this right. Knowing I couldn't have said anything worse.

That I'd wounded her in a way she couldn't afford.

Five minutes later, I heard the front door slam.

I didn't know why. I just knew. I just fucking knew.

I ran around to the front of the house.

Edie had a big bag slung over her shoulder, her arms crossed over her chest and her head dropped in humiliation as she trudged up the cobbled drive.

"Edie," I whispered the plea, before it turned frantic when she wouldn't look back at me.

"Edie."

She started to run.

"Edie, wait, please, wait."

She flung around, her hand a fist over her heart. Torment flowed from her mouth. "I can't believe you would do this to me. After everything I trusted you with. Just…stay out of it. Stay out of my life and my business because I can't trust you. Don't make this any worse than you already did."

A cab pulled up at the corner, and she sprinted away from me.

I fought to get to her.

To stop her.

She jumped in and slammed the door shut, her hands shaking as she fumbled to lock it right as I got there. She kept her head down, that halo of white covering her face, refusing to look at me.

"Edie!" I screamed. I banged at the window. "Edie!"

The car accelerated, and I ran into the street behind it as it pulled away.

Tearing away the last good piece of me.

"Edie, please!" I screamed at the night.

Please.

"Wait."

Torment wound and wound. That hollow place had come alive with the sour taste of death.

I shouldn't have been surprised.

That's what I did.

I took the good and I destroyed it. Crushed it in my hands.

Bitterness burned through my blood.

A hopeless mayhem.

"Leave at five," Baz warned. He was stuffing a bunch of shit in his bag, my brother packing for the last leg of their *Divided Tour*, one that would take us to six more cities.

This had been the tour that had defined them as a band.

The one that had given them fame.

Fortune.

But had it been worth it?

Because it was also the tour that had stolen Mark. The tour that had scored us in misery.

Of course, that had been before I'd seen the light.

Had been blinded by it, really.

Because now it felt like I was stumbling around in a pitch-black darkness. Knowing it would never end. That I was never gonna be okay. That my past, my mistakes, were always going to be right there waiting to catch up to me.

Julian. Julian. Julian.

His presence curled around me like wisps and vapors. Mocking me for my naivety. For the foolish belief that maybe, just maybe, I could find happiness.

That I could be good for someone. Give something back rather than take, take, take.

I bit back a resentful sound.

Because I had.

I'd found it.

Edie.

Then I'd turned right around and destroyed it.

"Got it," I returned. Didn't give two fucks where the roads led because I knew I'd only ever travel one direction.

Down.

But I had one last thing to do before I finally gave it up.

No one even noticed when I grabbed my brother's keys or when I took the fat wad of cash from the safe. Not when I showed up at that ghetto apartment, dealt the deal I knew would seal the asshole's fate, and sure as hell not when I snuck to his shithole house.

Kneeling behind his car, the pitted ground dug into my knees. I was quick to twist the screws holding on his license plate.

I tossed it behind a bush.

This isn't over.

His words rolled through me. The threat to my girl. One I was going to erase.

I held my breath when I slipped into his car and planted the baggies beneath his seat.

I dug around for a place to leave the note. For one unlucky bastard, it seemed I was full of it today, because the dumbass's wallet was hidden in the middle console. I slid the note between a five and a ten.

Three hundred dollars. Three hundred dollars more than you're worth. But hey, sometimes you have to pay the bitch.
And sometimes payback is the bitch.

Only solace I took in all of it was knowing when he saw the note, he'd know it was me, the words he'd so viciously cast at Edie repeated with a special *fuck you* just from me tacked on the end. My own little sayonara to send him on his way.

I hoped with every hope I had left that this would be enough to send the bastard straight to hell.

Maybe then he'd burn there with me.

I'd waited all day for the opportunity. Finally had it when the asshole had run back into his house like he'd needed to grab something. Like he was immune to all the world's consequences, he'd left his car idling in the drive.

One second.

One moment.

One mistake.

I guess that really was all it took.

From behind a wall, I watched him get in his car and throw it in reverse, pull out onto the street, and disappear at the end intersection.

I'd promised her I'd protect her.

And I was doing it the only way I knew how.

Five hours later, I stumbled onto the *Sunder* bus.

Fucking lost.

Hopeless.

Unable to breathe.

The guys filed off at the venue. Pumped for their show. Having no clue the devastation I'd caused.

I waited until they were gone before I broke into the cubby where I knew Mark had kept his dealer's number.

I texted for some oxies.

Anything to numb the pain.

To blot it out.

Desperate for the darkness.

Because after you stood in the light?

You no longer knew how to live without it.

thirty-six

AUSTIN

"Goodnight!"

The four of us threw up our hands and exited the stage. It felt like my feet weren't touching the ground.

Body floating.

Spirit soaring.

Screams, cheers, and a chant for more only served to heighten it further. Blood sloshed and pounded. I could feel the adrenaline consuming every cell in my body. Begging to be set free.

I itched.

I think it was that moment when I finally fully grasped the compulsion my brother had once tried to describe to me. When he'd tried to make me understand what it really was like to stand on a stage in front of thousands of fans. How it felt to feed the frenzy and how they just poured it right back into you.

As soon as we made it through the wall of curtains, Ash clamped his hands down on the back of my shoulders. Dude used me as a springboard to propel himself into the air, doing his own sort of flying. He landed with a clap of both palms on my back.

"Hell yeah, man. You kicked ass. Show was off-the-charts epic. Crowd was wild. They loved you, man. Seamless. Fucking seamless."

Seamless.

That's the way it'd felt.

Like I'd belonged in that stitching all along.

Lyrik gave me a jut of his chin in clear approval as he stalked away, black hair bobbing above the crowd he disappeared into. Zee offered a fist bump as he passed. "Did it, man. Knew you could."

But it was my brother who was waiting in the wings who slowed my steps.

His approval I sought.

He grabbed me by the shoulders. Shook me. Fingers digging into my skin. "So fuckin' proud of you, Austin. So fuckin' proud."

He pulled me into a tight hug, his fists at my back, and I hugged him back. Everything he'd ever done for me was right there, at the forefront of my thoughts and memories.

"Thank you for giving me this chance."

His words were thick. "Thank you for taking it."

My nod was slight, and my racing heart pounded a little harder as I relished it all for a moment more.

Then I let it go.

Focused on what had brought me back to L.A. in the first place.

The main reason I was here, even if I did feel as if I'd found a missing piece of myself along the way.

Paul had returned my text when I'd let him know I'd leave a backstage pass for him with will call, said he'd be there.

I was ready.

So damned ready to stand up and take the responsibility that was mine and make sure the bastard never had a stray thought toward my girl ever again.

I knew it'd be a fight.

One I refused to do anything but win.

Figured it'd only sting more when he stood in front of me,

thinking he was about to hit the jackpot when the asshole hadn't even played. Figured it'd hit him harder by bringing him here under the auspice of something great when things for him were about to go terribly wrong.

Agitation slid slow but strong. I searched the faces waiting in the wings, fully expecting him to step out of the shadows like the creepy motherfucker he was.

Then I would go back to Santa Cruz, find my girl, and confess it.

Tell her I'd gone and whipped up a mess of mayhem, the way I always did, in the end only making it worse.

Even when I'd just been trying to make it right. I knew I couldn't go on without getting him out of her way when he'd promised it wasn't over. But I realized now, it wasn't ever going to be until Paul was taken care of.

Anthony strode up. Confused, he looked around like he was hunting for someone. I didn't miss the worry that flashed on his face or the concern that shifted his feet.

"Hey, Ash," he called.

Ash had his arm around some chick, making her giggle as he whispered something I was sure was all kinds of obscene in her ear. Dude was always such a dog.

"Be back in a minute, darlin'," he said with that cocky lilt. He sauntered Anthony's direction. "What's up, man?"

Anthony hesitated, eyes darting around again. Something in my spirit made me latch on to whatever he was about to say, my body struck with a quiver of unease.

"Did you see your sister...Edie?"

Ash's expression went blank for the flash of a second. Like he was processing. Perplexed.

While my insides twisted.

"What do you mean, my sister?" he asked, shucking the aloof cloak he always wore. Something intense took him over.

"Your sister. She's here. Told her to wait in the VIP section backstage. Don't see her now."

Worry climbed into the clench of Ash's jaw. "My sister? You sure, Anthony? Don't fuck with me, man. Not about her."

Anthony shook his head. "Really think I'd mess with you about something like that?"

Their conversation became a dull hum in the back of my mind.

Everything shifted to overdrive.

My gaze flashed around the room. Searching the coves and recesses.

Panic lit in my belly.

Like the flick of a stove.

A ring of fire.

I stood in the middle of it.

Burning.

No.

Not again.

Fuck. Fuck. Fuck.

I dug into my pocket for my phone.

Fear swept vast and wide as I read the message I had waiting.

One from Paul.

Backstage. Ready to hear whatever it is you've got to say.

No. No. No.

I didn't even realize I was saying it aloud. My voice grew louder with each word that ripped from my tongue. "No...fuck...no. Edie."

I yelled it, spinning in a circle. "Edie!"

Ash hooked onto the frenzy buzzing through my bones.

Our eyes locked.

Like he knew.

I raced toward the back of the building where the after party raged.

Ash was right on my heels, talking the whole way. "Why do I get the sinking feeling you've got a fuckton of explaining to do and I'm not gonna like what you have to say?"

I didn't pause to give him an answer.

I just pushed through the people hanging at the back of the hall where the big room opened up, yelling for her the entire time.

Inside, a ton of assholes lounged around like they owned the place, girls ready to waste what they had on these losers just to get a little taste of the glitz and glam.

As if anyone the next day would even remember their name.

I scanned each of them.

She wasn't there.

Dread spread like the crawl of spindly branches.

Burrowing in and taking hold.

I nearly crashed into Ash when I flipped back around. I darted out into the hall. Both of us rushed deeper into the bowels of the old building, toward the dressing rooms and offices in the very back. We were flinging open doors, her name flying on a constant stream from our tongues.

Something close to hysteria rose up within me.

The thought of that bastard touching her...hurting her...

No.

Wouldn't let it happen.

Not again.

Coming up short, I spun around and hurtled back down the way we'd come, Ash taking up my side.

Didn't give a fuck I was literally shoving people out of my way as I barreled through.

Confusion reigned on everyone's expressions when we came back to the side of the stage, Baz, Anthony, and Zee staring back at us like they were wondering what to do, Lyrik now a part of the fray.

Frantic, my eyes scanned.

Everything seized when I saw the door to the left of the stage, hidden and forgotten in the hollows.

I ran toward it and grabbed the knob. I yanked it.

Locked.

Terror burned, suffocating, and I stepped back, lifted the sole of my boot so I could slam it against the door.

It rattled but stayed.

I did it again.

And again.

I just fucking kicked and kicked until it splintered and gave. It slammed open, and it collided against the inside wall. Without hesitation, I went bolting through.

Edie.

Violence clawed beneath the surface of my skin.

Paul had her pinned up against a big box pushed up on the far wall. In shock, he turned to look over his shoulder when he heard me crashing through.

But I knew.

There was no missing it in those terrified, aqua eyes, what the piece of shit had intended to do.

"Austin." My name left her on strangled relief, and she sagged when he spun around and released her.

Fuck, I hardly knew how to make sense of it. The fact my girl was here after the way I'd betrayed her the other night.

Rage tweaked my muscles and my hands curled into fists. Propelled by pent-up fury and unstoppable hate, I rushed.

I lunged right for the asshole.

Edie yelped and jumped out of the way.

Somewhere in the fog of my mind, I could hear Ash's voice cutting through the stifling air. "Edie...oh God...tell me you're okay. What the hell are you doing here? Edie."

But I couldn't process it. My focus was on the man at the root of it all. Full force, I rammed him.

I hit him in the stomach with my shoulder. On impact, I locked my arms around his waist and knocked him from his feet.

We flew.

It only fed the darkness, fueled the rage, my veins burning fire. We landed hard, a tangle of limbs and harsh, bitter grunts, an outright battle to come out on top.

I did.

Because I wasn't about to let this piece of shit win.

I knew Ash was right there, on edge, muscles tight. Tense

with adrenaline. At the ready to jump in. Having not the first clue what we were fighting for other than the fact the prick had his little sister locked away in a storage room.

That in itself would be enough to turn things south.

But if he knew how deep it went?

He would have lost it. Same way as me.

"Motherfucker." Paul's grunted curse was low, eyes wide with both confusion and shock.

Though maybe not as shocked as when I cocked back my arm and drove my fist like a hammer into his face.

I delivered two crushing jabs.

Skin split.

Blood poured.

I gripped him by the shirt, yanked him up, and slammed him against the concrete floor. "You fucking bastard. Did you really think I was going to let you get away with touching her again?"

"What the fuck is this?" he grunted, fighting back, fool just catching on to the fact he wasn't there to get a slice of *Sunder*.

But I sure as hell was gonna take a piece of him.

"Warned you I'd kill you," I seethed, my teeth gnashing, desperate to make good on the threat.

A hand flew free and clipped me on the chin.

Caught off guard, I rocked back, and he scrambled free, on his feet and coming at me, his laughter loud.

Maniacal.

"You want to go down for that little slut? Fucking bitch…sent me to jail for the last four years. She's gonna pay. One way or the other. Might as well take it out on you."

Dude had to be off-kilt mad throwing those words at me. And let's not forget Edie's brother was standing right the fuck there. Trying to make sense of the details.

Adding it up.

Knew it would only be a few seconds before he finally caught up.

Apparently the dickbag had missed the notice that a few years had passed. Because I sure as shit wasn't a scrawny kid anymore. The second he pounced, I knocked him back with a jab. A direct blow to his nose.

Cartilage cracked and blood gushed. It splattered across his face and the dingy floor. Didn't even give him time to cry out like the bitch he was before I was on him.

Boxes toppled over, glass shattering and metal equipment clattering where it spilled onto the floor as I drove him back like a battle ram. I pinned him to the wall. He struggled and my hold increased as I laid it out, words grit as I spit them toward his face, the shot of laughter that left me bitter. "You think Edie did this to you? That sweet girl you about destroyed? You really think it was her? Why don't you think about it a little harder, asshole?"

My voice went lethally quiet. *"Think about it.* Or didn't you have enough time to figure it out while you rotted behind bars for the last four years? Did that warped conscious of yours ever let you in on the deal? Did you finally *get* it…finally understand why *I* sent you there? Did you really think for one second I would stand aside and let you get away with what you did?"

A sob ripped from Edie. God, I wanted to crawl to her on my hands and knees. Beg her to forgive me for what I was doing.

Instead, I focused on the fear of losing her for good, directed all of it on Paul. The asshole whose eyes rounded on the impact of my words, the reality of my admission hitting him like an avalanche.

Bricks raining down.

"Tell me," I demanded.

"You," he spat.

"What the fuck…someone—" Ash's cringed desperation barely broke the red haze of hate that gripped me everywhere. My muscles ticked and that ugly, vile place inside screamed at me to just do him in.

End it.

"Yeah. *Me.* And I'd fucking do it again…a million times over. Wish I would've done more, because you and I both know four years of you gone won't undo what you did to her."

He sneered. "I did to her? She wanted it."

Violence skated the surface of my skin. I lifted him from the floor, pinned him high on the wall, everything pouring out. "It won't erase you from her skin or her memories. Won't erase her pain or erase her fear. Won't erase the fact her daughter is somewhere out there...being raised by someone else."

Edie wailed, and suddenly Ash was behind me, a ball of rage that blistered across the floor. "Someone needs to tell me what the fuck is happening and do it now because I'm about half a second from losing my shit."

Sobs.

My girl.

Angel.

My chest tightened so damned tight, and I winced. Blinked through the daze, realizing what I'd allowed to pass through my lips. The secret I was always supposed to hold.

Somehow this showdown had become a spectator sport, because I could feel the eyes, the barely contained restraint of my brother, Lyrik, and Zee, Baz's girl behind them.

Fuck.

"Edie," I whispered, wanting to soothe her. To calm her. To let her know it was going to be okay.

Set her free.

My words grated like broken glass. "Baby...it's okay...it's okay."

Baby.

There it was.

Out there.

For the first time offered up like a revelation.

Without shame or disgrace or scandal.

Without all the bullshit hiding.

A whimpered cry broke from her mouth.

Ash ripped at his hair, his expression tormented as he spun around and angled his attention at his sister, pointing a demanding finger Paul's way. "This piece of shit hurt you?

What did he do to you? Tell me what's happening, Edie. Tell me right the fuck now what Austin is talking about."

Paul laughed. "I didn't hurt her. She was begging me to fuck her."

Ash roared, and suddenly Lyrik and Baz were there, holding him back as he struggled against their hold. All of them knew if Ash lost it like this, things were going to get ugly and fast.

A cry erupted from Edie.

Excruciating.

Like that single sound had been harbored inside her for a billion years. A fiery boil of compressed magma that had waited beneath. Pressure building and building until there was no stopping the force and it burst free.

Edie's face twisted with disbelief. Hurt. And some kind of profound determination.

Courage.

The prick flailed. Fighting against my hands. Fighting for breath. Fighting a fight there was no use fighting for.

"You *stole* everything from me." Her words were a fractured whisper. "You stole my innocence. My future. You took advantage of *me*." She knocked her fist against her chest. "Violated *me*."

She gasped around a splintered breath. "And when I begged you for help, you laughed in my face. Shamed me. So don't you *dare* stand there and say you didn't *hurt* me."

He clawed at my wrist, breaking free long enough to spew the words. "You were begging me to fuck you."

I rammed him back down. "Shut the fuck up, asshole." I looked at my girl, urging her with my eyes to continue. To lay it all out. To get it out.

Maybe then she might finally be able to let some of this go.

Shimmery streams of tears streaked down her face. "No," she said, her voice growing bold. Like maybe it was the first time she believed it. "No. You're wrong."

My heart damned near seized.

So fucking beautiful.

Broken like me.

So many fractured, splintered pieces.

I felt each of them out there hovering at the fringes of our messed-up lives.

Quivering. Rattling in wait.

Like magnets repelled until they suddenly shifted and flew.

Careening as they sped.

Brought together by that unavoidable lure.

The energy and the force.

Crashing together to become one.

My mirror.

I slammed Paul back against the wall. My fists were balled up in his shirt, pressing under his chin. "She was *fourteen.*" The bitter accusation slid from my mouth below my breath, up close to his face where no one else could hear.

"Where I come from...that's called rape. When I had you meet me, I expected it to be just you and me. Figured we'd go round and round until one of us didn't get up. But considering we have an audience, looks like it's your lucky day. So listen closely, asshole...if you even breathe in her direction, ever again, I will *erase* you. You got me?"

Ash raged. Hooking onto the heart of it. Finally getting what really went down all those years ago.

Edie sobbed quietly in the corner.

I gulped around the guilt and fear in my throat. "I asked a question, motherfucker. Do you get me? Because I promise you, if I have to come for you again, it won't only be me knocking on your door."

Pussy's expression was riddled with fear. I suddenly released him and he slid to the ground. I landed a swift kick to his side.

Just in case the bastard needed an extra reminder.

Mouth wide open, he curled on his side, moaning as he rocked. He managed to climb onto all fours. He was barely able to stand when he pushed to his feet. He was gasping for pained breaths when he began to limp toward the door.

Lyrik lurched at him. Threatening as he past. An affirmation that what I'd been saying was true.

I wouldn't be the only one coming for him if he ever showed his face again.

Ash fought to break free, shouting as he raged. "Watch your back, asshole...watch your fucking back. You touch my sister?"

Paul didn't look up. Just slinked out like the pussy he was.

Bastards like that? They were always preying on the weak. Taking from those who couldn't defend themselves. Tucking tail the second someone with the *ability* stands up to hold the bitch accountable.

As soon as he dropped out of sight, it was instant.

The way the silence pulled and tugged so goddamned tight.

The distress hovering around us was enough to snuff out those bits of hope I'd felt when I'd stood on that stage feeling like a goddamned king.

Now I stood there a beggar.

Warily, my gaze shifted to Edie.

Her entire face twisted.

In disbelief.

In horror.

In this gut-wrenching sorrow I felt cut straight to my soul.

"How could you?"

Her hand pressed to her stomach. Like she was trying to keep herself from crumbling.

"How could you? My brother...oh my God."

Her head shook. "Twice, Austin. Twice I trusted you with my secret. And twice you gave it away. And then...t-t-then you've been *lying* to me? Acting like you didn't know anything about the texts when you were responsible all along? I *trusted* you. I believed in you. I came home for *you.*"

She blinked. Shaking. Disoriented.

She stepped back, knocked into a box.

Shocked.

"I can't..."

Baz broke through the torment. "Shea...baby...why don't you get Edie out of here? Think she needs some time and the rest of us need to cool down."

Shea gave him a quick nod, their eyes locking in a silent conversation as she edged into the room, her voice soft when she got close to Edie.

"Hey, Edie. I'm Shea." She brushed her fingers gently through my girl's hair. "What do you say we get out of here? Just the girls...you and me and Tamar. Get you some air."

Disconnected, Edie blinked, nodded, mumbled, "Okay."

Shea began to lead her out.

Ash's plea broke in pain. "Edie."

Shea slanted him a look that said *later*, Edie tucked into her shoulder, leaning against her as she led her out.

And fuck.

I wanted to run for her. Chase her down and drop to my knees. Beg for the forgiveness I knew I didn't deserve.

Instead, I stood there panting, my heart beating so hard I was sure it would break free of the confines of my chest.

Because if Edie was gone?

It was too.

Be careful with me.

That's all she'd asked.

And I'd fucked it up.

Took the good and crushed it in careless hands.

I stood staring at the empty doorway, before I warily looked over at Ash.

His back was to my brother's chest, Baz still gripping him by the arms, but he'd loosened his hold.

Tension bounced around the walls of the small room.

Ash's brow twisted in spite as everything slowly sank in. Penetrated his being. His entire face pinched when he forced out the words. "You were sleeping with her? With my baby sister...when I brought her into our house when she was seventeen? When I was the one who was supposed to be taking care of her? The one responsible for her?"

Emotion squeezed all over. Regret. Hope. Bright blips and flickers of unfound dreams.

The girl who'd awakened the dead places inside me. The one who'd breathed life back into the broken.

Firelight.

It glowed so bright.

Slowly, I shook my head, everything raw. "No, Ash, I wasn't sleeping with her. I was falling in love with her."

He shook his head, harsh, and Baz released him. He slanted his fingers through his blond hair, staring at the ground for a beat, before he looked up at me. "She had a kid?"

I nodded, not able to meet his eye. Didn't matter that the secret had already been betrayed.

Seemed wrong to be offering him the details.

"Fuck." He shouted it toward the ceiling. "How the fuck did this happen?"

Helpless, I looked at him. "That's something you've got to talk to her about. I've already said too much."

He pushed out a weighted breath, raked an agitated hand down over his chin. "You been with her the whole time? This whole damned time when I thought she was out there finding herself? Because that sure sounds a whole lot like what you've claimed to have been up to, don't you think?"

"No," I said, roughing a palm over my face. "No, man...she took off because that piece of shit found out..."

My fault.

Again.

"And I...I left to find myself. Because without her it felt like everything was missing. And somehow, in this great big world, we found each other."

Frustration shook my head. "But you know my MO, Ash. I'm given chance after chance, and every damned time, I turn around and fuck it up again."

Hesitation stalled me, and I warred with what to say. How to lay it out there for Edie's brother. Because I was so done with all the hiding. Done with treating what Edie and I had as something dirty and disgraceful. Not when it was the most beautiful thing I'd ever had.

A gift.

I looked him straight. "I love her."

It was the most honest thing I'd ever said.

"But I messed up," I continued. "I messed up bad. Should have just told her. Come clean about what I did and why I did it. But Paul? I don't regret it. He needed to pay. Needed out of her life for as long as I could possibly make it happen. And if I'm the one who has to pay the price by losing her, I'll swallow it. It'll fuckin' destroy me, but I'll swallow it."

His stare was riddled with guilt. "Why didn't she just tell me?"

Grief and affection clotted in my throat. "Think tonight was the first time she really accepted it wasn't her fault."

His mouth twisted, and he jerked his head. "Need to get out of here. Gonna crack."

Ash pushed around Zee who moved out of his way. I started after him. Lyrik set a hand on my chest. "Let him go, man. You just unleashed a shit storm. He needs some time to process what this all means."

Emotion crawled up and down my throat like a caged cat. I gave a hard nod, having no clue what I was supposed to do now.

Baz sighed. "Come on...let's get out of here."

Nothing was said while we packed up our things. Mood somber. We headed out back where Baz's truck was parked in the backlot. I set his electric guitar in the bed of his truck, climbed into the front passenger seat.

I kept checking my phone. Antsy. Feeling that missing piece aching out from within.

Baz turned the key in the ignition, backed out, and pulled onto the street. He kept stealing curious glances at me while he drove, like he was both fighting a grin and a lecture.

Knew it was difficult for him to give up on those days.

I scowled at him, a little bit pissed off. "Why the hell do you keep looking at me like that?"

Air puffed from his nose, and he let his grin go, his tone almost teasing. "So you and Edie Evans, huh?"

I sighed, rubbed my forehead, knowing this conversation was getting ready to take a nosedive. I wasn't sure I was ready to delve into those depths with him.

Not when I didn't know if the girl was mine or if she'd had enough of my bullshit.

My entire being recoiled at the notion.

He chuckled, accelerating from a red light. He tapped at the wheel, contemplating. "Funny…there were a bunch of times I would have sworn there was something going on between you two back when she was staying at the house up in the Hills. Tension thick as molasses every time the two of you were in the same room. But she was so damned shy, I thought better of it."

He looked over at me. "Guess I should have thought *worse* of it. I mean…what did I expect, leaving you to your own devices? All of us were wiser than that."

It was packed with innuendo.

I shook my head. "Told Ash I didn't sleep with her back then. Wasn't lying."

Wanted to.

God, I'd wanted to so damned bad my sight had gone crooked.

"And molasses? For real, man, you turning country on me or what?"

Laughter rolled from him, a grin pulling at his mouth. "Might have a girl or two who are rubbing off on me."

"Shea makes you happy, yeah?"

"Crazy happy."

Truth of the matter? It made me crazy happy that she did. "Good for you, Baz. Hope you know that. Know it was a rough time when I left. But I need you to know I did it as much for you and Shea as I did it for myself."

"Didn't at the time…but after a while, I did."

Silence stole between us. "Why'd you do it?" he finally asked.

Do *it*?

Start sneaking in her room?

Slip up in front of Paul the first time?

Set him up?

Try to cover it up when he again started sniffing around?

So many choices. Right or wrong, they'd all been made for one reason.

I sank further into the seat, my voice tight. "Because I love her."

Because I wanted to protect her.

To take care of her the way I was made to do.

Dubious laughter rolled from him. "Loving someone will be one of the hardest things you ever do, little brother. It will twist you up and hang you out to dry. It'll fill you with more worry than you think you can stand, then turn right around and fill you with the greatest joy. It's a fucking battle, Austin. A battle because you'll spend the rest of your life fighting to keep it. But if you know one thing? Know there's no better mistake than one you make in the name of love."

I laughed, though it lacked any amusement at all. "But sometimes those mistakes cut too goddamned deep, Baz. They sever and they break. Pretty sure this cut might have gone all the way through and I don't have the first clue how to piece it back together."

He blew out a breath between pursed lips. "Secrets will always come back around, Austin. Maybe you and I know that better than anyone else. Didn't matter how far Edie ran from that one, it would have caught up to her. You or someone else."

My head shook. "Betrayed her, Baz. She asked one thing of me."

His phone went off and Shea's face lit up the screen.

My insides twisted, and my pulse rate spiked, my body inclining toward the phone like it might bring me closer to Edie.

He grabbed it, pulled it to his ear. "Hey, baby."

I could hear the intonation of her voice, but I couldn't hear what she said.

"Okay...yeah...see you in a bit. Love you."

He ended the call and another bout of silence throbbed in the cab. Baz kneaded the wheel.

"What'd she say?"

Hesitation wrapped around him. Because that was Baz's way. Always trying to protect me from what he didn't think I could handle. "Not a kid anymore. No more of this bullshit…no more not saying what needs to be said."

A sigh filtered from his lungs. "Shea put Edie up at a hotel. Said she needs some time."

Pain crushed my chest. A million fucking tons.

He seemed to war with what to say. "Why don't you come to mine and Shea's place? Plenty of room."

I shook my head. "Just…take me to the *Sunder* house."

The place where I'd found her and she'd found me. Where I felt closest to her.

He gave me a short nod, and we drove the rest of the way in silence. He pulled to a stop in the drive.

"Thanks, Baz," I said as I opened the door and stepped out.

"You going to be okay?" he asked, and I paused, halfway out when I looked back at him, my smile grim.

"Loving her might be the best mistake I ever made."

His lips pressed together in a sympathetic twist. Like he got it. Figured if anyone could, it was Baz.

I slung my bag over my shoulder and grabbed the guitar that now belonged to me. I trudged up the walk that made up so many memories, stepped into the darkened house that shouted back the loneliness.

Slowly, I took the stairs, my breaths heaving from my lungs. I opened the door to my old room and switched on the light. It was exactly the same. The same furnishings and pictures. All my belongings in their rightful place.

Exactly the way I'd left it.

Crazy, because nothing about it felt right.

I backed out, my head dropped while I stood in the long, quiet hall.

Apprehensive.

But not even that could stop me.

Because I was drawn.

I moved, my footsteps quieted. Same as they'd been years

before.

Subdued.

Tempting *fate*.

Sucking in a breath, I snapped the latch and entered her old room.

I stood inside the darkness. The flowy, translucent drapes shimmered in the faint moonlight breaking through. The bed was made. The room clean. Ready for any guest who needed a place to sleep.

Didn't matter.

It still felt like her.

Smelled like her.

I set the guitar on the floor and let my bag slide off my shoulder and drop free, kicked off my shoes, and fell face first onto the mattress.

I breathed in the hurt, and I let the magnitude of the mistakes I'd made tumble through me like a wailing storm.

I couldn't even pinpoint where they'd started.

Maybe it'd been tonight when I'd exposed her secret to Ash.

Or when I'd lost myself on *our* birthday. When I'd been so fucking desperate for her to fill up the void the way only she could.

Could have been not confessing right off the bat when she got the first text from Paul.

Or possibly when I let her secret run away from my mouth the first time. Again fueled by my fury as I released her trust into the hands of the very person she was determined would never know.

Maybe it was sneaking in here the first time.

But I think there was a part of me that knew. Knew I could trace it all back to that day on the beach.

The day I'd ripped the other half of my spirit away.

My darkest day.

It was the day I'd been set off-balance. My equilibrium shot. One side weighted by the ugliest, grimmest dark, the void on that side making it too hard to stand.

It'd left me spinning in a downward spiral.

Forever falling into the depths of an unending pit.

I hugged a pillow. Buried my face in it.

"What do I do, Julian? What the fuck do I do? When will it ever end?"

I lay there in the darkness as the Santa Ana winds whipped through the city and pounded against the walls.

The window panes rattled.

And I prayed prayers I didn't have the right to pray.

"Please."

I drifted in and out of consciousness. Barely hanging on. My heart thundering in the well of my chest. This erratic boom, boom, boom I couldn't calm.

Energy shifted. Lifted and swelled.

I sucked in a breath.

The door creaked open and that power lit. A sliver of hazy light bled across the floor and onto the bed, and the tension bounded.

Thick and profound.

Suffocating.

Her footfalls were light. Slow and cautious.

I remained frozen as she silently crossed the room, my breath gone when her fingertips traced a path up the center of my back, tender as they brushed the skin of my neck and up under my hair.

Shivers slicked down my spine, tightening every cell.

I shifted, almost scared to look over my shoulder.

But there was no chance I could look away.

Because there was my girl standing over me.

Hair like ethereal flames.

A white halo around her head.

Aqua eyes shimmered in the night.

Diamonds.

Angel. Light. Life.

She said nothing, just climbed onto the bed. I rolled onto my back, and she straddled my waist.

Every inch of my body hardened.

I stared up at her. The girl a vision. "Edie," I murmured.

She said nothing, only lifted the dream catcher above me. The hoop twisted and spun where it was suspended over my head, the feathers cast in a slow wave.

I clutched her by the hips. The lump was so thick in my throat. Because I had no idea which direction this was going to go.

Her voice was wispy when she finally spoke, almost faraway. "The first night you came to me I was so lost. I was terrified to live, Austin. Terrified to feel. But you broke through all those barriers. You made me remember what it felt like to hope. What it felt like to believe."

I sat up, bringing us face to face. Her body burned against mine, her heart a constant pound, pound, pound.

I could barely get out the admission. "The first time I touched you was the first time I breathed."

Not since I'd been a little boy.

She cast her gaze down. "That's the way it's always been with us. Something brilliant and beautiful pitted against something ugly and dark. The two always at war."

She looked up at me beneath her lashes. That sea of blue toiled with emotion, staring straight at me. Into me. She was always the one who could see it all. "How will we ever win if we can't stop fighting it?"

I attempted to swallow, fumbling around inside for a way around the obstacles that continued to block our paths. The ones that always led us back to the other.

Gently, I cupped her sweet, trusting face. "Because I don't ever want to stop fighting for you."

Tears leaked out at the corner of her eyes, and her chin trembled, my girl chewing at her lip as she tried to keep it contained. "I'm so scared of *this*, Austin. Scared of us. Scared to be free with you because that might mean letting her go. I'm afraid of the way you fill up the emptiness. I'm terrified that one day…one day she'll walk right by me and I won't recognize her."

My thumb brushed her cheek. "And I am terrified that one

day…one day I won't feel him anymore. That if I don't ache, maybe I will no longer remember. That if I fill up the void, I'll forget."

I stared at her.

My reflection.

My mirror.

Fingers caressed my forehead and across my brows. Tender and soothing, *comforting me*, in the midst of all her pain. "What happened the other night…on the beach. I know it didn't happen because you didn't *care* if you were careful with me. I know you do, Austin. I know you care. I *know* it. *Feel* it. But it felt like I was losing the *choice*. That I was out of control, and I don't know how to handle feeling that way."

The shake of her head was slow. "And you stopped…stopped when I asked you to. But that's what scared me most. That I let myself get lost in you."

She blinked, her words emphatic as she offered them into the night. "I want to be her, Austin. I want to be the one you can touch. Without reservations because you know I'm yours because I've given myself to you. I want to be the one that you know will always be there for you. Always. In whatever capacity you need me. That I belong to you the same way you belong to me. I want to be *free*."

I framed her face in my hands. "I'm going to mess up, Edie. I'm going to make mistakes. Do things I wish I didn't. But you will always—*always*—be free in me. With me. I will always be there to support you in whatever choice you make. And I fucking hate it that I lost that control. But I promise you…I'd never hurt you on purpose. It kills me that I did."

Tears kept coming, like streamers of glinting light rolling down her cheeks. "I never thought I'd trust someone enough to put myself in the position where I might have that *choice* to make again."

She set a palm on her stomach, her expression haunted and brimming with hope. "But when I came here, I made the decision I don't want to be scared anymore."

Rasping out a relieved breath, I hugged her close and

buried my face in her chest. Right over her heart. I just needed to hear it beat. "Can't tell you how sorry I am about Paul. About letting it get out in front of your brother."

I could feel her head shaking. "I was upset. Hurt. But I knew, Austin. Sitting alone in the hotel room, I knew every single *choice* you'd made was for me. That all along, you've done everything you could to protect me."

We stayed like that. Rocking slow. The girl on her knees. Curled around and hovering over me.

My angel.

Slowly, I sat back, pulled her arms out in front of her, unwound the catcher she had clutched in her hand. I held it up. My attention darted between her and the hoop. My confession came on a ragged whisper. "Promised you this catcher would always hold your dreams. Chase away the bad ones and keep the good ones safe." I swallowed around the jagged rocks lodged in my throat. "But I never told you mine."

Aqua eyes flashed. "Tell me."

Softly, I spoke. "I dream about a life with you, Edie. One I live for you. With you."

I threaded our fingers together, brought her hand to my mouth, kissed across the knuckle of her ring finger. "Dream about putting a ring on this finger. About calling you my wife."

I laced the words with caution. Because I knew I was pushing through the last of the barriers that remained between us. My fingers brushed back the hair matted to her damp cheeks. "Dream about a little girl with your eyes...maybe one who has my smile. *Someday*, Edie, *someday*...I want all those things. I want them with you. Whether it's tomorrow or years from now...I want all of it with you."

If what happened on the beach the other day brought it sooner, I'd be there. With her. For her.

Together.

Just like I'd promised.

"I want it, Austin. *Someday*, I want it. With you. I want it all."

I hugged her to me, my face going back to her chest.

She weaved her fingers through my hair, her voice a whispered confession. "I saw you on stage."

Those old dreams flared. I swallowed hard, while her voice went soft as a song. "You were beautiful, Austin. Powerful. Mesmerizing. You were right where you belonged."

"I...I came here thinking that was the best way to get close to Paul. Hurt him more. Getting him as close to the band as I could. But being up there...it felt like...Edie, it felt like I was where I belonged. But bigger than that is the fact I belong with you."

She pulled back, her smile sincere and so, so sweet. "This...this is where *we* belong. I don't want to run, Austin. Not anymore."

Exhaling the weight, I pulled her arm to my face, kissed the inside of her wrist, the inside of her elbow, the cap of her shoulder.

"Firelight."

My confession.

My world.

The light.

Edie gripped me by both sides of the face. Her hold strong. Sure. "Make love to me, Austin. Make love to me forever. Never leave my heart. Don't ever let me go. *I choose you.*"

thirty-seven

EDIE

*M*orning light spilled into the room. A room so familiar. The boy wrapped around me from behind so right.

His skin burned hot against mine, his heart rate steady.

Strong.

Slowly, I untangled myself from his arms and legs, smiling down at where he slept.

The boy who made me believe.

The one who made me see I didn't have to be ashamed.

Careful not to wake him, I slipped into my clothes that Austin had left a messy pile on the floor the night before, and quietly tiptoed out the door. I edged down the stairs to the slumbering house below, everything so quiet.

I headed across the living space that looked out to the city shimmering with the sun. I pushed the double swinging doors open that led to the kitchen.

I froze just inside when I saw I wasn't alone.

A rustle of anxiety rushed through my nerves. I pushed them down.

You don't have to be ashamed. You don't have to be ashamed.

My brother stood at the counter facing away, wearing only

a pair of worn jeans, feet and chest bare, blond hair a disaster on top of his head.

"Ash," I managed, my word lame and useless, but I had no idea how to broach all that had transpired under Ash's nose. "You're up early."

He chuckled but there was no true laughter behind it. Missing was the casual ease he typically wore. He shrugged a single shoulder. "Couldn't sleep. But I guess no one could blame me, could they?"

I cringed, stayed quiet while he poured a cup of coffee. He waved the carafe my way. "You want one?"

I moved to the island, my entire body ill-at-ease as I leaned up against it. "No…thank you."

He spun, leaned back against the opposite counter, eyed me over the top of the mug. His voice was rough. "Didn't know you were here this morning."

I let my eyes dart up. A silent indication of the boy who'd drawn me here in the middle of the night.

Because I hadn't been able to sleep, either. I had only tossed and turned and fumbled through my emotions until I came to the most important one.

What glared and glowed within me.

I was in love with Austin Stone.

And the boy was in love with me.

Now it was on us to figure out the rest.

He nodded slow. "Baz dropped Austin here last night. And you came."

Another nod.

He pushed out a sigh, winding himself up, finding the strength to say the things that needed to be said. "You were pregnant."

"Yes." The admission caught in my throat like spiky barbs.

God. It hurt so bad to admit it aloud. Especially after I'd protected it for so long, the most priceless, perilous secret.

"Paul." He spit it.

My mouth trembled, but I didn't need to respond.

Looking at his bare feet, he shook his head, trying to figure it out. "When...how?"

"You took me to a party...right before we moved to Ohio."

His hands shot up to cover his face as if he'd been punched. Then he dropped them like they were bricks. "What?" He blinked as the memories assaulted him. "I took you to a party."

He said it like he just realized the fact.

"I begged you to."

Disgusted, he shook his head. "I took my fourteen-year-old kid sister to a party...and I...I left you alone."

He began to pace. "I took a little girl to a party like that? Left her alone with the vultures so I could get an easy piece of ass?" He sucked for air. "Shit. All of it...it's on me."

He gripped his hair at the sides of his head, guilt pouring free.

My mouth trembled. "It wasn't your fault."

He scoffed. "I've always treated life as nothin' but fun and games." Bitter laughter seeped free. "I didn't even give it all that much thought when you asked me to tag along. I had not one fuckin' clue what went down that night. I promise, Edie, I didn't know."

"Of course you didn't. I never blamed you, because it wasn't your fault."

"Why didn't you just tell me? Kills me that all this time...all this time I never knew."

Everything I'd repressed for so long broke free. "I...I was terrified Ash. I had no idea what to do. I went to Paul for help...he...he gave me money...three hundred dollars."

A gasp punched from him. "Motherfucker—"

I kept on, needing to get it out before I lost my nerve, my words a ramble of regret. "And I just ran. I hid and pretended. Because that seemed so much easier than facing it."

Emotion pressed down on my chest. "Mom finally figured it out when I was about five months pregnant. She convinced me to find an adoptive family. To keep it a secret. Not tell anyone so I could move on with my life afterward. She promised me over and over it was for the best...and somewhere inside...I knew it was. I *knew* it was. But that didn't change what I felt inside, Ash. It didn't stop the devastation. I loved her so much."

My big brother looked to the ceiling, trying to rein in his emotion. Sorrow. Grief for me. "I don't...kills me, Edie. Fucking kills me. I didn't even know. How the hell can that happen? Right under my nose? I'm over here thinking all is good...and you're hurting in the worst way. Alone."

My mouth trembled. "But he found me, Ash. He found me in the middle of it. And for the first time...for the first time I thought maybe it would be okay. Austin and I...we're probably all wrong for each other because we're *so* right."

He was my weakness and my greatest strength.

My turmoil and my greatest peace.

Peace.

I wanted it.

I wanted it so desperately, to sink into his warmth.

Forever.

"I spent so much time blaming myself. Taking all the responsibility. But I'm ready to let it go, Ash. Please understand that. I know it's new for you, but this is something I've been dealing with for a long, long time. And the time's come for me to finally truly deal with it. Face it. Accept it. And that means if I'm going to stay here, I need you to accept it, too."

"And I'm guessin' that staying here involves staying with him?"

I raked my teeth on my bottom lip, gave a slight nod. Nervous but hopeful.

Ash stalled, before he finally cracked one of those too-wide grins, but there was something sincere behind it. "So you're telling me I don't get to kick Austin's ass?"

Soggy laughter slipped free. "No...you don't get to kick his ass." I sobered. "I love him, Ash. I love him so much it hurts. But it's the good kind of hurt. I don't ever want that to go away."

Ash set his mug on the counter. "Come here, baby sister."

He pulled me against him, his chin on top of my head, his arms banded around my waist. "Don't ever take off again. You don't have to hide anything from me. Not now. Not ever. You understand me?"

Out of the blue, he chuckled. "And if you're ever in need of some ass kickin'? First order of business is to let me know. You do realize that's what big ass, awesome big brothers are for?"

I laughed. "I don't doubt that."

I stepped back, looked up at him in all seriousness. "I really missed you."

He hooked his knuckle under my chin. "I missed you, too."

We both looked to the side when the door swung open.

Austin stood there, shirtless, his hair an utter, perfect mess from my hands tugging at it all night.

Desire.

Devotion.

Love.

Hope.

They were all there.

Reflected back in his smile.

"Hey," he said, voice rough with sleep.

"Hi."

Ash sighed dramatically. "Ahhh...I do believe that would be my cue. A guy knows when he's no longer wanted." Shooting me a wink, he grabbed his mug, sauntered toward Austin. He stuck out his fist as he passed. "Take care of my sister, man, though it sounds to me like you've been doing a damned good job of it all along."

Austin bumped it. "Always."

Ash kept moving, heading through the double doors, before he paused half way out and peeked his head back in. "Oh...and just so we're clear...I'm official ass-kicker. Baby girl has an issue with you? You've got an issue with me. Got it?"

It was all a tease falling from a cocky smirk.

"Not gonna be necessary," Austin said, glancing at him and

slanting me a smile.

Ash cracked a grin. "Young love. Suckers. Whole lot of you." The door swung shut behind him, and his voice echoed back through the walls. "Everyone around here has lost their ever-lovin' minds. First my beautiful Shea then my Tam Tam." His volume rose, crestfallen and fake, before the words began to fade as he walked away. "Then my baby sister. Heart. Broken."

And Austin stood there, staring at me, before he was moving. Winding me in his arms. Relief in his kiss. A promise in his hold.

No more shame.

No more hiding.

Just the future waiting out ahead of us.

thirty-eight

AUSTIN

Water lapped at the shore, a soft tumble reaching out as it staked its claim up the beach.

As if fingers were stretching out.

Calling to me.

That presence never far.

A haunting voice.

A distant memory.

My chest tightened in sync with the tightening of her hand where it burned against mine.

"Are you ready?" she asked, her own voice a tremble.

I squeezed her back. "Yeah."

Crazy that she was the one hauling me along, my girl dipping her toes in the cold waters that lined my old neighborhood. The place we used to play. And I could almost see him where he splashed and laughed, a strike of white hair against the sun, smile so bright.

So much life.

A tangle of remorse twisted in my heart and tugged at my spirit. The same spirit that was somehow propelling me forward.

A wave eased up around Edie's ankles, our hands entwined. She turned back to look at me. She watched me with all that encouragement and understanding

Filling me up the way only she could.

I sucked in a breath. I fucking froze when I dipped in a toe.

I tried to swallow, to keep in the emotion that ran amok, a wild stir of old hurt and sorrow, the guilt I'd born for so damned long tumbling through my insides.

"I've got you," she said, and fuck, if I didn't want to weep, this girl standing at my side. Just like I was never gonna stop standing at hers.

Winter wind gusted, blowing in low, a groan that howled as it beat against my chilled flesh.

I took another step deeper.

Drawn.

Trembles rolled, and I was at her side as the cold water consumed us to our waists.

We stood there.

Together.

Waves rushed around us, our hands entwined, the sun glinting at the horizon as it slowly told the day goodbye.

Edie glanced at me with those aqua eyes that blazed their warmth. Then she released my hand and turned to look out over what seemed an endless expanse of water, the ocean deep.

She lifted the dream catcher to her chest, tightly held it there as her words flew from her in a whisper.

In a confession.

In a prayer.

"I will always love you and my heart will always hold you. There will always be a place for you waiting within my soul. But I'm letting you go. I'm letting you live this beautiful life knowing you're loved. That you're cared for. That you're adored. If you ever decide to come back to me, to find me, I'll be *waiting*."

She pressed the hoop to her lips, a frenzied, hallowed kiss, before she squeezed her eyes and threw it with all the strength she had, releasing it into the embrace of the waves.

It landed, not far from where we stood.

It bobbed gently, twisting and turning as it floated. Before it tipped and was swallowed by the waves.

Taken to the depths.

Nerves shivered through me. Grief and guilt and my own belief.

Belief built by the strength of this girl.

Belief somehow found in *his* presence.

I clutched the tattered, grungy monkey to my chest. The one he'd taken with him everywhere he went. The one he'd slept with all his days.

His comfort.

His safety blanket.

I held it to my lips where my words fell on a whisper.

My confession.

My prayer.

"I love you, Julian. My brother. My twin. The other half of my soul. Please forgive me for stealing all your tomorrows. For robbing you of the chance to live out the days you should have lived. I didn't mean to. God, please, believe me. I didn't mean to."

I choked on the sorrow clotting my throat and forced myself to continue. "Now I've got to let you go. You can't stay here and I can't go on trying to keep you here. I won't ever forget you. Please don't forget me." I squeezed my eyes closed, the words a tight rasp. "I'll see you on the other side. I know you'll be *waiting* for me."

I fisted the monkey.

Held on tight.

Before I let it go.

It landed just where Edie's hoop had gone.

It floated. Waved its green, furry arm just above the waves, bobbed up and down. It grew heavier with the weight of the water.

Consumed.

Taken under.

Edie threaded her fingers through mine.

wait

A new web woven.
Love. Peace. Life.
Hope set right in the middle of it.
Shining bright.
Firelight.

epilogue
SOMEDAY

*E*die wailed and her head pressed back into the pillow. Her face lifted toward the ceiling as she released a cry.

Her husband squeezed her hand almost as fiercely as she squeezed back.

"You've got it, Edie. You've got it. One more push. One more push and you're all done."

Emotion gripped her everywhere.

Her instincts alive.

Sweat beaded on her brow, and she bore down, her teeth gritted.

She pushed.

And everything went silent.

Her heart stopped.

A tiny shattered cry.

A tiny perfect body.

Her heart took off at a sprint.

Love.

Love.

Love.

And she pushed up to sitting, hands reaching, fumbling for

the child. "Please," she whimpered. And *she* was there, placed in her arms, swaddled in a small white blanket, a blue and pink cap on her head.

Lips red.

Eyes swollen.

She blinked a stony gray.

He looked down at them. Tears soaking his face.

Awe and love.

Endless adoration.

A big hand cupped Edie's cheek, and he pressed a kiss to her forehead, his lips whispering his belief at her skin. "You did it, baby. You did it."

And their hearts. They tumbled and spun. Swelled and grew.

Overflowed.

Two empty lives that had been so hollow.

Two lives that now brimmed so full.

the end

Stay Prologue

WILLOW

We rarely know when our lives are about to change. When the direction we've been traveling will shift. When the stagnant comfort we've cut out for ourselves will take a sharp turn south or when everything we know will come to an abrupt, excruciating end.

Maybe I should have known it then. When the bell jingled above the door.

I guess I'd been too absorbed in my work. Lost to the feel of the wood beneath my hands as I shaped and sanded away the rot and decay to expose the true beauty hiding underneath.

Maybe I should have taken the way my heart suddenly sped as a premonition. As an omen. As a warning to steel myself for the debris littering the road just ahead.

But instead, I took it head on, my eyes squinting against the blinding rays of late-afternoon sun that spilled in like a flash flood behind the man who suddenly took up the entirety of the

340

doorway.

A concealed figure cast in shadows and silhouettes.

A mystery rimmed in the brightest fire.

Maybe I should have braced myself for impact.

For the collision I never could have anticipated.

He took a single step forward and into my direct line of sight.

He stared at me for the longest time, taking me in as if he knew me, before he tilted his head and slanted me the cockiest grin. One that had the power to plow through me with the force of a speeding truck that'd lost its brakes.

Maybe I should have prepared myself.

Maybe I should have been stronger.

Maybe I should have clung to the promise I'd made to never allow myself to get burned.

Not ever again.

Little did I know I was now standing in the flames.

MORE FROM A.L. JACKSON

Bleeding Stars
A Stone in the Sea
Drowning to Breathe
Where Lightning Strikes

The Regret Series
Lost to You
Take This Regret
If Forever Comes

The Closer to You Series
Come to Me Quietly
Come to Me Softly
Come to Me Recklessly

Stand-Alone Novels
Pulled
When We Collide

More Bleeding Stars Novels Coming Soon
Stay
Stand

ABOUT THE AUTHOR

A.L. Jackson is the New York Times and USA Today bestselling author of contemporary and new adult romance.

She first found a love for writing during her days as a young mother and college student. She filled the journals she carried with short stories and poems used as an emotional outlet for the difficulties and joys she found in day-to-day life.

Years later, she shared a short story she'd been working on with her two closest friends and, with their encouragement, this story became her first full length novel. A.L. now spends her days writing in Southern Arizona where she lives with her husband and three children.

Connect with A.L. Jackson online:

www.aljacksonauthor.com
Facebook (www.facebook.com/aljacksonauthor)
Twitter: @aljacksonauthor
Instagram: @aljacksonauthor
Newsletter http://smarturl.it/NewsFromALJackson
For quick mobile updates, text "ALJACKSON" to 24587

Download the App:
http://smarturl.it/ALJacksonAuthorApp

Made in the USA
Middletown, DE
14 January 2017